ALSO BY GREG BEAR

Hegira
Beyond Heaven's River
Strength of Stones
Psychlone
Blood Music
Songs of Earth and Power
Eon
Eternity
Legacy
The Forge of God
Anvil of Stars
Queen of Angels
/ (Slant)
Heads
Moving Mars
Dinosaur Summer
Foundation and Chaos
Star Wars: Rogue Planet
Darwin's Radio
Vitals
Darwin's Children

COLLECTION

The Collected Stories of Greg Bear

EDITOR

New Legends

DEAD LINES

GREG BEAR

BALLANTINE BOOKS • NEW YORK

This is a work of fiction. Names, characters, places, and incidents are the products of the author's imagination or are used fictitiously. Any resemblance to actual events, locales, or persons, living or dead, is entirely coincidental.

A Del Rey® Book
Published by The Random House Publishing Group

Published in the United States by The Random House Publishing Group, a division of Random House, Inc., New York, and simultaneously in Canada by Random House of Canada Limited, Toronto.

www.delreydigital.com

Cataloging-in-Publication Data is available from the Library of Congress.

ISBN 0-345-44837-5

Book design by Susan Turner

Manufactured in the United States of America

First Edition: June 2004

10 9 8 7 6 5 4 3 2 1

FOR

J. Sheridan Le Fanu.

Henry James.

M.R. James.

Arthur Machen.

H.P. Lovecraft.

Shirley Jackson.

Fritz Leiber.

Richard Matheson.

Kingsley Amis.

Peter Straub.

Bruce Joel Rubin.

Ramsey Campbell.

Dean Koontz.

Stephen King.

Scary people, all.

DEAD LINES

A ghost is a role without an actor.

Ghosts are like movies—the story goes on, but nobody's home. Like dead skin, under normal circumstances, a ghost lingers just long enough to protect the vulnerable flesh of the living.

Not all that rarely, people are born with nothing inside, or lose what little they have—living ghosts. And when they die, sometimes even before they die, a hole opens up and a bit of the dark world creeps in.

We were all there in that city that draws its paycheck from the manufacture of ghosts. We were there when one man started handing out free talk. And we are there now, sad little dolls made of dust.

Your friends, if only you knew. If only you were smart enough to care. Maybe now you'll listen, though you never have before.

You'll join us soon enough.

You're next.

CHAPTER 

PAUL IS DEAD. Call home.

Peter Russell, stocky and graying, stood on the sidewalk and squinted at the text message on his cell phone, barely visible in the afternoon sun on Ventura Boulevard.

He lifted his round glasses above small, amused eyes, and brought the phone closer to see the display more clearly.

Paul is dead. He flashed on his youth, when for a week he had sincerely believed that Paul was dead: Paul McCartney. *I am the walrus.* But he had misread the phone's blocky letters. The message was actually *Phil is dead.*

That shook him. He knew only one Phil. Peter had not talked with Phil Richards in a month, but he refused to believe that the message referred to his best friend of thirty-five years, the kinder, weaker, and almost certainly more talented of the Two Ps. Not the Phil with the thirty-two-foot Grand Taiga motor home, keeper of their eternal plans for the World's Longest Old Farts Cross-country Hot Dog Escapade and Tour.

Please, not that Phil.

He hesitated before hitting callback. What if it was a joke, a bit of cell phone spam?

Peter drove a vintage Porsche 356C Coupe that had once been signal red and was now roughly the shade of a dry brick. He fumbled his key and almost dropped the phone before unlocking the car door. He did not need this. He had an important appointment. Angrily, he pushed the button. The number rolled out in musical beeps. He recognized the answering voice of Carla Wyss, whom he had not heard from in years. She sounded nervous and a little guilty.

"Peter, I just dropped by the house. I took the key from your bell and let myself in. There was a note. My God, I never meant to snoop. It's from somebody named Lydia." Lydia was Phil's ex-wife. "I thought I should let you know."

Peter had shown Carla the secret of the bronze Soleri bell, hanging outside the front door, after a night of very requited passion. Now, upset, she was having a sandwich and a root beer from his refrigerator. She hoped he didn't mind.

"Mi casa es su casa," Peter said, beyond irritation. He tongued the small gap between his front teeth. "I'm listening."

Carla's voice was shaky. "All right. The note reads 'Dear Peter, Phil died. He had a heart attack or a stroke, they aren't sure which. Will let you know details.' Then it's signed very neatly." She took a breath. "Wasn't he another writer? Didn't I meet him here in the house?"

"Yeah." Peter pressed his eyes with his fingers, blocking out the glare. Lydia had been living in Burbank for a few years. She had apparently made the rounds of Phil's LA friends. Carla rattled on, saying that Lydia had used a fountain pen, a folded sheet of handmade paper, a black satin ribbon, and Scotch tape.

Lydia had never liked telephones.

Phil is dead.

Thirty-five years of kid dreams and late-night plans, sitting in the backyard in old radar-dish rattan chairs on the dry grass between the junipers. Shooting the bull about stories and writing and big ideas. Phil hanging out on movie sets and model shoots—not so selfless—but also helping Peter carry his bulky and unsold wire sculptures to the dump in the back of the old Ford pickup they had often swapped.

Only the truck, never the women, Phil had lamented.

Slight, wiry Phil with the short, mousy hair who smiled so sweetly every time he saw a naked lady. Who longed for the female sex with such clumsy devotion.

"Are you okay, Peter?" Carla asked from far away.

"Heart attack," Peter repeated, lifting the phone back to his mouth.

"Or a stroke, they aren't sure. It's a very pretty note, really. I'm so sorry."

He visualized Carla in his house, locked in her perpetual late thirties, leggy as a deer, dressed in pedal pushers and a dazzling man's white dress shirt with sleeves rolled up and tails pinned to show her smooth, flat tummy.

"Thanks, Carla. You better leave before Helen comes over," Peter said, not unkindly.

"I'll put the key back in the bell," Carla said. "And Peter, I was looking through your files. Do you have some glossies of me that I can borrow? I have a new agent, a good guy, really sharp, and he wants to put together a fresh folio. I'm up for a credit card commercial."

All of Carla's agents had been good guys, really sharp; all of them had screwed her both ways and she never learned. "I'll look," Peter said, though he doubted cheesecake would help.

"You know where to find me."

He did, and also what she smelled and felt like. With a wave of loose guilt, Peter sat on the old seat in the car's sunned interior, the door half open and one leg hanging out. The hot cracked leather warmed his balls. A cream-colored Lexus whizzed by and honked. He pulled in his leg and shut the door, then rolled down the window as far as it would go, about half way. Sweat dripped down his neck. He had to look presentable and be in Malibu in an hour. His broad face crinkled above a close-trimmed, peppered beard.

Peter was fifty-eight years old and he couldn't afford to take ten minutes to cry for his best friend. One hand shielded his eyes from sun and traffic. "Damn it, Phil," he said.

He started the car and took the back roads to his home, a square, flat-roofed, fifties rambler in the Glendale hills. Carla was gone by the time he arrived, leaving only a waft of gardenia in the warm still air on the patio. Helen was late, or maybe not coming after all—he could never tell what her final plans might be—so he took a quick shower. He soon smelled of soap and washed skin and put on a blue-and-red Hawaiian shirt. He picked up his best briefcase, a maroon leather job, and pushed through the old French doors. The weedy jasmine creeping over the trellis had squeezed out a few flowers. Their sweetness curled up alongside Carla's gardenia.

Peter stood for a moment on the red tiles and looked up through the trellis at the bright blue sky. He pressed his elbow against a rough, sun-battered post, breath coming hard: The old anxiety he always found in tight places, in corners and shadows. When events fell outside his control or his ability to escape. A minute passed. Two minutes. Peter's gasping slowed. He sucked in a complete breath and pressed the inside of his wrist with two fingers to check his pulse. Not racing. The hitch behind his ribs untied with a few solid pushes of cupped fingers under the edge of his sternum. He had never asked a doctor why that worked, but it did.

He wiped his face with a paper towel, then scrawled a note for Helen on the smudged blackboard nailed below the Soleri bell. Reaching into the oil drum that served as an outdoor closet, mounted high on two sawhorses, he tugged out a lightweight suit coat of beige silk, the only one he had, a thrift-store purchase from six years ago. He sniffed it; not too musty, good for another end of summer, soon to turn into autumn.

PETER LET THE old Porsche roll back out of the garage. The engine purred and then climbed into a sweet whine after he snicked the long, wood-knobbed shift into first gear.

Last he had heard, Phil had been traveling in Northern California, trying to unblock a novel. They hadn't seen each other in months. Peter tried to think why friends wouldn't stay in touch from week to week or even day to day. Some of his brightest moments had been with Phil; Phil could light up a room when he wanted to.

Peter wiped his eye and looked at his dry knuckle. Maybe tonight. But Helen might drop off Lindsey, and if he started crying with Lindsey around, that might rip open a wound that he could not afford to even touch.

Numbness set in. He drove toward the ocean and Salammbo, the estate of Joseph Adrian Benoliel.

CHAPTER 2

THE SUNSET BEYOND the hills and water was gorgeous in a sullied way: lapis sky, the sun a yellow diamond hovering over the gray line of the sea, dimmed by a tan ribbon of smog. Peter Russell pushed along in second gear, between lines of palm trees and golf-green lawn spotted with eucalyptus. Flaubert House cast a long cool shadow across the drive and the golf-green approach. Crickets were starting to play their hey-baby tunes.

Salammbo covered twenty acres of prime highland Malibu real estate. She had survived fires, earthquakes, landslides, the Great Depression, the fading careers of two movie stars, and tract-home development. In more than thirty years in Los Angeles and the Valley, Peter had never encountered anything like her—two huge, quirky mansions set far apart and out of sight of each other, looking down descending hills and through valleys rubbed thick with creosote bush and sage to Carbon Beach.

Here was illusion at its finest: the fantasy that peace can be bought, that power can sustain, that time will rush by but leave the finer things untouched: eccentricity, style, and all the walls that money can buy. Life goes on, Salammbo said with sublime self-assurance, especially for the rich. But the estate's history was not so reassuring.

Salammbo was a nouveau-riche vision of heaven: many mansions "builded for the Lord." The lord in this case had died in 1946: Lordy Trenton—not a real lord but an actor in silent comedies—had risen from obscurity in the Catskills for a good twelve-year run against Chaplin, Keaton, and Lloyd. His character—a drunken aristocrat, basically decent but prone to causing enormous trouble—had palled on audiences even before the onset of the Depression. Trenton had gotten out of acting while the getting was grand. One grand, to be precise, which is the price for which he had sold all rights to his films in 1937.

During the Depression, Lordy had invested in sound equipment for the movies and made big money. In the mid-thirties, he had built Flaubert House and then started to erect what some architectural critics at the time referred to as Jesus Wept. Trenton's friends called it the Mission. The Mission featured a huge circular entry beneath a dome decorated with Moorish tile, high vaulted ceilings, bedrooms furnished in wrought iron and dark oak, an austere refectory that could seat a hundred, and a living room that by itself occupied two thousand square feet. It consumed much of his fortune.

In the early forties, beset by visions of a Japanese invasion of California, Lordy connected Flaubert House and the Mission with a quarter-mile underground tramway, complete with bomb shelter. He lined the smoothly plastered stone-and-brick tunnel with a gallery of nineteenth-century European oils. At the same time, he became involved with a troubled young artist and sometime actress, Emily Gaumont. After their marriage in 1944, she spent her last year obsessively painting full-sized portraits of Lordy and many of their friends—as clowns.

In 1945, during a party, a fire in the tunnel killed Emily and ten visitors and destroyed the tram. Four of the dead—including Emily, so the story went—were burned beyond recognition.

A year later, alone and broken by lawsuits, Trenton died of acute alcohol poisoning.

The next owner, a department-store magnate named Greel, in his late sixties, acquired a mistress, allegedly of French Creole descent. To please her, he spent a million dollars finishing the Mission in Louisiana Gothic, mixing the two styles to jarring effect. The name Jesus Wept acquired permanence.

Greel died in 1949, a suicide.

In 1950, the estate was purchased by Frances Saint Claire, a Hitchcock blond. Blackballed by the studios, her career ruined by allegations of leftist sympathies, Saint Claire had married a savvy one-time pretty boy named Mortimer Sykes. Sykes, playing against type, wisely invested her money and endlessly doted on her. In 1955, they built the third and final mansion of Salammbo, the trendy, Bauhaus-inspired Four Cliffs. In 1957, just six months before Saint Claire's death from breast cancer, a grove of eucalyptus trees caught fire. The flames spread to two of the mansions. Four Cliffs burned to the ground. Most of Jesus Wept survived, but the refectory lay in ruins. A police investigation pointed to arson, but friends in local politics hushed up any further investigation, suggesting there was already enough tragedy at Salammbo.

In 1958, Sykes put the estate up for sale and moved to Las Vegas. A broken man and heavily in debt, he tried to borrow money from the wrong people. Two years later, hikers discovered his body in a shallow grave in the desert.

The estate lay vacant for five years. In 1963, Joseph Adrian Benoliel became Salammbo's newest master. A lifelong bachelor, Joseph had made his fortune producing beach flicks and managing a chain of real-estate franchises.

And between 1970 and 1983, he had secretly financed four of Peter's titillation movies; lots of nudity but no actual sex.

PETER PARKED THE car, got out, and pulled his coat down over a slight paunch. Broad-shouldered, he carried the extra weight well enough, but he was starting to look more like an aging bodyguard than an artist. No matter. The Benoliels didn't care.

Peter lifted and dropped the bronze fist on the striker plate mounted on the huge oak door. A young man with short black hair, dressed in an oversized blue sweater and beige pants, opened the door, looked him up and down, then held out something as if making a donation to the poor. Peter had never met him before.

"Here, Mr. Benoliel doesn't seem to want it," the young man said in a clipped tone of British disappointment. "They're free. Who are you?" He pressed a black plastic ovoid into Peter's hand and stood back to let him in.

"That's Peter," Joseph said. "Leave him alone." He walked into the entryway with a persistent poke of his rubber-tipped cane, moving fast for a man with a limp. "I hate the goddamned things." He did not sound angry. In fact, he smiled in high good humor at Peter. In his early seventies, with a football player's body gone to fat and the fat carefully pared away by diet, the flesh of Joseph's arms hung loose below the short sleeves of his yellow golf shirt.

Bandy legs weakened by diabetes stuck out below baggy black shorts. His bristling butch-cut hair had long since turned white. "Hate them when they beep in restaurants. People driving and yakking. Always have to be connected, like they'd vanish if they stopped talking. There's too much talk in the world already." He waved his hand in a gesture between permission and irritated dismissal. "If you take the damned thing, turn it off while you're here."

"They don't turn off," the young man explained to Peter, drawing closer. His wide blue eyes assessed Peter's character and the size of his wallet. "You can turn the ringer down, however."

Peter smiled as if at a half heard joke. "What is it?" he asked.

"Free talk," Joseph said. "But it doesn't work. Where's Mishie?"

"She told me to get the door," the young man said.

"Well, hell, Peter has a key. Mishie!"

The young man regarded Peter with newfound but uncertain respect.

Mishie—Michelle—walked out of the hall leading back to the drawing room. "I'm here." She smiled at Peter and hooked her arm around Joseph's. "Time for his lordship's monkey nut shots," she announced with thespian cheer. "Come along, dear."

Joseph stared gloomily at the small elevator to the left of the long flight of stairs, as if doom awaited him there. "Don't ever leave me alone with her, Peter," he said.

"You two fine young bucks wait in the drawing room," Michelle instructed primly. "We'll be down in a whiffle."

"I'm *down* now," Joseph said. "If there's anything I hate, it's monkey nuts." He patted Peter's arm in passing.

"NICE COUPLE," THE young man said as they sat in an alcove looking over the west lawn. The wistful last of the day faded far out over the cliffs and the ocean. "They *were* joking, weren't they?"

"I think so," Peter said. "I'm Peter Russell."

"Stanley Weinstein."

They stretched out of their chairs and shook hands. Chairs throughout Flaubert House were always set shouting distance apart from one another.

"Scouting for an investment?" Peter asked.

"An invest*or*," Weinstein corrected. "One million dollars, minimum. A pittance to finance a revolution."

"In telecom?"

Weinstein cringed. "Let's please avoid that word."

Peter raised the plastic ovoid to eye level and twisted it until he found a seam, then tried to pry it open with a thumbnail. It wouldn't budge. "If it's not a phone, what is it?"

"We call it Trans," Weinstein said. "T-R-A-N-S. Plural, also Trans. Invest a little, and you get one to use. Invest a lot, and you get more to hand out to friends. Very chic, extraordinarily high tech, nothing like them on the market. Feel that weight? Quality."

"It's a cell phone," Peter said, "but not."

"Close enough," Weinstein agreed with a lean of his head. "They'll be free for the next year. Then we go public and open booths in every shopping mall in the world."

"Joseph won't invest?" Peter asked.

Weinstein shrugged. "Our demo did not go well. Something seems to be wrong with the house."

"There's a steel frame. Lots of stone."

"Trans will work anywhere from the center of the Earth to the moon," Weinstein said, puffing out his cheeks. "I don't know what the problem is. I shall have to ask my boss."

"And your boss is . . . ?"

Weinstein held his finger to his lips. "Mr. Benoliel trusts you?"

"I suppose," Peter said. "He trusts me not to hit him up for money too often."

Weinstein looked funny at that, then wiggled his finger in the air. "Monkey nuts?"

"That *is* a joke," Peter said. "I do stuff for them. I'm nobody, really."

Weinstein winked. "You have influence. They trust you, I can tell," he said. "Keep the unit. In fact, let me give you more. Hand them out to your friends, but if you would, please give one to a good friend of Mr. Benoliel's, or better yet, Mrs. Benoliel's."

Peter shook his head. "I already have a cell phone," he said. "I get calls every week about new service plans."

"What about *no* service plan?" Weinstein thrust out his fingers like a magician. "A Trans unit lasts for a year, and then you replace it with another, price yet to be established—but less than three hundred dollars. Unlimited calling day or night, anywhere on the planet. Better than digital—in fact, pure analog sound quality, just as God intended. Do you like vinyl LPs?"

"I still have a few." In fact, Peter had hundreds, mostly jazz, classical, and 1960s rock.

"Then you know what I mean. Lovely, like a soft whisper in your ear. No interference, just clean sound. If you can convince Mr. Benoliel we're on to something, you'll get free units for life. You and five—no, ten of your friends."

Peter gave a dry chuckle. "And?"

Weinstein lifted an eyebrow. "Five thousand shares, IPO guaranteed to be set at twenty-three dollars a share."

Peter raised his own eyebrow even higher. He hadn't survived a career in films for nothing.

Weinstein grinned devilishly. "Or five thousand dollars, up front, your choice, payable when Mr. Benoliel invests."

"How about ten thousand?"

Weinstein's smile remained, tighter but still friendly. "Okaaay," he said, mimicking Joseph's deliberate drawl. "Pardner." He pulled a folded piece of paper from his pocket and began scrawling on it with a fountain pen. "Do you have an agent?"

"He hasn't heard from me in a while." Peter examined the short, neatly penned document. The address was in Marin County. He would probably need to go north anyway, for Phil's funeral—if there was going to be one. He asked for the fountain pen and signed. "What the hell," he said. "Joseph rarely changes his mind."

Weinstein excused himself and returned a few minutes later with a white cardboard box. In the box, buried in layers of foam, were ten plastic ovoids in various cheery colors. "All active and good for a year. Push the help button for instructions."

"How do you open them?" Peter asked.

Weinstein demonstrated. Pressing a barely visible dimple on one side released the upper half, which swung aside with oily smoothness. There were no buttons. A screen covered most of the revealed face and lit up pearly white with black touch keypad and letters, different from his Motorola. The unit was neatly made and felt just right in his hand, slightly warm, slightly heavy.

"It's not a gift from aliens, is it?" Peter asked.

"It should be," Weinstein said, chuckling. "No, it's entirely human. Just . . . people."

Weinstein handed Peter the box and looked around the drawing room. "Quite a place," he said. "Have you worked here long?"

Peter smiled. Joseph did not like to be talked about, in any fashion, by anybody.

Weinstein turned serious. "Get this done, Mr. Russell, and you'll rate a visit to our new headquarters, as well as your bounty money. Then you'll meet the man behind Trans."

Peter folded shut the top of the box. "I'll put these in my car," he said.

"That lovely old Porsche?" Weinstein asked. "Is it a replica?"

"Nope," Peter said.

"Then it's older than I am," Weinstein said.

AFTER WEINSTEIN'S DEPARTURE, Peter followed Michelle up the long curve of marble stairs to the second floor. Flaubert House was huge and quiet, as solid as a tomb but cheerful in its way. "That was awkward," Michelle murmured. "Joseph knew someone's daddy way back when. Now one of his boys sends a salesman to hit him up for ten million dollars."

Peter walked beside her for the last few steps, silent. It had taken him into his forties to realize that the true art of conversation was saying almost nothing.

"Joseph's been a little down. I mean, not that he's ever a ball of fire, you know? But a little less twinkle."

In truth, Joseph had never struck Peter as being capable of twinkle. Blunt honesty, sharp conversation, an uncanny ability to pin down character—and a good joke every now and then—defined his few charms. Over the years, Peter had come to like Joseph; honesty and the occasional joke could make up for a lot.

Michelle looked tired. "Says he has a palooza of a chore for you. Won't tell me what. Man stuff, do you think?" Her long legs carried her more quickly over the thick Berber carpeting in the broad hallway.

"Monkey nuts," Peter said.

Michelle smirked. "I'll tell him you're here." She left him standing between walls covered by framed glossies of movie stars. Most of the stylish portraits were autographed, souvenirs of Joseph's days as a producer. Peter recognized them all: beautiful or soulful people brooding or sunny, feigning humor or dignity, looking inaccessible or seductive, but all seeking approval no matter what attitude they copped. Long ago, he had realized an almost universal truth about actors. They became real only when they were being witnessed, when they were on-screen. Hidden behind doors, alone, or looped around a reel and locked in a dark metal can ... For an actor, not being seen, not having an audience, was worse than limbo.

"All right," Michelle said, returning. "He's decent." She opened a door near the end of the hall. "Joseph, it's Peter."

"Who else would it be, Eliot Ness?" a voice bellowed in the dark beyond.

Michelle sighed. "Ten percent bonus if you leave him a contented man."

"I heard that!"

Michelle sighed loudly and closed the door behind Peter.

Joseph sat in a huge leather chair near full-length windows opening onto a false balcony about a foot deep and faced with black wrought-iron railing. Lights from the front drive and the last of the sky glow drew him in broad grainy strokes like chalk on velvet. The room also contained an antique oak bar from a saloon in Dodge City, so the legend went, and two brown leather couches separated by a square black granite table. "Goddamned awkward," he said. "Did Weinstein try to suck you in?"

"Yeah. Ambition," Peter said.

"In spades."

Peter nodded. His eyes adjusted slowly to the twilit gloom.

"Offer you stock to convince me?"

"And cash."

Joseph chuckled. "They've been yammering at me for a week. Goddamned things don't work. You'd think they would check that out before they try to hit up a rich old fool." There was a strange set to Joseph's words. "Old trumps rich," he murmured. "And fool trumps old." He was staring fixedly through the windows. Peter stood about six feet from the chair. "Anyway, I'm glad you're here. I need you to go see a woman. Interested?"

"For you, always," Peter said.

"She may be the most charismatic female on the planet. Certainly one of the smartest. If I went personally, she would play me like a farm trout. You, however . . . You know women better than any man alive. You'll survive."

Peter gave a small, dubious laugh.

"Well, you will. You've made it with over two hundred women, photographed maybe two thousand, and Michelle genuinely likes you. That's a résumé no other man in my experience can equal."

"Who gave out my track record?"

"We've known each other a long time," Joseph said. "I did some research before bankrolling your films."

"A bit exaggerated," Peter said. "I never kept count."

Joseph lifted his hand, spread his fingers, then let it drop back to the chair arm. "Before she met me, Michelle used to know a lot of photographers. Long-haired sacks of fermented pig shit. That's what she called them. But not you."

"I'm respectable?" Peter asked.

"Not if you work for me, you aren't." Joseph shifted in his chair. "This woman you're going to meet is seventy years old. She's the most beautiful woman I've ever seen, bar none. I've watched her on TV. Her teeth aren't perfect, but she smiles like some sort of Eastern saint, whatever you call that."

"Kwan Yin," Peter offered.

"Yeah, maybe. Her name is Sandaji. Used to be Carolyn Lumley Pierce. She's from the Bay Area, started out as a New Age groupie, but I checked up on her, and she's been through hell and come out wiser. Amazing story. She's holding meditation seminars in Pasadena."

Joseph's voice became a low, assertive bellow. "I want you to drop a roll of money, ten thousand dollars in hundred-dollar bills, into her collection plate. Then ask her my question. Bring me the answer tomorrow morning."

Peter's errands for Joseph were varied and often peculiar, but he had never done anything like this. Peter was not fond of New Age types, followers or leaders. They had disappointed him.

"Directions. Loot." Joseph held out a folded piece of paper and a thick roll of money. "Don't tell Michelle. She's still mad at me for paying a quarter of a million dollars for a watch last week."

"Jesus," Peter said involuntarily.

"It's a good watch," Joseph said with petulance. He pulled back his sweater cuff to reveal a wide flash of platinum. "Maybe I'll will it to you when I die."

"I'm a humble man," Peter said.

"Well, Michelle's already in my face, so don't tell her how much this time, okay?"

"All right." He pocketed the money and the directions. The money pushed against the Trans.

Joseph shuddered. "Goddamn, it's cold in here. Peter, you look gloomy. Worse than me, and I feel like an old cabbage. What's up?"

"My friend died. A writer named Phil Richards."

"Sorry. Friends ... can't afford to lose them." Joseph's eyes moved beyond Peter to the far corner of the room. "Water out there somewhere, reflecting moonlight," he murmured. Peter looked up over his shoulder and saw a dim, milky flare play across the ceiling. Then it was gone.

"What should I ask her?" Peter asked.

"I've arranged for a private audience. You will absolutely not tell anyone else. I trust you, Peter ... but I want you to promise me anyway. Swear to me as much as one atheist can swear before another, all right?"

"Cross my heart, hope to die," Peter said.

Joseph seemed to accept this. He folded his hands in his lap like a schoolboy about to recite. Peter had never seen him so vulnerable. "Ask her if she believes it is possible for someone to live without a soul. Ask her in private, not in front of all those salivating white-collar geeks she cultivates."

"Someone, live, without a soul," Peter said.

"Don't mock me, Peter Russell." Joseph's voice was hard and clean. In the glow of the rising moon, his face was the color of an expensive knife.

"No disrespect, Mr. Benoliel," Peter said. "Just getting my lines straight."

"HE HAS BEEN such a *lemon* lately," Michelle said in the entry, holding the door. The veranda lights cast a dull golden glow over the stonework. "Please make him feel better."

"Isn't that your job?" Peter asked.

"You're short tonight," she observed.

"My best friend just died," Peter said.

"Oh, shit, really?" Michelle was shocked and saddened. On her face, the effect was of a curtain drawing open to a new play. She stood straight and let go of the door. "How much time do you have?" she asked. "Time for a drink?"

"You know I don't drink."

"A small glass of sherry for me, ginger ale for you," Michelle said with studied grace. "We'll toast your friend."

They went into the huge kitchen and Michelle sat Peter at the marble-topped counter. Only the counter lights were on and the rest of the kitchen fell back into olive-colored shadows. Peter felt as if he were under a spotlight. Michelle poured two glasses as described and sat at the corner next to him. "To your friend," she said, lifting her sherry.

"To Phil," Peter said, and felt his shoulders make a quaking motion. He sucked the ginger ale down wrong and started to choke. He used that to disguise the tears, and coughed until the impulse was almost gone.

Michelle gave him a napkin to wipe his eyes. "Want to talk about him?"

"I don't think there's time."

"Your appointment isn't for another hour and a half," Michelle said. "Was he famous?"

"Not really," Peter said. "He was a better writer than me. Maybe a better man."

"Do you still write?" Michelle asked.

"When I need the money," he said.

"I admire people who do something with their talents." Michelle put down her glass. "What did you think of Weinstein?"

"A hustler," Peter said. He reached into his pocket and took out the Trans. It slid smoothly past the roll of hundred-dollar bills. "Haven't tried it."

"Give me your number," Michelle said. "Weinstein left a box of them. I'll pick out a nice blue one."

"Do they even work?"

"Not in the house, apparently," Michelle said. "But I need to get outside more. Besides, Weinstein will pay you if we convince Joseph . . . won't he?"

Peter smiled ruefully, tilted his head, and nodded. He opened the unit and read her the number from the screen. It was odd, seven sets of two digits separated by hyphens.

Michelle wrote the number on a slip of paper. "See?" she said, and patted his hand. "I was hard up once. Cast adrift. I know how life goes. It isn't easy finding a safe harbor." She shook her hair and shoved out a hand toward the kitchen walls, as if to push them back. "I just get lost here. It's been thirteen years with Joseph, and I still haven't explored all the rooms." She shook her head. "Half aren't even furnished. I can do whatever I want with the houses, but it's just the two of us, and you, and the cleaning people once or twice a week. Joseph doesn't want servants living on the estate."

"It's quiet," Peter said.

"Very quiet," Michelle said. She took Peter's Trans and opened it. "Weinstein explained it to me a few days ago, before he spoke with Joseph," she said. "Is this the only one you have?"

"He gave me nine more," Peter said. "Should I throw them away?"

"No, no. Maybe it's the weather and they'll work inside the house later. We'll just spread them around. They're no use sitting in a box. Then I'll talk to Joseph again and try to convince him. For your sake, not Weinstein's."

Peter leaned forward. "I don't know what to say. You're treating me like a brother."

"You might as well be a brother," she said. "You know your boundaries. You give me more respect than my real brothers ever did. You understand that I have a tough job, but it's one I intend to stick with. We've seen a lot of the same old world, from different sides of the fence. And we both mean what we say."

"Wow," Peter said. "That's something I can, I don't know, cherish."

Michelle's lips twitched. "You're my project, Peter Russell." She sipped her sherry. "When you toast the dead," she said, "they feel comforted and don't bother you, and you have only good thoughts about them."

"You sound like an expert," Peter cracked.

Michelle smiled. "That's what my grandmother told me when I was a little girl. She was French, from Louisiana."

Peter took up his glass and they toasted Phil again.

"May he sleep tight," Michelle said.

CHAPTER 

JOSEPH'S MAP TOOK Peter into Pasadena and down a series of narrow streets. The summer evening air oozed through the half-open windows, filling the car with the green odors of juniper and eucalyptus cut by the sweetness of honeysuckle. Sticky jacaranda flowers filled the gutters with purple rivers. Old-fashioned street lamps dropped puddles of dim yellow light. He drove slowly, looking for a restored Greene and Greene home, a classic wood-frame bungalow with Japanese touches.

Can't miss it, Joseph had written on the map. *Numbers hidden. Guidebook says it's fronted by a huge river rock wall. Bamboo garden inside.*

JOSEPH AND PETER'S last picture together, in 1983, had been *Q.T., the Sextraterrestrial*, Peter's biggest budget production—half a million dollars. Too old-fashioned, the film had gone straight to late-night cable.

The hard-core porn revolution had punched heavy-gauge nails into Peter's film career. Whatever his morals, Peter had been more of a gentleman than his competitors. He had cared for his ladies. It had been tough watching them waltz off to shoot hard-core. Some had ended up sadly; others had become underground legends.

Movies had never left his thoughts, however, and in the early nineties, while visiting Benoliel to drum up support for a low-budget horror feature, Peter had discovered a new element in Flaubert House: Joseph's young wife. They had been married two months. Michelle had taken an immediate liking to Peter and had talked up his screenplay, but Joseph had refused to lay out good money for bad horror. Persistent almost to a fault, Michelle had asked Peter if he could do other work. Down to his last few hundred dollars, he had agreed.

Gruff, never easy to get along with, Joseph Adrian Benoliel could turn on the charm when he wanted to, but only if he needed something. Worth half a billion dollars, he rarely admitted to needing anything. Under Michelle's tutelage, Peter had become his more charming face.

"You're a gem, you know that?" she had told Peter at the beginning of his new role, as she had walked ahead of him, a slight, wiry figure in shorts and halter top, her lambent contralto and slapping zoreys echoing across the marble-lined entry of Flaubert House. "You won't believe the weirdoes trying to take advantage of Joseph. You're just what he needs."

For thirteen years now, Peter had toted, met with, dismissed, couriered, and kept mum. He had made more money from helping Joseph and Michelle than he had ever earned from his movies. In the end, Peter had become a decent factotum, fed his family, and acquired a loose sort of freedom from want.

Now he was locked in, wary of trying anything new, of making another wrong move and losing the last important things left in his life.

A fair number of people in LA now knew Peter only as Joseph's dogsbody.

So had ended his big dreams.

PETER SPOTTED A river rock wall nine feet high and thirty feet long, then found an open space across the street just big enough to fit the Porsche. Beside the wall, twin red cedar garage doors were illuminated by hyperbolas cast by jutting tin-saucer lights fitted with clear glass bulbs. Authenticity meant a lot in Pasadena.

He walked along the rock wall, knuckles brushing the jutting boulders, until he came to the cedar gate. Somewhere deep within the night behind the wall, chimes tinkled. A breeze stirred dry leaves and they made a sound like little hands rubbing together.

Peter found a small ivory button mounted in green bronze above the standard NO SOLICITORS sign and rechecked the description. Nothing else like it on the block. He pushed the button. Security lights switched on within the yard. Two minutes later, a thin woman of sixty or so peered through the gate with intense black eyes.

"Yes?" she said, leaning to look behind him.

"My name is Peter Russell. I'm here for a private meeting with Sandaji."

"Representing yourself?"

"No," Peter said.

"Who, then?"

"I was told to come here and you'd know everything you needed to know."

"Well, identification would certainly help," the woman said. Peter produced his driver's license. She held out a small flashlight and examined it with wrinkled brow. "You make a good picture," she said, and then stepped back. The gate pulled open on a metal track. To either side of a slate walkway, bamboo formed an undulating curtain, up to and around a stone lantern. Through the stalks, he could see a porch and dimly lit windows.

"Come in, Mr. Russell," the woman said. "My name is Jean Baslan. I'm Sandaji's personal assistant. She's very busy this time of year. We always love coming back to this house. A peaceful place." Her voice had a pleasant ululation to it, accompanied by a trace of Nordic accent.

Peter followed her up the winding walkway.

"We've cleared this hour for you," Jean Baslan said. "If you plan on taking less time, please let us know. Have you met Sandaji?"

Peter said he had not.

Baslan smiled. "You have a treat in store, Mr. Russell. We're all totally devoted to her." With a gentle wave, she guided him through the front door into the living room. Dark wood and exquisite built-in cabinetry set off antique furniture and handwoven oriental carpets. Tiffany lamps sat contented and elegant on long tables of solid bird's-eye maple. Peter recognized Morris chairs that looked genuine, and the books within the glass cases were rich and interesting: leather-bound sets of Voltaire, Trollope, Dickens. He wondered what kind of women had lived in this house when it was first built: no doubt lovely, their dresses ankle-length, stepping like young deer with charming hesitations and subtle glances. He could almost smell their perfume.

"We're here to help needy people," Jean Baslan said, "people living in pain and confusion, who desperately need Sandaji's message of hope. What sort of question did your friend, your employer, have?"

"Well," Peter said, "it's private."

"Is he elderly?"

"In his seventies," he said.

"A friend as well as an employer?"

Peter tilted his head to the left. "We respect each other," he said.

"Is he married?"

Peter smiled. "Mostly I run errands and take meetings. That sort of thing."

"How intriguing . . ." She lifted her hand. "Sandaji will know what to tell him, I'm sure."

They had passed through a dining room and into the rear portion of the house. He saw a sleeping porch with two women sitting in warm darkness on wicker chairs. Their eyes glinted at him as he passed. For a moment, he half imagined them in long silken dresses. The effect was at once charming and disconcerting.

"You know what our greatest difficulty is?" Baslan asked. "Discouraging proposals. For marriage, you know. The men who come to Sandaji find her so comforting. But then, she is beautiful, very much so, and that confuses many."

Peter said he was looking forward to meeting her. Personally, however, he had never found age much of an aphrodisiac.

The house was a work in progress and in these back rooms, it looked more like a middle-class grandma lived here than a very rich aunt. Past the dining room, tables, couches, and chairs were not antiques. The jambs and rafters still supported decades of paint, rather than being stripped to native wood as in the restored sections.

The first thing Peter noticed as Jean Baslan opened the last door was the scent of freshly crushed herbs: thyme, rosemary, and then spearmint. *Aromatherapy,* he thought. *Oh, goodie.*

Sandaji was pressing her dark velvet gown down over her hips, having apparently just stood up from a plain wooden chair. Peter saw her first, and then the room she was in. Later, trying to remember the room, he would be hard-pressed to describe what was in it. The rest of the house remained clear, but from this moment, all he truly remembered was the woman. She stood six feet tall, hair a gray curly fountain tamed by clips and a ribbon to flow down her back. The black gown she wore ended at mid-ankle and she was barefoot, her feet bony but well formed, like the rest of her; hips protruding, though she was not excessively thin, roll of tummy pronounced but not obtrusive, faint nubs on not particularly small breasts. As Peter's eye moved from bare feet to shoulders, he received the impression of a willowy college girl, and then Sandaji turned her head to face him, and he saw the mature woman, well past her fifties but surely not in her seventies, observant eyes relaxed in a face lightly but precisely seamed by a subset of whole-life experiences. Her lips, still imbued with natural color and utterly lacking in lipstick, bowed into a knowing Shirley Temple smile. She seemed wise but mischievous, awaiting a cherished playmate, inviting speculation that she might be won over to a deeper friendship; his eyes moved down in reappraisal. The black gown covered a trim, healthy body, promising rewards beyond the spiritual. She enjoyed his appreciation.

Peter had met many beautiful women. He knew what they expected, the charming dictates they imposed on all their unequal relationships. Somehow, however, he did not think his experience would be much help with Sandaji.

"This is Peter Russell," Jean Baslan announced. "Representing Mr. Joseph Adrian Benoliel."

Sandaji narrowed her eyes like a cat settling in for a coze. "How is Mr. Benoliel?" she asked, and looked back at the table. "It's a pity we will not meet this evening. I understand he has a question."

"He does," Peter said.

Sandaji looked around the room, pink tongue tipping between her lips. "That's a good seat," she said, and pointed to the forest-green couch against the wall, beyond the glass-topped table, all of which Peter now noticed. "Please feel at ease."

"I'll leave you two alone for a few minutes," Jean Baslan announced with a wink, as if she were a liberal-minded duenna leaving her charge in the trust of a gentleman. She closed the door behind her.

Peter sat on the green couch, knees spread comfortably, and rested his big, dry hands on them; an easy workman's way of sitting, not a gentleman's, and for once, he was acutely aware of the difference. Sandaji pressed her gown again with a downward stroke of her hand and returned to the plain wooden chair. She sat straight and with knees together, not as if manner dictated, but equally in comfort. Her long fingers continued to shape precise smoothing motions, drawing the clinging velvet down an inch as she made a small contraction in the corner of her mouth. Human, that contraction said; no matter what else you see or feel, I am merely human.

Peter was not so sure. He could not take his eyes off her. She seemed utterly at peace. Her eyes remained fixed on his.

"I do odd jobs for Mr. Benoliel," Peter said. "He told me to come here."

Sandaji obviously appreciated the effect she had on men and probably on other women, but it did not in the final balance seem to mean a lot to her. She raised her brows with an expression that said, *how nice.* "There's so much pain to be soothed, so much confusion to be guided into useful energy." Her voice was tuned like a cello. Peter could imagine himself swimming in that voice.

"I'm sure," he said. Then, without willing it, he added, "My best friend died today."

Sandaji leaned forward and she held her breath for an instant before exhaling delicately through her nose. "I am so sorry to hear that," she said.

"He was a writer, like me," Peter added.

"You both have qualities," Sandaji said. "You are valued, that I can see. So many people—women in particular, I think—have placed an astonishing faith in you. That is something special, Peter."

"Thank you. I like women," he said. "They seem to like me. And around me, well ... I can't ..." He could not stop talking. Embarrassing. His hands clutched his knees.

"I understand," Sandaji said. "I commit only to my work now. That confuses some who need the kind of love we can't afford to give, for different reasons."

Peter chuckled uncomfortably. "Well, it isn't because I'm successful and devoted to my work."

"No?"

"More like I've never grown up."

"There's a charm in youth, and a sting," Sandaji said. "We let go of youth for a great price. Life does not offer the price to all."

Ah, Peter thought, and felt a measure of control return. *I'm getting her range. She's very good, but she is not impenetrable. Still, she is very good.* "Sorry. That just slipped out. I'm not here to talk about me."

"I see."

"My employer has a question."

"We have time."

"Michelle told me that earlier. Mrs. Benoliel."

A wrinkle formed between Sandaji's pale brows. "She worries for her husband."

"All rich wives worry," Peter said, feeling defensive now and not because of the implied analysis of Michelle. He could feel the spotlight of Sandaji's attention moving around his personal landscape, touching points he might not want illuminated.

She looked to his left, then leaned back in the chair. "Your daughter," she said, and the wrinkle between her brows deepened.

Peter stiffened until his neck hurt. "I didn't ask about my daughter," he said.

Sandaji opened and closed her hands, then folded them on her lap, dimpling the black velvet. She seemed agitated. "I assure you, I'm not a psychic, Mr. Russell."

"I'm here on Mr. Benoliel's behalf. Why bring up my daughter?"

"Please ask ... your question." She looked up at the ceiling, frowning self-critically. "I'm so sorry. I did not mean to intrude. Please forgive me."

Peter looked up as well. Light flickered there, as if reflecting from a pool of water somewhere in the room.

Sandaji moved—jerked, actually, as if startled—and the light vanished.

That, and mention of his daughter, and Sandaji's unexpected discomfiture, made Peter nervous. The house was no longer welcoming and Sandaji's enchantment had evaporated. She suddenly looked fragile, like chipped china.

It was time to get this charade over with.

"Please," Sandaji insisted. "The question."

"Mr. Benoliel asks if a man can live without a soul."

She dropped her gaze to look over his shoulder, then slowly returned her focus to Peter. "He asks if *a man* ..." The wrinkle between her brows became a dark valley. She was starting to look all of her years, and more. "Live without a soul?"

"No," Peter corrected himself, getting flustered. "He said 'someone,' actually. Not 'a man,' but 'someone.' "

"Of course," Sandaji said, as if it were the most obvious question in the world. Peter blinked. For an instant, a shadow seemed to fill the room, sweeping across walls and ceiling and then hiding behind the furniture.

Sandaji appeared shocked and frightened. She stopped smoothing her gown. "I beg your pardon," she said. "I did not expect ... I am not feeling well. Could you call my assistant?"

Peter started to get up from the couch. Before he could reach for her, she slumped forward like a dying ballerina. Her hands fell limp against the worn oriental carpet. A copper bracelet dropped and lodged around her wrist. Her gray hair slipped and pooled. Peter kneeled, decided it would not be wise to touch her—she appeared stunned, half conscious.

He shouted, "Help!"

Jean Baslan entered with a prim, pale look and together they lifted Sandaji back into the chair. "No, this isn't very comfortable," Baslan observed, her face a tight mask of concern. They picked the woman up by her arms and helped her to the couch, where she lay back gracefully enough, skin waxy and hair in disarray.

"Of course," Sandaji said as she opened her eyes.

"What happened?" Baslan asked Peter.

"She just spoke a few words and fell over," Peter said. "She must have fainted."

"I saw *her*," Sandaji said. She angled her head to stare straight-on at Peter. Her green eyes were intense. "I am not a psychic," she repeated. "I do *not* have visions."

"Did you slip her something?" Baslan accused Peter. "In her water?"

"Water? No, of course not," he insisted to her steady glare.

"Did you see *her*?" Sandaji asked. Both women stared at Peter.

"There was a reflection," he said. "That's all I saw."

"It's time for you to leave, Mr. Russell," Baslan said.

Sandaji made an effort and sat up. "I'm so sorry. This has never happened before. I'm usually a strong, healthy woman." She tried to resume control, but it was a poor effort.

"Let's go," Baslan insisted to Peter. She took his arm and started to drag him away.

"No, his question," Sandaji said.

"It can wait," Baslan said. Peter nodded, eager to get out of the house, away from this nonsense. He wondered how much was being staged. It would not have taken much digging to find out about his children. A good conjurer or medium was always prepared.

"No, it's a good question. I should answer." Sandaji sat upright on the couch and took a deep breath. She lifted her shoulders and arched her neck, then slowly let out her breath. She looked at them with renewed deliberation and her voice resumed its rich cello intonation. "Many live on without souls," she said. "They are intense in a way most cannot understand. They are driven and hungry, but they are empty. There is nothing you or I can do for them. Even should they try for enlightenment, they are like anchorless ships in a storm." Her lips moved without sound for a moment, as if practicing a line, then she concluded, "A curious question, but strangely important. My beloved guru once spoke long on the subject, but you're the first who has ever asked me. And now I wonder why."

"It was the wrong question." Baslan glared at Peter.

"I am feeling much better," Sandaji said, attempting to stand. She fell back again with an expression of mild disgust. "I am so sorry, Mr. Russell."

"You have your answer," Baslan insisted.

"We are polite, Jean," Sandaji remonstrated softly. "But I *am* tired. And the evening started so well. I think I should go to bed."

Baslan brusquely escorted Peter to the front door. "The gate will open automatically," she said, her face still tight and eyes narrowed, like a mother cat protecting kittens.

Peter walked onto the porch and down the steps, then turned and looked back as the door closed. He stood there for a moment, the anxiety returning, and the shortness of breath. For an instant, he thought he saw something dark in the bamboo, like an undulating serpent. Then it was gone; a trick of light.

He reached into his pocket and felt the smooth plastic phone—Trans, he corrected—and the roll of hundred-dollar bills.

The donation.

For a moment, he thought of just walking on and pocketing the money. Otherwise, what a waste. He could pay a lot of bills with ten grand, Helen's bills in particular. Lindsey was starting school soon. She needed clothes. He would tell Joseph and Michelle that Sandaji's people were lying, that he had given Baslan the money.

But he had never stolen money in his life. Not since he had been a little boy, at any rate, lifting coins from his mother's change bowl. And he was not a good liar. Perhaps for that reason, he had always hated liars and thieves.

His feet again made soft cupping noises on the porch's solid wood. He knocked.

Baslan swiftly opened the door.

"How is she?" he asked.

"Some better," she said tersely. "She's gone upstairs to rest."

"I asked her a question on behalf of Mr. Benoliel. I got an answer. That's why I came here. No other reason. Anything like a personal *reading* was uncalled for. You do her research, no doubt. I resent you telling her about Daniella. I just wanted you to know."

He held out the roll of money. Baslan, her face coloring to a pale grape, took it with an instinctive dip of her hand. "I do not do *research*," she snapped. "I told her nothing. Sandaji does not do readings or communicate with spirits. We don't even *know* you, Mr. Russell." She bobbed left to put the money aside. He heard the clinking of a jar or ceramic pot. "We are not charlatans. You can leave now."

With Baslan out of the doorway, Peter had a clear view through an arch to the dining room, about thirty feet from the porch. A little boy in a frilled shirt and knee stockings stood there. He looked sick; not sick, dead; worse than dead, unreal, unraveling. His face turned in Peter's direction, skin as pale and cold as skim milk. The head seemed jointed like a doll's. The grayish eyes saw right through him, and suddenly the outline blurred, precisely as if the boy had fallen out of focus in a camera viewfinder.

Peter's eyes burned.

Baslan straightened. She gripped the edge of the door and asked sharply, "Do you need a receipt?"

Peter's neck hair was bristling. He shook his head and removed his glasses as if to clean them.

"Then good night."

When he did not move, Baslan looked on with agitated concern and added, "We're done, aren't we?" She prepared to close the door. Her motion again revealed the arch and the dining room. The boy was no longer visible. He couldn't have moved out of the way, not without being seen.

He simply wasn't there. Perhaps he had never been there at all.

Baslan closed the door in Peter's face with a solid *clunk*.

Peter stood on the porch, dazed, face hot, like a kid reacting to an unkind trick. He slowly forced his fists to open. "This is crap," he murmured, replacing his glasses. He had not wanted to come here in the first place. He walked quickly down the steps and along the winding stone path between the bamboo to the gate. The scuff of his shoes echoed from the stone wall to his left. The gate whirred open, expelling him from the house, the grounds: an unwanted disturber of the peace.

On the street, he wiped his forehead with a handkerchief, then opened the car door and sat. He started the car, listening to the soothing, familiar whine, and tried to recall the answer Sandaji had given to Joseph's question; despite everything, it remained clear in his head. He repeated her words several times, committing them to memory before putting the Porsche in gear.

Slowly his breath returned and the muscle binding in his chest smoothed. The back of his eyes still felt tropical, however, as if they were discharging a moist heat into his skull.

They were charlatans after all. Why go through that awful charade in the back room, then trot out a little boy in a Buster Brown outfit? Both had been stunts to gull the shills, trick the unwary into asking more questions, paying more money. That was as reasonable an explanation as any.

PETER WAS HAPPY to leave Pasadena. His thick, powerful hands clasped the wheel so tightly that he had to flex his fingers. "Ah, Christ!" he shouted in disgust once again at all things New Age and mystical. There was life and this Earth and all the sensual pleasures you could reasonably grab, and then there was nothing. Live and get out of it what you could. Leave the rest alone. That other sort of madness could kill you.

Then why did I reach out for Phil?

Driving alone, his work done, the traffic on the 210 blessedly easy for this time of night, going back to his home in the hills, he pictured Phil's rueful, ingratiating smile. On the highway, his tears flowed. His shoulders shook.

And a pretty little girl in a blue sweater, pink shorts, and a tank top. Don't forget her. Ever.

The loss and the old, much-hated self-pity just piled up and spilled. It was all he could do not to break into a mourning howl.

All he could do, almost, not to spin the wheel and drive right off the freeway.

CHAPTER 4

PETER ROLLED OVER in the tangled sheets and opened his eyes to an out-of-focus bedscape. He blinked at a blur of satin trim coming loose from his brown wool blanket, then rubbed his eyes and closely observed another blur spotted with white: a rumpled pillow leaking feathers through its seams. He was still half asleep.

His hand fumbled on the bed stand for his glasses.

A shaft of sun fell across one corner of the room from the skylight, reflected from the full-length mirror, and beamed over the space beside his bed. He made out dust motes in the beam. The motes danced with a puff of his breath.

Nice to just sink, let sleep win. His head fell back onto the pillow.

Eyes closed. Delicious blankness.

Birds sang in the backyard.

He opened his eyes again, arm twitching. The beam had shifted and the dust motes were swirling like spoiled cream in coffee. As he watched, bleary, they took a sort of elongated shape. He thought he could make out two legs and an arm. Small. The arm lengthened, adding a hand-shaped eddy. A face was about to form when he opened his eyes wide and said, bemused, "All right. I'm waking up now." He leaned over and waved his arms through the sunbeam. The motes dissipated wildly.

His jaw hurt. He was a mess and he stank. He got out of bed and straightened, hooking a temple piece around one ear.

The night had been disjointed, filled with scattered flakes of dream, memories drawn up from a deep sea like fish in a net. The dreams had all possessed a jagged, surreal quality, as if scripted by restless demons, pent up for too long.

"Art, sperm, and sanity don't keep," Peter said to the face in the mirror.

He thought about that for a moment, then padded into the bathroom to turn the hot-water tap for a shower. The old white tile in the stall was cracked and creased with mildew. The room smelled of moisture. It was a good thing the air up in the hills was dry or the floor would have rotted out a long time ago.

As he dressed, his clothes became a kind of armor, like blankets wrapped tight around a child's eyes. The waking world was filled with traps designed to make him feel bad and he did not want to feel bad anymore.

He stepped into old slippers and shuffled into the kitchen to make coffee in a French press, the only way he liked it. As he pushed the red plastic plunger down through the grounds, a bell-like tone came from the living room, not his house phone and certainly not his cell phone, both of which sounded like amorous insects. He finished the plunger push and went to look. Big throw pillows in Persian patterns covered an old beige couch. Two graceful sixties chairs made of parabolas of steel wire and slung with purple canvas supported massive green pillows, like alien hands offering mints. The big front window looked out over a garden left to itself the last nine months, and doing fairly well without Peter's attention. Jasmine and honeysuckle vied with Helen's old rosebushes to scent the air, and the splashes of red and yellow and pink in the late-morning sun were cheerful enough.

The bell toned again. He peered back through the now-contrasty and dark spaces of the living room. Then he remembered. He had left the box of Trans on the table by the French doors. He had also carried one with him into Sandaji's house in Pasadena.

He opened the door, stepped out across the brick pavers to the upright oil drum closet, and fished out his coat. The unit was still in the coat pocket. He opened it and the display lit up at his touch.

"Hello?" he said into the tiny grill.

"Peter, it's Michelle. Seven rings. Hope I didn't wake you."

"Just getting cleaned up."

"Good. Weinstein left a map. It led me to ten more phones in a box hidden behind the couch. Is that cute, or what?"

"Pretty cute," Peter said.

"So I have fourteen phones now. I was trying to remember which one you put in your pocket. Did I dial the right number?"

"You probably didn't *dial* anything," Peter said, looking at the circle of shaded graphic lozenges on the touch screen, numbered from zero to twelve.

"Yeah, right. Smartass. Well, I'm standing outside the house, on the drive. It seems to work out here."

"Great," Peter said, longing for coffee.

"Joseph's curious to hear what that woman told you."

"I could come over now," Peter said, hoping his sincerity sounded thin.

"He's taking hydrotherapy. How about noon? He'll be ready by then and relaxed, and besides, you know that noon is the best time of his day."

"I'll be there," Peter said, and stifled a small urge to say, *I's a-comin', with bells on.*

"Are you glad to hear the phone works?"

"Trans," Peter corrected. "Delighted. I'll tell what's-his-name."

"Weinstein. No, I'll tell him, once I convince Joseph. And I'll tell him *you* convinced me."

Peter was picking the other units out of their box, just to give his hands something to do. Each was a different color: opalescent black, dark blue, red, a trendy metallic auburn, and the one he held, dark metallic green. They looked like props in a science fiction film. Something from the parts catalog in *This Island Earth.*

"It's our little conspiracy," Michelle said. "Besides, it won't hurt you or me to help Joseph make another pot of money."

What few telecom stocks Peter had owned had gone south long ago, leaving his retirement scheme in a shambles. "Never mind," Peter said. "I'll talk to Weinstein when the time comes."

"If you insist. Noon, then. How do you end a call with this thing?"

"Shut the cover," Peter suggested.

"Right."

A click, then silence. Peter pulled the unit away, then raised it to his ear again. The quiet in the room seemed to deepen. He tried the other ear. Same thing.

Actually, he *was* impressed. He had never heard voices so clearly on a phone. Michelle could have been right there in the house.

Maybe Weinstein was on the up-and-up.

* * *

AS HE DRANK coffee and ate a bowl of Trix, Peter opened up the green Trans on the counter and punched the single button marked "Help" below the circle of numbers.

Welcome to Trans, the display said. The message scrolled across, then shrank to fill the touch screen, with arrows pointing left and right at the bottom.

Trans has voice recognition. Ask a simple question or say a key word.

"Dial," Peter said in a monotone. He had worked with computers enough to know the drill: Talk like a robot and the unit might understand.

Would you like to dial a number?

"How do I dial?" Peter asked.

Trans works with a base-12 number system: 10, 11, and 12 are treated as integers. Every Trans unit has an individual identification number seven integers long. There are no area codes or country codes. To communicate with another user, dial the ID number of the unit you wish to connect to. Remember, a hyphen before 10, 11, or 12 means you should push one of those buttons rather than entering the component numbers (1 or 0 or 2) on separate buttons. Trans is base-12!

Peter made a *hmph* face and wondered if anyone other than computer geeks would ever catch on to that. "What's my number?" he asked.

The number of your Trans unit is -10-1-0-7-12-3-4. Your unit has been used once to receive one call. You have not yet made any outgoing calls. Please use Trans as often as you wish to place a call anywhere on Earth. Don't be shy! There are no extra charges with Trans.

"My own personal Interociter," Peter murmured, lifting the unit and looking at it from above and below. There were no holes for a recharging plug or an earphone. Except for the top of the case, the unit was seamless.

The Soleri bells gonged loudly outside the front door. Still in his robe, Peter marched across the slate floor to the door and peeked through a clear section of glass. Hank Wuorinos—thirty-one, buff, his close-cut gelled hair standing up like a patch of bleached Astroturf—stood on the patio. He reached out one tattooed hand to play with a drooping branch of jasmine. Peter undid the locks and opened the doors.

"Hey!" Wuorinos greeted. "I'm on a flick, a Jack Bishop film. I'm off to Prague. Wish me luck."

"Congratulations," Peter said, and stood back to let him in. Hank had gotten a start as a teenager handling lighting for some of Peter's more decorous and ornate model shoots. The girls had nicknamed him Worny, which he had hated but tolerated, from them. Now he was a full-bore professional, IATSE card and all.

"Got some coffee?" Hank asked.

"Half a cup. I can make more."

"Beggars can't be choosers." Hank followed Peter into the kitchen. He poured himself what was left from the French press and filled it to the brim with milk, then slugged most of it down with one gulp. "I've never been to Europe. Any advice?"

"I've never been to Prague," Peter said.

"I hear it's fatal sensuous. Beautiful women eager to get the hell out of Eastern Europe."

"Look out for yourself," Peter advised with some envy.

Hank waggled his extended pinky and thumb. "No worse than your average day at Peter Russell's house."

"Did Lydia tell you about Phil?"

Hank's smile faded. "No . . . what?"

"He died yesterday."

Hank was too young to know what to say, to feel, or to actually believe. "Jesus. How?"

"Heart attack or stroke."

Death was new to Hank. He tried to find something appropriate, some sentiment, and his face worked through a range of trial emotions for several seconds. "You going to the funeral?"

"I haven't heard about a funeral yet," Peter said.

"Lydia will want one," Hank said with assurance. "Or at least a wake. But I'm leaving tomorrow. I won't be able to come . . . I could . . ."

Phil had introduced Peter and Hank. Hank had stayed with Phil and Lydia for a few weeks as a teenager. It had been a seminal moment for Hank Wuorinos, young runaway from Ames, Iowa. Lydia had probably shoplifted Hank's virginity. Phil had never much held it against Hank. Lydia was what she was. A real Hollywood career, after such an introduction to Los Angeles, was a sign of persistence and genuine talent.

"Go to work," Peter said. "Phil would understand."

"Besides, I couldn't face Lydia," Hank said.

"She'd want you to stay over and console her," Peter said.

"Shit," Hank said, crestfallen. "She would. You know she would."

Peter held up the cardboard box. "You'll need one of these to keep in touch," he said. "Take your pick."

Hank peered. "What are they, Japanese Easter eggs?"

"They're called Trans. They're like cell phones but they're free. You'll love them. They use a base-12 number system."

"Wow! They actually work?"

"I just took a call on one."

Hank picked the red unit and twisted it with delight in his hands. Hank's dark emotions were wonderfully transient. He had a job, he was about to see the world, and that easily trumped the death of poor, hapless Phil.

"No long-distance charges?"

"Not so far. They're demos."

"Let's try."

Peter indulged him. Just being around Hank cheered him. Peter showed him the help button and they took down the numbers of all the phones on two pieces of paper. Then they tried calling the different units from various rooms in the house, like boys with cans on strings. The sound was crystal clear. Hank was thrilled.

"They are so *cool*," he said. "They're like Interociters."

"That's what I thought," Peter said.

"How many can I have?"

Peter overcame an odd twinge of greed. "Take two," he said. "One for your girlfriend."

"I don't have a girlfriend," Hank said seriously, "but I will find one in Prague. I've been reading Kafka just to get in the mood. The tourist brochures say Prague is supposed to be the most haunted city in Europe. City of ghosts. A church made of bones. That's what the DP told me. Who ya gonna call?" The dark emotions returned and Hank picked up his cup of coffee in a toast. "To Phil. Is this what it's like to get old, your friends start dying?"

"Something like that," Peter said.

AFTER HANK LEFT, Peter checked his answering machine in the kitchen. A red 1 flashed on the display. He rolled back the tape—it was a very old unit, he seldom bought new appliances—and listened.

It was Lydia. She had a voice like the young Joanne Woodward, honey and silk and baby's breath. She told him she was already in Marin—she had taken the train—and she had finalized arrangements. She said she would be at Phil's house and gave his address and phone number. The wake would be late tomorrow. "No funeral. Phil wanted to be cremated. Just a few friends, mostly from the time we were married."

He listened to the message again. Double whammy: Lydia had used a phone, and Phil had a house in Marin.

"Who'd of thunk it?" Peter asked. His voice sounded childish, even petulant, as if he were resentful that Phil had kept secrets. Phil had kept secrets from his best friend and then ditched him.

He went to pack his bag.

CHAPTER 

JOSEPH STRETCHED OUT on a lounge chair with a florid towel spread over his legs. He listened to Peter's report with a gray, still face. Not even the sun shining through the sunhouse glass over the pool could improve his pallor. He looked impassive, like an old king who has seen and done it all.

When Peter finished, Joseph started to tap his thumb on his draped knee. Peter did not tell the rest of the story. He still had not made any sense of that part of the night's events.

"Sandaji took my money?" Joseph asked.

"Her assistant did," Peter said.

"All God's children need money," Joseph said with yielding disappointment. Peter had never heard such a tone of defeat coming from the man.

"Actually, I forgot to hand it over and had to go back," Peter said. "I thought about just keeping it." Sometimes Joseph was cheered by confessions of human greed and weakness.

"I would have," Joseph said. "What did she mean by that answer?"

Peter shrugged. "I'm not much on this soul business, you know that."

"I didn't used to be. I'm giving it some real thought."

"We're getting old," Peter sympathized.

"Hell, you can still jog around the house and fuck when you want. For me, just going to the bathroom is a thrill."

"Bull," Peter said, shading his eyes.

"Yeah," Joseph said. "Old man bullshit. I can still get it up, but I don't know that I want to anymore."

They sat for a minute.

"I've led a wicked life, Peter," Joseph said. "I've hurt people. Messed around and messed up every which way. Despite it all, here I am with the sun and the sea and the hills and the cool night breezes, living on twenty acres of paradise. Makes you think. What's the downside? Where's the comeuppance?"

Peter left that one alone. He was not in the mood for discussing ultimates.

"Where do we all *go*?" Joseph asked in a husky whisper.

"I'm going to Marin," Peter said. "To a wake. That's sober enough, isn't it?"

"Was your friend a good man?"

Peter shrugged. "A better man than me, Gunga Din."

Joseph cracked a dry smile. "Was he your water bearer?"

"He saved my life when I was at the end of my tether. And he braved many an insult for a chance to peer at the ladies."

"Sounds like he had at least one good friend," Joseph said, softening. Right before his eyes, Peter thought, the sun was melting this chilly man with the gray face. The sun and the thought of a wake.

"You'd *love* what I saw last night," Joseph said, apropos of nothing. He stared at the horizon, the hazy blue sea beyond the grass and hills. "Do you believe in spooks, Peter?"

"You know I don't."

"I hope I never see them again."

Peter shivered involuntarily. He did not like this.

Another silence.

Joseph grimaced as if experiencing a stomach pain and waved his hand. "I'll tell Michelle to give you a five-hundred-dollar bonus. Come say howdy when you're back."

Peter prepared to leave. Joseph spoke out from across the pool. "Michelle tells me those damn plastic thingies actually work. She's passing them around to her friends. Maybe I booted that whelp son of a bitch too early."

Joseph waved his hand again. All was square.

* * *

MICHELLE WAS UNUSUALLY quiet as she handed Peter five hundred dollars in cash in the foyer. It was eleven o'clock. The whole damned house felt sad, Peter thought.

"When are you going to use a checking account?" she bugged him, a favorite topic. Peter had cut up all his credit cards and never carried a checkbook. He had a small savings account and that was it. He was now strictly cash-and-carry, paying his bills in person when he could, and having Helen write his tax and other checks when he visited to make child-care payments.

"When I deserve to be a yuppie again," he answered.

"You can be such a *pill*," Michelle said.

As he left, she gave him a quick peck on the cheek and a friendly pat on the buns and wished him a good trip to Marin. "Don't let it get you down," she warned.

Peter had already put his bags in the Porsche. He descended the winding road to Pacific Coast Highway and turned left into light traffic. He had had his share and more of grief, of unbearable loss and hopeful speculation. After his lowest moment, when manic anguish and drink had almost killed him, he had come down firmly on the side of teetotaling skepticism. Put on armor, wrapped himself in blankets.

Now, for reasons he could not fathom, people were trying to poke him through the blankets. First Sandaji, and now Joseph.

"Blow it off," he suggested. Then he glanced in the rear-view mirror, looking into eyes made cynical by the rush of warm air. He puffed his upper lip into a feline pout and said "Spooks" several times, mimicking Bert Lahr's Cowardly Lion in the forest of Oz.

Fifty miles north of the Grapevine, driving north on 5, lulled by the road, he felt an oddly comforting, bluntly selective silence fill the Porsche. He could still hear the slipstream, the whine of the engine, the rumble of tires on the grooved freeway. Still, the silence was there. Sometimes that happened. He would be in a quiet room and the ambient noise would flicker, replaced by a distant, high-pitched hum that faded slowly into a new silence. He remembered listening to the whine of the air as a boy, back when his ears had been far more sensitive.

He instinctively patted his pocket and felt the green Trans.

His thoughts wandered as the traffic grew sparse and the freeway straight and monotonous. Someday, he mused, before all passion was spent, in this world of high-tech communications, his own final true love would call him and her voice would rise above the ambient noise of all the other women. That was Peter's one supernatural quest now: the perfect woman, a beauty who watched him with cool amusement from behind his thoughts and memories, elusive and brazenly sexy.

Peter had met only one woman that came close to that impossible ideal, a model and sometime actress named Sascha Lauten. Buxom, smart, cheerfully supportive, Sascha had been sufficiently vulnerable and sad about her life to make his heart puddle. Phil had warned him about Sascha. "She sees right through you," he had said. "Your charms do not soothe her magnificent breasts." Sascha had ultimately turned down his proposal and married a skinny-assed salesman with bad skin. They now lived quietly in Compton.

He stuck his hand through the half-open window to feel the speed. Over the wind he sang, "I hate this crap, burn up the road, I hate this *shit*, burn up the ROAD."

CHAPTER 

PETER CROSSED THE Golden Gate Bridge at midnight and climbed the long hill into Marin before turning inland. Somehow, he missed a turn. Sitting at a gas station, he used the Trans to call Lydia. When she answered, her voice was like a little girl's. She gave Peter the final directions to Phil's house in Tiburon. "The place is filled with boxes," Lydia said. "God, was he a pack rat."

Peter was tired. He thanked Lydia and closed the Trans. He had long wondered where Phil had stuck all the books and old magazines and movies that he had bought over the decades. Apparently, for some years Phil had been hauling his worldly goods north in the Grand Taiga, following through on a long-planned final escape from Los Angeles. And he had not told Peter about any of it.

The last few miles he followed a winding, dark road beneath a black sky dusted with ten thousand diamonds. Shadowy grassland and expensive houses flanked the road. Beyond lay more hunched hills. When he found the last turn, onto a cul-de-sac called Hidden Dreams Drive, he looked south and saw San Francisco lit up like a happy carnival on the far shore of the Bay.

The house cut three long, inky rectangles out of the starry sky between silhouettes of knobby, pruned-back trees. Peter drove up beside a new-style VW Beetle. As he set the parking brake, he saw Lydia sitting on a front porch swing, short, bobbed hair like a dark comma over her pale face. The orange bead of a cigarette dangled from her hand. She did not wave.

Jesus, Peter thought. *The lot alone must be worth a million dollars.* He stood on the gravel at the bottom of two wooden steps. "Nice night," he said.

"I'm not staying," Lydia announced. She got up from the porch swing and stubbed the cigarette into a tuna can. Then she tossed the butt into the darkness. Peter jerked, thinking she might start a fire or something. But that was Lydia.

"Should I go in?" Peter said.

"Up to you. He'd probably want you to," Lydia said dryly, "just to sort through his stuff. Last hands pawing what he wanted most on this Earth. He sure didn't love his ladies worth a damn."

Peter did not rise to the bait. Lydia stretched. At forty-eight, she still had a pruny grace. Low body-fat since youth—and wrinkles from smoking—had diminished her other native charms, but the grace remained.

Peter hauled his one suitcase onto the porch. She handed over three keys on a piece of dirty twine. The twine was tied to a small piece of finger-oiled driftwood. The driftwood dangled below his hand, swinging one way, then another.

"The medical examiner found my address in Phil's little black book," Lydia said. "Some cops came to visit me. They said he had been dead for a couple of days." She opened the screen door for him. "Did you know he had this place?"

Peter shook his head and entered the dark hallway. He set down his suitcase.

"He sure as hell didn't tell me," Lydia went on. "It didn't turn up on the divorce settlement. What do you think it's worth?"

"I have no idea," Peter said.

"Ancient history," Lydia said. "Anyway, I got him into a crematorium in Oakland. I think maybe the mailman found him. He had been dead for a few days."

"You said that," Peter said, grimacing.

"The mortuary will bring him back tomorrow. Hand delivery. We'll hold the wake in the backyard. I've invited some folks who knew Phil. And some of my friends. For backup."

"When did you get up here?" Peter asked.

"This morning. I left everything the way I found it. Peter, I hope you understood him. I hope somebody understood Phil. I sure didn't."

Peter did not know what to say to that.

"You know, despite everything, he was the sweetest guy I ever met," Lydia said. She poked Peter in the chest. "And that includes you. See you tomorrow around one. If they deliver Phil early, just put him on the mantel over the fireplace. And, oh . . ." She held out her hand. "I have no idea where he kept his money. I paid for everything. Donations cheerfully accepted."

Peter removed his wallet. He pulled out the five hundred dollars Michelle had given him in Malibu. He was about to peel off several of the bills when Lydia dipped her hand with serpentine grace and snatched the whole wad.

She counted it quickly. "That doesn't cover even half the cost," she said. She patted his bearded cheek. "But thanks." She walked across the gravel to the VW, her bony, denimed hips cycling a sideways figure 8.

The car vanished into the dark beneath the stars.

That left Peter with ten dollars, not enough to pay for the gas to get home.

CHAPTER 

THE HOUSE WAS quiet and still. Outside, not a breath of air moved. A hallway beyond the alcove led past the living room, a bathroom, and the kitchen, to three rooms at the back.

He switched on the lights in the alcove and the hall and stepped around two neatly taped boxes Magic-Markered with names and dates: *UNKNOWN WORLDS 1940–43, STARTLING MYSTERY 1950–56.* Handmade pine shelves filled with paperback mysteries and science fiction covered the wall behind the door, arched over the door, around the corner, and into the living room, where more shelves framed the wide front window. Beneath the window, records and old laser discs occupied a single shelf. He could make out still more shelves marching back into the shadows of a dining room, and stacked boxes where a table might have been.

In the living room, a single threadbare couch faced a scarred coffee table and the wide window. The coffee table, seen from above, had the outline of a plumped square, like the tube of an old black-and-white television set. In the fifties, those conjoined curves had been the shape of the future. Peter thought about Indian-chief test patterns, the Monsanto House of the Future at Disneyland, and how such curvilinear dreams had become part of the deep and forgotten past.

Their past.

Phil liked old black-and-white movies best. His taste in music was even more conservative than Peter's: Bach and Haydn and Mozart, no rock, just big bands and fifties jazz up to early Coltrane. No Monk, even.

For some reason, it was taking time to get used to the idea that he had the house to himself. He kept thinking Phil would show up and grin and apologize, and then show him around, pulling books from shelves, removing their plastic bags to fondle his many little treasures.

Materialism, with a difference. *Give me ideas, stories, music. Forget booze and diamonds, forget women. Pages filled with printed words and grooves in vinyl are a guy's best friend.* So Phil had once told him.

Peter found the kitchen. He filled a plastic glass with water from the tap. The sideboard was neatly piled with clean dishes. No cats or dogs, that was a blessing. Phil had never been enthusiastic about pets. Most of the cupboards in the kitchen were stuffed with old pulp magazines, *G-8 and His Battle Aces*, *The Shadow*, thick compound issues of *Amazing Stories*. One small corner shelf was reserved for cereal boxes and three more plastic glasses. The refrigerator held a six-pack of cheap beer, vanilla pudding cups, yogurt, clam chowder in plastic pouches. White foods.

Phil loved mashed potatoes.

Peter searched for coffee or tea. He needed something warm. Finally, he found a jar of instant coffee and a mug, right next to each other on the windowsill over the sink. He put on a saucepan of water and set it to boil. Then he pulled up an old-fashioned step stool and sat with a *whuff*, wiping the long drive from his eyes with a damp paper towel. He did not want to sleep in the house, but there wasn't enough money left for a motel. The couch did not look inviting. Peter could not just sleep anywhere these days. His muscles knotted if he lay down wrong. Finally, cup in hand, he turned on all the overhead lights in the kitchen and hall and the back bedrooms, inspecting each one until he came to Phil's. More shelves, mostly new and empty, as if waiting to be filled. It was not a mess; it was actually pretty neat. Spartan. Someone had made up the queen-sized bed.

Phil never made his bed.

Peter gritted his teeth. Lydia did not say where they had found Phil. The room did not smell. Still, he decided against sleeping in here. He took blankets from the hall closet and reluctantly settled on the couch. The window looked slantwise across the Bay at San Francisco, framed by two willow trees farther down the road. It was a beautiful view.

"Jesus Christ, Phil," Peter said. "If you come back, I'll punch you. I swear to God I'll punch you right in the face. You should have told me you were sick."

He was so tired. Against all his intellectual rigors, all his best intentions, he was still hoping to find Phil somewhere in the house. Hoping to grab one last minute together. "Where are you, buddy?"

He finished the cold coffee. Caffeine had little effect on him, but he doubted he would be getting much sleep tonight. "Come on, Phil," he cajoled, his voice like a small bird in the big living room. "One more time. Show up and give me a heart attack. Don't ditch me."

Peter leaned back and pulled up a small wool blanket. He kept rolling around on the old cushions, pushing his legs out as his knees felt antsy. Sleep came, but it was uneven. Finally, awake again and bladder full, he got up, stumbled around the boxes, and walked down the long hall. *Never afraid of the dark. Never have been. Empty dark.* He touched his way along the wall to the bathroom door and turned right.

A small plug-in night light illuminated a claw-foot tub, a round-mouthed porcelain toilet, and a stand-alone corner sink that must have dated from the teens or twenties. He lifted the toilet lid, unzipped his pants, and peed. Sighed at the relief from the sharp incentive nag. Not as bad as some his age, but still. Jiggled the stream around with childish intent, roiling the water. The little things we do when facing the big things, the imponderables. Peter softly sang a Doors song, *"This is . . . the end . . . beautiful friend."*

His stream finally faltered and he shook loose a few drops, harder to get the last dribble out, a small indignity, meaningless in the face of that awesome and final one.

"My only friend . . . the end."

Something passed the open door, black against a lesser dark. Peter's last squirt splashed on the floor. Half asleep, he stared in dismay at the puddle, zipped quickly, then bent to dab it up with a folded piece of toilet paper.

What?

Glancing left, he lowered the lid. His fingers slipped and the lid fell with a loud clatter on the ceramic bowl.

Crap. Tell the world.

He poked his head through the doorway and looked up and down the hall. His eyes were playing tricks. He wished Lydia, somebody, anybody, would pop out and go, "Boo!" just to show him how ridiculous he looked and sounded. How much he was betraying his vows to be skeptical.

He might be doing it again, deceiving himself, hoping beyond hope, beyond the material world, and if it kept on this way, sliding into this painful, hopeful retreat from the rational, he knew where it could all lead: straight into another case of Wild Turkey.

Trying to find the one who did it. Asking for Daniella. One last conversation with my daughter, oh my God.

Something moved again in the hall, making not so much a distinct sound as a change in the volume of air. Now Peter was sure. Someone had come into the house while he was sleeping—not Phil, of course; a burglar. He reached into his pants pocket, feeling for the knife he sometimes kept there, and did not find it. It must have slipped out in the car or on the couch.

He pushed open the bathroom door with a—this time—deliberate bang and stepped into the hall, looking both ways. Dark left, dark right. "Whoever you are, get the hell out," he called, hands clenched.

Peter had no tolerance for burglars. He had been robbed often enough—the house four times, his car three times. People who stole deserved no mercy as far as he was concerned.

He found an antique button switch and pushed it. The hall light came on. Empty. The door at the end of the hall, leading into Phil's bedroom, was open just a crack. He stood for a moment, listening.

Someone crying. The sound could have come from outside, from another house. But there were no houses close enough, not here at the end of Hidden Dreams Drive. Peter could feel heat rising again behind his eyes, steamy. Tropical. Such a weird sensation.

He realized he was making little hiccuping gulps as he finished his walk toward the end of the hall, Phil's bedroom. The door's closing had been blocked by wire hangers hooked over the top. He was astonished by how clearly he saw everything in the light of the hall fixture: wallpaper pastel flowers in diamond patterns, dark-stained baseboards, antique oak floor, worn oriental-design runner rucked up and curling on one side, boxes on the left stacked almost to the ceiling, *WEIRD TALES 1933–48,* the bedroom door and the hangers again, the darkness beyond the crack.

It sounded like *a woman* crying, soft, silky sobs, voice like dusty honey. Not Phil, then, of course, and probably not a burglar. A lost little girl, maybe. Some out-of-it doper marching around late at night. Peter forced his breath to slow. Maybe it was someone Phil knew, a lover come back to pick up her toothbrush, her underwear, her jewelry, as unlikely as that might be—Phil had kept so much to himself.

Peter assumed a fencer's position in the hall, *En garde.* "I'm out here, and I won't hurt you," he said, hand outstretched. "Don't be afraid. It's okay." He knew, could feel it as a tangible fact, that the bedroom was empty, but he could still hear the sobbing through the door.

Slender lines of darkness gathered in the periphery of his vision like smeared ink. As he tried to focus, they blended into corner shadows like wisps of spiderweb. Still, outside his direct gaze, the smudged lines flashed toward the bedroom door, wriggling like dark, blurry eels anxious to get in.

I'm having a stroke, just like Phil.

But he did not feel ill. Physically he was fine; it was the house, the bedroom, that was not fine.

It was the bedroom that was crying.

Peter was not a coward. He knew that about himself. He could feel fear and still act, but what he felt now was not fear; it was an unwillingness to learn, and that was very different. Some things that you discover—infidelity, the death of loved ones—you cannot turn back from. What you suddenly know changes you, chops you up into little pieces.

He did not want to learn what was in the bedroom.

Still, he poked the door open with a stiff finger. He leaned slowly into the bedroom and fumbled to push the button switch. The ceiling fixture slowly glowed to sterile yellow brightness. Shadows fled across the bedroom like little cyclones of soot.

Peter grabbed the doorjamb.

A woman stood at the foot of Phil's bed. She had buried her face in gray hands, but Peter could tell who she was by the dark comma of bobbed hair and the honey-silk quality of her weeping. "My God," he said, and his shoulders slumped. He let out his breath and started to smile. "Lydia. You scared me."

The woman's hands dropped. She turned, head cocked, listening; slowly turned and listened some more, as if to far-off and unpleasant music.

All of a sudden, through his relief, Peter's tongue moved involuntarily, and he bit into it. His head exploded in pain. Eyes watering, gasping, he felt vulnerable and very, very foolish. Through his tears, he saw that the woman's face was like a flat sheet of mother-of-pearl. Her eyes opened to quizzical hollows. Less than solid, she resembled a paper doll frayed by careless snipping. Peter could actually see her edges ripple. Trying to back out, he thumped against the door, closing it, and for an instant, felt something tug at his head, his throbbing tongue, his nerves.

Her blank and empty eyes vibrated. They seemed to point not quite in his direction, but through and beyond him. The image filled out like a balloon, assuming a counterfeit and temporary solidity.

Not Lydia. But it looks like her.

The image moved its lips. As if pushing through gelatin, the sound arrived late at his ears. "Phil, how could you do this, how could you just *die*?" came the high-pitched silken wail, only a little louder than the buzzing of a fly.

The eel shadows swooped through the door and into the bedroom like descending hawks. He could feel them brush his shoulders like the tips of cold, damp fingers. The figure jerked in a horrible simulation of fear, trying to escape, dodging faster than flesh, like a bad film edit. But escape was impossible.

Peter's mouth went stone dry. He wanted to look away, block his vision with a hand. Instincts old and deep instructed him that he was about to bear witness to something private, a sight no living human should ever have to see; but he could not stop himself.

He stared. Pity held him. And curiosity.

The eel shadows swarmed and lanced and worried the image, snatching away scalloped bites and crumbling pieces. It lifted its hands in weak defense, shuddering with an astonishing, dry simulacrum of pain. Whatever it was, its time had come. As the likeness of Phil's ex-wife diminished and deflated, its wailing turned tinny and desperate. It unraveled drastically, peeling and dissolving in shreds like a tissue-paper cutout dipped in a bowl of water. In a few seconds, the last of its murky outline disintegrated and fell away. Sated, the shadows fled, draining like water around his feet. The room seemed to shiver off the last of them, leaving just the bed, neatly made and undisturbed, and the threadbare carpet and empty shelves.

The image, the delusion, the reflection or copy of Lydia—whatever it might have been—was gone. Peter leaned his shoulder against the doorjamb. He could not move. For the moment, he could not even turn his head. Blood pounded in his ears. His calf cramped and he gritted his teeth. Even in his worse days of besotted grief, he had never seen anything remotely like this.

Pitiful, something left behind, dropped like an old Kleenex.

His heart slowed. The heat behind his eyes cooled. Finally, he had to blink. That instant with his eyes closed terrified him and he felt his neck tense and intestines curl.

Nothing came. Nothing touched him. Quiet and still. The room was innocent.

Nothing had actually happened.

Nothing *real.*

Peter was finally able to turn. He put out one foot as if rediscovering how to walk, then another, and slowly left the bedroom, reaching back with numb and inept fingers to close the door. The hangers caught. He could not close the door all the way, so he angrily slammed it. The hangers jangled. One fell and bounced off the wood floor with a tinny resonance. The whine of the hanger wire made him grit his teeth; it sounded too much like the *voice.*

He gave up and walked on what felt like tingling stumps to the couch in the living room. Sat on the couch with hands folded on his lap. Did not even try to relax. Watched the carnival of the city across the water, darker now in the wee hours. His neck knotted and stayed that way.

He was still alive and wasn't sure he wanted to be, not if he had to think about what he had just seen.

PETER WATCHED THE dawn light gather slowly over San Francisco, then burst forth along the eastern hills, reflecting gold against skyscrapers and banks of fog, the most beautiful sight of all: day.

He was making a big, grown-man decision. There was only one way to react—it must have been a bad dream—and two things to do. He walked into the kitchen and poured himself a bowl of Cheerios, chewing reflexively each milky mouthful. The milk had been in the fridge since Phil's death and was on the edge of spoiling, but served well enough.

He forced himself to take a shower in the big bathroom, removing his clothes with catlike caution, climbing into the claw-foot tub, and drawing the curtain around on its pipe, tucked inside just enough to keep water from spraying on the floor, but with a clear view of the open bathroom door. This took tremendous will but it had to be done, and just this way. The water was set hot and stung his back. Phil did not believe in wimpy showers; no water inhibitor valves for him.

No Bergson valves.

As Peter scrubbed using Phil's rounded block of Ivory soap, he tried to recall what a Bergson valve was. Something he had picked up reading *The Doors of Perception* in the sixties.

This is the end . . . beautiful friend.

Aldous Huxley. Something about drugs opening doors, or was it spigots? Letting the taps of reality flow free. He'd look it up when he got home. Or maybe Phil had a copy.

After toweling dry, he dressed in the living room, putting on his good wool slacks and a black long-sleeve shirt and the thrift-store suit coat to get ready for when they delivered Phil, or when—and he did not know how he would react to this—the real Lydia turned up again on the porch.

Peter washed the bowl in the sink and suddenly started snorting with laughter. It didn't last long; it wasn't funny, really. It was sad. "I see live people," he said, and started snorting again until he had to take off his glasses to wipe his nose and his eyes.

His best friend's wake was today and he couldn't keep his act together long enough to get a good night's sleep. He had to start seeing things. Peter the screwup, two nights running. Maybe he was hoping to draw attention to himself; poor Peter, maddened by loss once again.

Really sad.

The self-hatred built like bad clouds before a storm. Then it burst and went away. Peter's ground state was a mellow kind of cheer, high energy at times, but usually slow to blame or anger. Sometimes he just reverted to the ground state when things got really bad, without explanation, but no solution, either; the bad clouds inevitably returned. He would have to deal with them. Just not now.

"It did not feel like a dream," he told himself. He was clean and well dressed, wearing his beige silk coat. He had become a figure of calm masculine dignity, gray-bearded, with wide-spaced and gentle eyes and glasses, lacking only a pipe.

Bring it on.

He sat on the porch swing, relishing the sun, the cool fresh air.

"What a great house, Phil," he said. "Really."

A dark blue unmarked panel truck came up the road trailing a thin cloud of exhaust and dust. It parked on the gravel beside the Porsche and a man in a dark brown suit got out, carrying a square cardboard box.

"Is that Phil?" Peter called from the porch.

"Delivery for Ms. Lydia Richards," the man said, holding out the box in both hands. He had thick, theatrically wavy gray hair and walked and spoke with a jaded but professional dignity. Peter had once known a stripper who had married an undertaker. It was all about flesh after all.

"I'll take him," Peter said.

"Are you authorized by the family to receive the mortal remains of Mr. Philip Daley Richards?" the dignified man asked.

"I'm family," Peter said, and signed for Phil's ashes.

CHAPTER 

PETER GINGERLY PLACED the box on the mantel of the fireplace. It barely fit.

The morning's explanations weren't making much sense now.

"Lydia, where did Phil die?" he rehearsed out loud, standing before the fireplace. "Lydia, I don't think he died in the house. Did *you* die in the house, Lydia? Because it wasn't Phil who showed up this morning, in the dark."

He rubbed his lips as if to wipe away that potential conversation. Best to just let the wake roll on. Unlike Peter, Phil had not become a teetotaler. He would have appreciated a few drinks hoisted on his behalf. But solemn speeches and rows of furtive people dressed in black would have bummed him.

Peter looked down at his hands. They were trembling. He was not cut out to lose people. He was not cut out to face the death of loved ones, and he had loved Phil. Maybe he was not meant to be a friend or a husband or a daddy or any kind of serious human being. He had been at his happiest, he thought with a real twinge, facing the softer truths of young flesh, bawdiness and bodies live, parties on sets that sometimes turned into happy orgies. So much joy and laughter, walking around with a large pad of newsprint and a marker, wearing a wide floppy Shakespearean hat and nothing else, sketching his actors while orating like Richard Burton; loose easy conversations and kisses and oral sex and gentle, easy fucking and food, just between friends.

In the sixties and early seventies, he had stayed well away from the serious and somber.

He would have loved to go on that Old Farts Hot Dog Tour, had there been time; that would have been something he could have done well with Phil. This, he did not think he was going to do well.

"Lydia, do you burn incense, practice astral projection?"

Peter gave it up.

At noon, still alone in the house, pacing, glancing at the mantel, Peter realized that the cardboard box was not decorous. He walked up to the fireplace and lowered the box to the brick hearth. Inside, a bronze-colored plastic urn looked both cheap and better. He lifted the urn from the box and centered it, creating two urns, one on the mantel, one in the mirror above the mantel. Phil and anti-Phil. Through the looking glass.

By one o'clock, Peter was irritated and not in the least nervous or worried about what he would say. By two, he was furious. He opened a can of baked beans from the back of the cupboard and ate them cold. He spooned up the sweet smoky beans and the little lump of pork fat and thought of all the potluck food Lydia would no doubt bring.

As he finished the last bite, the Trans chimed in his pocket. He answered.

"Yeah?"

"Have I reached the party to whom I am speaking?"

"Who is this?" Peter asked.

"Stanley Weinstein. Mrs. Benoliel told me you were in the Bay Area. I'm calling to say thanks."

"For what?"

"For convincing Mr. Benoliel to invest in our company."

"Did I?"

"You did. And he did. We're bubbly. I'm inviting you to come to the Big House and meet the crew. We have some of your reward, and if you're interested, we might have some work for you. I've been doing my research. I didn't know I was meeting a famous man."

Peter stared out the window at the city. "Where are you?" he asked.

"Michelle says you're somewhere in Marin. We're not far, if that's true—and I don't otherwise know, because a Trans unit cannot be located, it is completely private."

"I'm in Tiburon," Peter said.

"That's grand. We're less than half an hour away. Let me give you directions. You can't miss it, actually. Do you know where the old San Andreas prison is?"

"I've never been there."

"Now's your chance. California Department of Corrections closed the prison three years ago to sell the land. Very posh, four hundred and fifty acres, great Bay views."

"I didn't know that," Peter said.

"We lease space in the condemned wing. It's right next to the gas chamber. When can you get here?"

"There's a wake today. Maybe tomorrow?"

"I was sorry to hear about your friend."

"Thanks," Peter said.

"You'll need some time, obviously. Why don't we get together at eleven tomorrow morning? If that's not too soon."

Peter realized he could use the money, if any, to get home. "Thanks. I'll be there."

Weinstein gave him his Trans number and the backup landline office number. "We're still having some glitches," he explained. "Just temporary."

Peter wrote the numbers on a piece of scrap notepaper with a ballpoint pen.

"Looking forward to it. I think you'll enjoy the whole experience." Weinstein ended the call. The cutoff was noiseless. The silence next to Peter's ear just got deeper. He closed the unit, then turned over the paper. Phil had cut an old typed manuscript into smaller pieces. Always thrifty.

He read the truncated bit of dialog.

"Do you play any games?" Megan asked him, licking her lips.
"Not really, not very well," Carlton replied huskily.
"Why? Do you have something against rules?"

Peter folded the scrap and put it in his shirt pocket, then walked down the drive for the fifth time in the last two hours to see if cars were coming. For a moment, he wondered if Lydia had died in an accident and he actually had seen her ghost last night. Perhaps she had committed suicide, taking his five hundred dollars and driving down the road to the beach and drowning herself in the cold waters of the Bay. That was crazy. Crazy thinking. Here he was, seeing things, almost flat broke, hoping for a payout from Stanley Weinstein because he didn't have enough money to get home.

His imagination had slipped into a tense, angry riot when he finally saw cars driving up Hidden Dreams Drive. The first one, a green new-style Beetle, carried two people. The driver was Lydia. Behind the Beetle came three more cars.

Peter straightened his coat and walked back to the house.

What the hell, he thought as he climbed the porch. *Phil, you might have liked this. I sure don't. But it has your touch, somehow.*

CHAPTER 9

LYDIA LOOKED TIRED and pale but vital, and she certainly behaved as if nothing untoward had happened. She introduced the guests to Peter. Two he had met long ago, writers from a group Phil had belonged to for almost thirty years, the Mysterians. Peter had attended several meetings and liked them well enough. Mystery writers, reporters, a couple of cops. The two Mysterians that Lydia had invited were both male, portly, and in their sixties. Peter had the impression they were gay and lived together.

Two women Peter did not know—matronly, in their early forties—carried Tupperware bowls of potato salad and green salad and a foiled tray of lasagna up the walk and into the kitchen. Four other unfamiliar faces drifted by and were introduced, all male and in their mid-to-late fifties. The guests shook hands with Peter, stood awkwardly in the living room, and circulated past the bronze plastic urn, giving it sidelong glances.

"I'm glad Phil showed up," Lydia whispered to Peter in the kitchen. Peter watched her closely. "They had him for two days before they called me," she said. "I don't know why they didn't call you."

"You kept his last name," Peter said. Lydia brushed his shoulder with her arm. She smelled cool and nervous, beneath the haze of tobacco. If she had not smoked for thirty years she might still be beautiful. She faced him square and her expression turned to concern. "You look bad, Peter. Maybe you shouldn't have stayed here last night."

"It was not a comfortable evening," Peter admitted.

"Spooky?" she asked, piquant.

He awarded her a thin smile for the jab.

"I doubt it was Phil," Lydia said. "He's long gone. This world never did suit him. *I* didn't suit him. But you know, even so, I kind of lost it yesterday," she suddenly confessed, her eyes bright. "I had a little fit. I started shouting his name, in the empty house. Isn't that strange? Just blew out my grief. I felt better after. I didn't know I still gave a damn."

Peter's eyes turned warm again. "Where were you when that happened?"

"In his bedroom. Looking at all the empty shelves. Why?"

"Standing at the foot of the bed?"

"What does it matter?"

"It doesn't," Peter said.

"Let's get this over with," Lydia said with a shrug.

She called the guests into the living room. The room was not crowded. Three of the men stepped up to the mantel and offered half-accurate descriptions of Phil, short, false literary tributes. The second called him a neglected talent. The third spoke fondly of a short story that Phil had not in fact written.

Lydia thanked them quietly. Peter spoke for a moment about their friendship, saw eyes glaze, and felt his throat get thick with emotion. None of them had known Phil well. Phil was not famous enough to want to suck up to, not in town often enough to make a strong impression; and none of them had known about the house.

They then stood around eating sandwiches and potato salad on chipped plates from Phil's sideboard. The two gay male writers took the opportunity to step out on the porch to smoke.

The four men Peter did not know left quickly when they realized there was to be no liquor. Phil would have left as well, Peter thought. The two on the porch returned and wanted to look around the house, examine the artifacts and old mystery pulps and Phil's books, but Peter politely put a stop to that by saying the best of the collection was in boxes now, not much to see. Phil would not have liked strangers pawing his prize possessions. They seemed mildly affronted. Lydia politely accompanied them down the drive, back to their car.

The matronly younger women stayed to clean up. Peter helped stack the old plates on the drying rack beside the sink. Only then did they introduce themselves. The redheaded woman with a plump, pleasant face was Hanna; the mousy-haired one with an expression of peaceful vacancy was Sherry.

"We only knew him to talk to a few times," Hanna said. Sherry nodded. "He was nice. Sherry wants to write, but neither of us have published much."

"We keep journals," Sherry said.

"We don't write real books, like Phil," Hanna said.

Lydia returned to the kitchen and sat on the stool. "That's that," she said.

"Where did Phil die?" Peter asked.

"Does it matter? Jesus, Peter." Lydia stared at him with large, expressionless eyes. "They didn't tell me—the ME's boys, I mean. Neither did the cops." She tongued her upper teeth, picked at a piece of lettuce with a fingernail, then concluded softly, "Not in any of these rooms, I guess."

Hanna and Sherry regarded each other with bowed lips.

Peter took Lydia aside, into the living room. "Did you do anything here yesterday I should know about?" he asked.

"Another odd question. You look *odd*, Peter."

"Humor me."

"I made arrangements. I told you. I had my moment, my grief thing, then got ready for what has turned out to be a truly sad little shindig. By the time you arrived, I was completely worn out. What is *wrong* with you?"

"I don't know," Peter said. Hanna and Sherry exchanged glances in the dining nook.

Lydia shuddered. "Don't creep me out anymore," she said. "This house already feels weird with a beard. I don't want to stay any longer than I have to."

Peter could feel it, too. The same quality that he had sensed, or not sensed, while driving north in the Porsche. The deeper silence that made quiet seem loud.

"Do you think *Phil is still here?*" Sherry asked softly, trying for delicacy and not succeeding. Her cheeks pinked.

"He might have wanted to stay with his books and magazines, wouldn't he? It's such a fine collection," Hanna observed.

"The house is quiet, not noisy. Right, Peter?" Lydia asked.

"Mostly," Peter said.

Lydia squinted at him. "Whatever Phil was, he was *not* quiet," she said, walking to the mantel. She touched the urn with a long finger. "If he was here, he'd be talking our ears off about this and that."

They returned to the kitchen, where the matronly women gathered up the bowls and dishes of leftover food. "All done," Hanna said, seeing boredom in their near future. She folded and draped the dish towel. "We should be going. I came with Lydia, but I can go back with Sherry."

"Go on ahead," Lydia said. "I need to talk some more with Peter."

CHAPTER 18

THE DUSK SKY over the hills faded through shades of peacock blue, distant and serene. After the curious pair had left, Lydia took a seat on the porch swing and lit up a cigarette. Peter stood by the rail.

"He didn't leave a will," Lydia said. "I never heard about any family. I don't know who this stuff belongs to. I suppose the state will take it all eventually. So you should pack up whatever you think is rightfully yours. I could try to sell his books in the city and send the money to whoever you think should get it. Myself, I don't want any of it—books or money."

Peter had never made out a will and did not blame Phil for the oversight. "You should hire a lawyer," he suggested.

"I'm his ex, not his wife. I suppose some of this is community property, but I don't know what, and certainly not the house. I never saw this place. I just want shut of it."

"I understand," Peter said.

"You should look around. Maybe there's a little key or a combination on a piece of paper. Maybe he left a document in a bank box somewhere and it all belongs to you. That would be great. A load off." She waved her cigarette in the gathering dark.

"Something is just not right here," she added a minute later. "Don't take this the wrong way, Peter, but . . . is it *you*? Because the house did not feel this way before you arrived."

Peter shook his head. "I'm just a screwed-up old friend of the deceased," he said.

Lydia glared at him in the gathering dark. "So what did you think I was doing here, casing the joint? Waving my juju wands to exorcise poor Phil and move in?"

"I'm sorry I asked. It was a rude question."

"I have a lot of baggage, but none of it has to do with this house. Just with Phil. We were not good for each other. But you asked for a reason. I know you well enough, Peter."

Peter could not bring himself to describe what he had seen. So he compromised. "I felt your grief here last night," he said. "I'm not psychic, but it was here. Pretty obvious, too. That's all."

"Well, I'll be darned, Peter Russell. You're a sensitive man after all."

"I actually went to a medium once," Peter said sheepishly, digging the hole a little deeper.

Lydia stubbed out the cigarette. This time, she left the butt in the sand-filled can. "Really?" she asked, savoring this breach in Peter's wall. "Do tell."

"It was a long time ago."

"After Daniella?"

"Yeah."

Lydia nodded. "We learn our lessons. Phil was one of my lessons. I do not do well with nice, nervous little men. Mean and self-assured, that's my style."

"Hank Wuorinos came over to visit yesterday. He's off to Prague on a film shoot."

Lydia's face hardened. "Why mention him?"

"He remembered you and Phil."

"Did he tell you I fucked him?" she asked.

"No," Peter said.

"I was crazy, Peter. I hated Phil. I hated men in general. Phil talked about nothing but your goddamned movies and model shoots and being your guest at the Playboy Mansion, that stupid cartoon thing, you introducing him to Hef and meeting Miss October or whatever. That was the high point of his life. Do you know what that made me feel like?"

"No," Peter said, folding his arms.

"Like spoiled leftovers. Then this innocent, beautiful young man comes into the house, I don't know where Phil found him, but we put Hank up, and he was so sweet. I told myself I could start all over again, I could feel something with this boy. It was a bad season, Peter. I hope Hank remembers me fondly, because that was the beginning of the end for me and Phil."

"I'm sorry," Peter said.

"Poor Phil," Lydia mused, pushing out her lips. "Having to ogle all of Peter Russell's naked ladies." She took a smoker's dialog beat, picking at a flake of tobacco on her tongue. "How could anyone compete with *your* fantasy life?" She said this with a sad but radiant smile. He had never seen her like that, glowing with the short-lived brilliance of a bulb about to burn out. She stood and hugged him. "You charming bastard," she whispered in his ear. Then she jogged down from the porch. "It's all yours, Peter." She opened the door to the Volkswagen and turned to wave cheerily at the house. "Goodbye, Phil! TTFN. Ta ta for now."

With two quick honks Lydia backed out, spun around, narrowly missing the Porsche, and roared down the road and around the willow trees.

The stars came out.

Peter pushed back from the porch rail and puffed out his breath. He could not stay in the house, not another night. He had been taken by an idea, however, listening to Lydia: not a pleasant idea, but more than a hunch. Before he left, he had to explore.

He walked down the steps, his shoes tapping hollow drumbeats in the dark.

He knew where Phil might have gone to die.

THE LAND BEHIND the house stretched for a hundred yards before meeting a wobbling wire fence, the end of the property, Peter presumed.

The night was beautiful, not very cold. Peter left his suit coat in the car.

The rough ground behind the house was covered with oat grass and scrub. A packed-dirt drive skirted a run-down toolshed and pushed up to a large old barn, slant-roofed, gray, and rickety. Someone had once kept horses on the property. Behind the barn rose low hills and a broad sweep of stars around a brilliant orange rising moon.

Peter followed the rutted drive, noting dark oil stains on the center hump. The old Grand Taiga had always been incontinent. He found the motor home parked behind the barn, out of sight from the house and half covered by a blue tarp. The exposed rear half gleamed white. Peter had always possessed good night vision, despite being nearsighted; he could make out the license plate number, the long awning rolled and tucked up against the roofline, the door. A long strip of plastic police ribbon lay discarded before the door.

Now he was sure. Phil had walked out here to die. Or perhaps he had planned to sleep in the motor home before making another trip south to pick up more stuff. A few days later, perhaps the mailman had knocked to deliver a package, and discovered that the house door was open. Even in Tiburon's countryside, leaving a door unlocked was not wise.

The mailman had called out several times, walked around the house to check the back . . .

Peter could piece together the rest of the story.

The Grand Taiga's cold metal door handle turned easily. He swung the door wide and held his breath for a moment, then sniffed. The interior smelled musty, faintly ripe, as if the sewage tank had not been emptied. He pulled back and leaned against the metal side, thinking.

The door swung closed on its piston.

Peter looked across the field to the house. A breeze from the Bay was rapidly cooling the land. Out in the long oat grass, insects tried to muster some enthusiasm.

He opened the door again, then grabbed a vertical metal grip and hoisted himself inside. The smell wasn't so bad. More like a weak fart. Certainly not strong enough to drive him out. He switched on the interior lights. Muddy boot prints and straw had been tracked on the floor. Phil had always kept the motor home immaculate. These, then, were police tracks. Coroner, medical examiner. The official violators of a privacy no longer needed, abandoned with the body. *Go ahead. Look. It's official; I'm out of here.*

The smell was stronger in the nook behind the stove and refrigerator. Stronger still as he moved forward, toward the big blue-corduroy upholstered captain's chairs.

He unlocked the driver's seat with his foot and rotated it. Blotches marked the lower cushion, darker than water stains and more suggestive.

Peter closed his eyes, letting go of the dream, laying to rest the Hot Dog Tour and Escapade. He slumped into the passenger seat and rubbed his short beard. Peered through the windshield. The motor home creaked from cooling off. The interior was still warm after sitting in the sun all day. How long had Phil sat propped behind the wheel, dead? How long did it take him to die?

Peter pushed up from the seat. He didn't have the heart to look for papers. It was all over. He just wanted to get away from the Grand Taiga, away from the house with its reminders that when you died all your precious stuff had no value to you; he simply wanted to get back into his car and drive somewhere, anywhere. He was about to open the metal door when he spied something on a small desk beyond the kitchen, hidden in deep shadow. Phil had often kept his typewriter there when he worked in the motor home. Peter found another switch. A small lamp glowed warm orange in the short corridor. As he stepped toward the rear, he saw that the desk supported not a typewriter, but a wooden game board and chess set.

He remembered the set. It had been one of Phil's favorite possessions, had cost most of the advance on a book: a Dale Enzenbacher original cast in bronze and silver, depicting the archetypal heroes and villains of pulp fiction. On one side, cast in silver, stood the heroes: the king, a stalwart adventurer in boots, jodhpurs, and waist-length double-breasted jacket, clutched what might have been a blaster or a long-barreled pistol. The queen was Dejah Thoris in all her naked pulchritude. Knights were private eyes, fedoras slumped low and collars pulled high, guns bulging in their tiny pockets. Bishops were bald, wise Asian priests in long robes, hands folded in Asian humility, no doubt waiting to torment and train the cruel and headstrong Lamont Cranston. Rooks were squat pyramids topped by radiant, all-seeing eyes.

The pawns on the hero side were all ghosts, specters and litches, and for the first time Peter found that odd. Spooks on the side of the heroes?

The villains, cast in dark-patinaed bronze, consisted of Ming and another princess, probably Ardala. She wore a spoiled, sulky expression and little else. Bishops were mad scientists, monocled and clutching tiny crystal beakers; knights were evil henchmen, dwarfish and hunched; rooks, castles mounted on hills and surmounted by lightning strokes. The pawns on this side consisted of tentacled and bug-eyed monsters, no doubt moving above and around our normal set of dimensions.

Pages of manuscript had been shoved up behind the game board—Phil had always preferred a typewriter to a word processor. Peter pulled down the last few pages and read them with a squint. Phil's great crime novel, talked about over the years: a young FBI agent investigating corruption in Salt Lake City. The last page ended in the middle of a sentence.

Phil could type over ninety words a minute on his old Olympic portable. And where was that essential tool? Peter glanced into the rear bedroom. Minus its silver-gray case, the typewriter had been deposited in the middle of the bed. The police, Peter suspected, had left these things untouched, eager to close a fairly obvious case file. Tag ends of a life too short and too disorganized by half.

Peter returned to the desk and the chess set. He stood with hands on hips, trying to figure out the extent and path of the rearrangements, based on Phil's habits. Above the desk was a small cupboard in which Phil had kept pencils and paper clips. Peter pulled the cupboard open. Inside were two shot glasses half filled with amber liquid. He carefully lifted one glass and sniffed it: Scotch. He put the first glass down in the middle of the chessboard, beside a leering monster, and lifted the second, finding underneath a page ripped from a notebook or bound diary. In Phil's crabbed handwriting:

Peter:

That you, bud? I hope you find this and not the cops or whomever. My last will and testament. Take whatever you want. I won't need it anymore. Leave whatever you don't want in the house.

I finally figured it out. This world is awful—it's bad art. Some of us don't fit because we're always trying to look deeper. There's something underneath, something wonderful and full of color. It's happy and it makes sense. I can feel it. Some hifalutin, cruel god has painted over an ancient masterpiece filled with joy. Well, I've run my course. I'm going exploring.

See you later, old friend.

Phil had always found the world of fiction—heroes and monsters, villains and exotic women—far more comfortable than reality. And for that matter, so had Peter. Phil had known he was dying, had known it for at least an hour. He had come out here to finish the job, given to drama even in his pain, leaving clues stuffed in the cubbyholes of their rolling clubhouse.

Peter reread the message, tears in his eyes.

Both of us just disappointed kids.

Finally, he folded the paper and slipped it into his shirt pocket. He then lifted the glass from the game board, toasted the empty air, and tossed it off neat. Even after sitting for days, the Scotch tasted great—smoke and fire and peat, a touch of vanilla oak—and immediately produced a far too pleasant effect. The second glass looked tempting. It was not his to drink, however. Something truly for the ghosts. He left it in the cupboard and closed the door, then rummaged in the kitchen and found a small box.

One by one he placed the silver and bronze Enzenbacher pieces in the box, wrapping them in tissue paper from the bathroom.

He had always liked that chess set.

PETER PUT THE box into his suitcase and carried it out to the car. He pulled the Trans from the pocket of his jacket, which he had left slumped in the Porsche's passenger seat.

The unit lay pretty and green in his palm.

The night air was chilly. He slipped on the jacket and hefted the Trans, thoughtful. Everything had sounded properly quiet in the Grand Taiga, but now, once again, below the quiet lay a deeper silence. Another illusion? Maybe he could ask Weinstein about that tomorrow.

Peter returned to close and lock up the house. Something flickered in the corner of his eye. He looked left into the darkened living room. Pools of light played across the walls, danced in the mirror above the fireplace, reflections, it seemed, shining through the front window. But it hadn't rained in days and the ground outside was dry. No puddles. Besides, the moon was too high to be playing tricks.

The lights gleamed in the mirror, glinted off the urn.

Phil's ashes. The last bits.

Peter stepped forward and picked up the urn, resolute. He would scatter the ashes somewhere nice. Absent a real will, he knew that was what Phil would have wanted, to sow him into the waves at Big Sur.

Put his carbon back into the Earth's recycling bin.

Let me go choke a fish.

He could almost hear Phil saying that; it sounded right. Well, good, then, he had a little bit of Phil's voice inside him still. Urn under one arm, Peter stood for a moment by the door watching the reflections. His face went quizzical. It took him twenty seconds to see that the lights were near the walls, not on them, and floated just below the ceiling in the middle of the room.

They weren't reflections at all. They moved with far too much freedom. They were will-o'-the-wisps, making almost inaudible *shoosh-woosh* sounds, like large moths.

Watching them was like slugging back a jolt of coffee; he felt connected, energized, curious. But the lights faded. The room turned dark and empty. Now he just felt lonely. The energy of a moment ago was replaced by something gray and unpleasant, like coming down off a high. He thought about going back and finishing Phil's drink. Or looking for the bottle. Phil wouldn't mind. A few minutes of solace . . .

Peter closed and locked the door behind him, then replaced the house keys on a nail up under the porch rafters. He walked to the car, wedged the urn beside his suitcase, closed the hood with a *clunk* and then leaned to latch it shut.

Only when he was about to switch on the ignition did he realize Lydia had not told him about the nail, or where it might be, or that the keys belonged there. The nail was not visible unless you looked from a certain odd angle.

He had just known.

And so had Lydia, apparently.

CHAPTER 12

THE NIGHT WAS cold in Marin and he did not fancy a drive south, only to return in the morning. Besides, he would have to conserve his scant ten dollars. So he stopped at a gas station and asked the night attendant, a young Asian woman locked in a fluorescent-blue booth, how to find San Andreas.

She stared at him speculatively from her bright little island. "The fault, or the prison?" she asked.

"I'm going to the prison tomorrow," Peter said.

She cocked her head to one side, coquettish. "You not look like a bad man," she said. "You mature, not punk." She added, "Prison closed. They build."

"Right," Peter said. "High-tech office buildings."

"I not know." She looked up the directions in a Thomas Brothers guide, glad to have company this late at night, and apparently glad it was Peter. He often had that effect on people, and especially on women. Lydia had nailed him. He might have led a different and more productive life if he had been a little less charming.

"Also, I need a good beach," he said. "Nice waves."

"This the Bay, no waves," the woman said.

Peter shrugged. "Anywhere close?"

"Maybe Point Reyes."

"That's good. Is there a YMCA nearby?"

"YWCA more fun, maybe?" She shook her short black hair and covered a giggle with her hand. "But I think one in San Rafael. I find." And she looked that up by going to the Web on her booth computer. "It get so boring here after ten, I go nuts," she said. "I travel all over the Web. Owner not mind. He my brother. You think he set me up with some nice man? No! I work work work long hours. Get off late." She glanced hopefully through the bulletproof plastic.

Peter rewarded her with a wry smile. "My friend's ashes are in the trunk," he said. "I'm taking him down to the beach."

That sobered her right up. She watched owlishly as he returned to the car with directions to the YMCA on Los Gamos Drive.

First, however, with the moon still up and the night still bright, and enough gas in his tank, it was time to send the last of Phil back to nature.

CHAPTER 13

THE WIND OFF the Pacific lifted sand from the beach in translucent sheets and sent it shushing through scrub and low trees. The moon was at its highest point and Peter could clearly make out the waves, long rough rollers grumbling in from an unhappy ribbon of black sea. Sand got in his eyes. He had thought of standing on a rock and dispensing fistfuls of his friend's ashes to a wide swath of ocean, but that clearly was not going to be practical. "Let's choke the fishes, not me," he murmured, pulling up the collar of his coat to keep the sand out of his eyes.

Carrying Phil's urn, he walked down as close to the waterline as he thought practical, then danced back as the spume hissed forward with unexpected energy. After a few tries, he found a good compromise position, stooped, unscrewed the thick plastic lid, and waited for the foaming burble of ocean to creep back. The best technique, Peter thought, would be to apply Phil a dollop at a time. Pouring out the contents of the tub all at once would leave a gray wet lump to be worked over like the stub end of a wet cigar. Not good.

Peter dispensed the gritty ashes in small handfuls. After five minutes, his ankles and knees ached. He thought of all of Phil's maladies: Heartburn, the beginnings of emphysema from so many years of smoking—Phil had smoked like a chimney, said it made him feel normal. A mole on his chin and beside his nose. An attack of shingles. Nerves in social situations.

In 1987, Phil had been a joyous, leering wreck at the Playboy Mansion. To calm him, Peter had sat him down at a table and pulled out a sketchpad. Together they had performed dueling cartoons until well past midnight. Phil's characters had been quickly sketched Everyman nebbishes with long noses and knowing eyes. Peter had drawn more detailed, world-weary devils with little horns and wry expressions. Right and left, cartoons had been handed out to a growing crowd of beautiful women and envious men. Hefner had sat with them for a few minutes, and later had published several of the cartoons. The checks had totaled over six thousand dollars. Phil had called that his finest moment.

He had suffered from obsessive-compulsive disorder. Not washing his hands over and over, but making sure light switches were turned off, appliances that might overheat were unplugged. Peter had once waited twenty minutes while Phil had checked his apartment, unlocking and then relocking the door ten times. Coffeemaker, TV, space heaters, all had to be off or unplugged, because you never knew where an electrical fire might start, and Phil was fanatic about protecting his stuff.

Peter tossed another fistful into the foam, staying out of the blowback as wind sang over the waves. He then crab-walked down the beach, another dollop, another step.

He had researched cremation for the horror film that Joseph had refused to finance. In older crematoria, bodies often had to be turned and poked and rearranged to be burned clear to ash. It was a tough, low-paying job, taking tongs and turning the hot, smoking bodies. Sometimes the heart, a tough hard lump of muscle meat, had to be picked out and hammered or ground up separately.

Or so some funeral planners had told him over drinks at a bar on Cahuenga.

"Jesus," he murmured, and bent to let the spume wash his hand. "The things I've done for you, Phil. I swear."

But it felt right. It was worth it. He could imagine Phil liberated from nerves and pain and bad memories. But the waves were also dissolving Phil's weird, crackpot humor and eyes gleaming as he talked about finding a rare pulp in excellent condition at Collector's Bookstore. The cold salt water, filled with breaking, hissing bubbles, was also sucking up the Phil that had waved his arms and laughed as they had discussed the stops on their Old Farts Escapade and Tour. "Pismo Beach. *Albakoykee,* Lompoc, and *Cuc-A-MONGA-a.*"

Gone also, the inner experience that had driven Phil to express himself about Peter's loss, tears rolling down his cheeks. "Shit, Peter, you never deserved anything this bad, never." Peter had almost quaked himself apart with grief in Phil's arms. Two grown men, hugging and crying.

The spume glowed pale as it drew the muddy last of Phil out to sea. Peter wiped sand and spray and fresh tears from his eyes and trudged back up the beach to the parking lot. It was four in the morning. Except for the Porsche, the parking lot was empty. He was too tired and wrung out to make it to the YMCA. He drove the car out of reach of the salt spray and sand and parked on a bluff. Then he curled his arms up in the tight bucket seat and leaned his head against a small pillow he carried to sometimes sit on.

With Phil gone, he had almost nobody to talk to. Being alone for this long was the worst kind of failure, something he had always tried to avoid, usually with considerable success. Before his marriage, there had of course been lots of women, but also lots of friends. And quite a few who had been both.

Phil, however, had always been there for the worst times. No more. No more.

He dreamed in vivid jerks about the keys on the string. They hung before him, suspended from someone's hand, a man's, not Lydia's, as clear as could be, caught in golden light. Even the dirty string was Titian red.

Then he woke and turned to see dawn glowing over the hills behind the freeway. His glasses lay folded on the dash. All the world outside was a blur. The ocean looked blue-gray and cold. His mouth tasted foul. He stank of salt water. There were cars on the road now. He couldn't just step outside and pee.

He heard a knock on his window, as light as a tapping fly. A grizzled old man bent to peer in at him.

"Nice car," the old man was saying.

Peter blinked and rubbed his eyes. "Thanks," he murmured, reaching for his glasses. They slipped from his fingers and dropped between the seats.

"Porsche, right?" The old man's voice sounded miles away.

"Yeah," Peter answered, neck hair pricking. He was feeling that tug again, the same wrench of demand he had sensed emanating from the image of Lydia in Phil's bedroom.

"She's a beauty, such a cutie, and from the rear, she looks like bootie. How about a ride?"

The old man kept talking. It took several seconds for Peter, still unable to find his glasses, to realize that while the background of the parking lot, the ocean, and surrounding trees was blurred, the old man was in fact crystal clear, almost painfully etched with detail. Behind him stood three children. The children were waifs, thin and pale, hardly there at all.

One of them climbed on a guardrail and did a balancing act, then jumped into the air and blew away like smoke.

"Young'uns grow three by three," the old man observed, "hang like monkeys from a tree."

Peter frantically felt between the seats while at the same time trying to keep his eyes on the old man, who smiled with sardonic benevolence.

"Lonely out here, ain't it?" the old man said. "What I need is some of that ol' Smoky Joe, twist, cut, or blend. Got some for a dear old friend?"

Peter felt the tug now sharp as a fishhook snagging his chest. His hand found his glasses and he straightened his knees, shoving himself hard upright in the seat.

"Tough old world. Smoky Joe. Helps you see what you should know."

Peter pushed the glasses over his nose, nearly poking his eye with a temple piece. The scene outside did a sickening reverse—the landscape became sharp and clear, but the man and the children suddenly lost detail. They looked ragged, not in dress but in form—dead but not decayed—not in the least like corpses, more like marble statues, faces worn smooth by long years of acid rain.

The old man's eyes were gray shadows, the nose a cartoon bump.

"Go away!" Peter shouted. His voice cracked. "You aren't there!"

The old man jammed shapeless clay hands flat against the window. The tug hauled Peter so hard against the door that he bruised his arm.

"Come on, *Peter*," the gray man said, his voice like insects trying to slap through the glass. "Give us a break, don't be slow. Give me that ol' Smoky Joe. *We all know what you don't know.*"

Then he started over again, exactly like a scratched and dirty record skipping to the beginning of the same old song.

"Nice car."

The waif jumped up on the guardrail, did a balancing act, blew away like smoke.

They were about to repeat the whole scene, with all the same lines, all the while tugging, tugging, sucking on what he was and what he knew like a lollipop, getting off on the sugar, the sweetness. Peter's thoughts turned slow and cold. He needed to get away, needed to chill the heat behind his eyes before it scalded.

He turned the key. The motor sounded like an old oil can rolling and rattling in a drum. Each cylinder laboriously ascended its round well, compressing a spume of gas, then—*BANG*—trudged down to expel a dead fume.

He could make out every slowly working piece of metal in the sequence. His ears felt as if they were stuck in Jell-O.

As he slipped the car into reverse and let out the clutch, the figures performed a frame shift, swinging beside him like transparent overlays on a theater screen.

Adrenaline kicked in. Time sped up. The tires spun and dug in and the Porsche's rear end waggled, kicking up a rooster tail of gravel. Peter toed hard on the pedal and roared and bucked onto the freeway, narrowly missing a red pickup and a big old Buick. The drivers honked and flipped him off. He did not care. He drove fast—eighty, ninety miles an hour—for ten miles, weaving through the early-morning traffic with squealing tires and drifts of rubber smoke, very unlike Peter Russell.

Two more near-collisions brought him to his senses.

At an old-fashioned garage with four rounded pumps and an antique red Pegasus, he pulled over and stopped, grabbed the shift into neutral, set the parking brake, and tried desperately to stop shaking. He strained at the shoulder harness.

The motor chugged and whined steadily behind him. Little puffs of blue smoke curled from the end of the tailpipe. He would need oil soon, he thought. The mundane world was returning, but now it had a real edge. The whole car smelled rank. He could not go to a business meeting like this. He was soaked. Gratitude for small favors—he had not shit his pants. Still, he was breathing okay. He was intact, not scattered across the freeway, with bits and pieces ground under the tires of an eighteen-wheeler.

He was alive.

He had to make himself presentable. His brain worked at high speed, using energy left over from the fear.

Taking up the Trans, Peter spoke a number—a phone number—from memory. He had to say it twice, his voice was so shaky. Desperate times called for humiliation and retribution, in that order, probably.

A woman's throaty, sleepy voice answered.

"Jessie, it's Peter. Forgive me. I need your help."

"Forgive you?" Jessie responded, her words languorous, as if she were lying back in bed. "Never. You are an unutterable creep. Where are you?"

CHAPTER 

SHOW BUSINESS HAD long ago taught Peter that some men and women should not get old. Perhaps it was looking in the mirror and predicting trends that had pushed Marilyn and Elvis into drugs and death: critical inspections of neckline, midsection, upper arms, tummy, thighs. For the heartachingly beautiful, too reliant on the love of a fickle public, putting on a few autumn pounds for the coming winter was more horrible than being nailed into a coffin.

She's fat.

She's dead.

Dead was better.

For a woman like Jessie EnTrigue, the rules did not apply. Personality had trumped age. Peter had known her when she had been the loveliest nineteen-year-old in the exploitation-film business, a fresh face with a suppliant, beautiful body and sufficient brains to pick a decent agent and move on to some decent films. She had grown nicely from a soft-core princess to establish a lasting reputation as a scream queen.

In 1970, she had starred in one of Peter's better youthful efforts, *Rising*

Shiner. They had lived together for six memorable months, and then she had packed up and moved on to better roles and better directors. "Things just aren't piggy anymore," she had told him.

By "piggy" she had meant interesting and a little perverse.

Decades later, growing large in thigh and bosom, she had played mature as an asset and became the sexiest horror-movie matron in town. Then she had quit altogether, when she could still claim it was her decision. Roles were still being offered. Peter had met her several times since at psychotronic film festivals—the last venue for old talent or talent that had never quite made the cut. They had exchanged Christmas cards once or twice.

Even now, standing in the doorway of the small, freshly painted tract home in one of the least expensive neighborhoods in Marin County, Jessie was aging beautifully. But then she lightly waved her arm to invite him in; just that, and it did not matter how old she was. Teenage boys still posted her pictures on their bedroom walls. Charisma only improved with age.

"How have you been?" she asked, swishing into the living room in a purple-and-orange caftan.

Peter followed her at two paces. "Up to now, fine, but I think I'm going nuts," he said.

She eyed him cautiously. "You stink like you've been in a fight," she said, not unkindly.

"I need to borrow a shower," he admitted.

"Jesus, Peter. It's nine A.M. Of all the showers in all the world, it has to be mine." Jessie said. "Like some coffee?"

TWENTY MINUTES LATER, she watched him like a bored cat, as he sat down on her large, comfortable couch. Peter had washed his hair and now his head was chilly. He was wearing her long, thick velour robe. He kept his hands folded politely in his lap. She had taken his shirt and underwear at the bathroom door. Even now the damp clothes were rolling and ticking in the dryer.

Jessie's half-friendly demeanor was not providing much warmth. "Someone after you?" she asked.

"I've been to a wake," he said. "I'm going in for a job interview. I needed to clean up. Thank you, by the way."

"De Nader, as they say at General Motors. Who died? Anybody I know?"

"Phil."

"Phil Richards?" Sympathy crossed her face, but the expression quickly lapsed into watchfulness.

Peter nodded. "I spread his ashes at Point Reyes last night." He fumbled into the story with eyes averted, not wanting to tell it and start crying. He explained about Lydia and his money but left out the sandblasted man and the three transparent kids. "It was rough."

"I remember Phil," Jessie said. "Nice fellow. Hungry eyes. He didn't know how to hit on women, but he wanted to. Oh, did he want to."

"He was my best friend," Peter said with a flat simplicity that surprised both of them. He looked away.

"Rough to lose friends. He was your age, wasn't he?"

"Two months younger."

Jessie was six years younger than Peter. "I'm going down to Oakland for a film festival later this morning," she said. "But I'll make you breakfast. Stoke you up for this interview. Then you have to go." She sauntered down the hall. Peter leaned back. He would have paid good money to watch her walk; it was pure music.

From the laundry room, she called out, "Is it show business?"

"Not really," Peter said. "Promotions, maybe more commercials. Telecom company. I'm going to prison."

"San Andreas? Don't try that joke around the natives." She returned and handed him his dry clothes, then gave him a look and thumbs-down. "All those telecom guys should go to prison for real. My retirement is shot."

She fixed him eggs and toast while he dressed in the bathroom. He looked at himself in the bathroom mirror as he shaved his cheeks and neck with her electric razor and recombed his hair. Presentable enough. He was starting to feel human again, if not confident.

Jessie sat on a stool at the pass-through kitchen bar and rested her chin on her hands and her elbows on the Formica. She still had the greenest eyes, and she watched him eat the way a sated cat watches a canary. "Why should I forgive you?" she asked. "What's to forgive?"

Peter pretended he could not talk with his mouth full. Finally, into her expectant and patient silence, he replied, "It just popped out."

"I left *you*, remember? Ran away with—"

"I remember," he said.

"You were a guy who needed variety. I could see that."

"I didn't, really."

"You're not here to try to hook up again, are you?"

Peter shook his head.

"Because I have a guy. A pretty good guy, a few years younger than me. Met him at a film festival. He thinks I'm a goddess. Chubby lights his fire. Isn't that wonderful?"

"It is," Peter said.

"Back then, I knew that for you, brains were everything, as long as they came with long legs and a nice pair of tits. Something told me I wouldn't be growing old with you." She waved her hands past her ample bosom and hips, *Look at me now.*

"That's not fair to either of us," Peter said.

"No, but I *do* forgive you." Now she had a distance in her eye. The visit was wearing. He was not piggy enough. "Tell me about why you're going nuts," she said.

Peter took off his glasses and wiped them with the clean paper napkin. "No," he said.

"Ingrate," Jessie said, but blew him a kiss across the counter. "Now get out. Gerry doesn't like me to consort with known photographers."

"I've been seeing things," he said. Again, the desperation; he did not want to be alone, anywhere. That frightened him almost as much as the old man and children.

"Oh?" The piggy gleam brightened in Jessie's eyes.

He told her about seeing the simulacrum of Lydia in the Tiburon house, and then, more reluctantly, he talked about the morning visitors at Point Reyes.

Jessie was very into it by the time he finished. Peter was becoming a diversion, a story she could tell her friends. She stared at him intently, green cat eyes searching. "That's wonderful," she said matter-of-factly as she took his plate to the sink. "Phantasms of the living. Doppelgangers. I made a film about that once."

"Am I crazy?" Peter asked.

"Beyond a doubt," Jessie said, then screwed up her face in disdain. "Peter! Come off it. You're not crazy."

"Then what am I?"

"People see things all the time."

"I never have," Peter said.

She shrugged that off. "Ghosts of the living are called wraiths. Ghosts of the dead are specters. I wish *I* could see something. Life is a bore around here. Maybe you can take Gerry and me out to Tiburon. We could hold a séance. On second thought, never mind. Séances are a *real* bore, and Gerry's an atheist."

She walked around the counter and gave Peter a quick hug. "Now really. Time for you to go." He appraised her bulk through the caftan and wondered about Gerry, trying to picture him.

As they walked to the door, Peter peeked down the narrow hallway, looking for he knew not what. Residues of bad times, perhaps. Wraiths of Gerry crying out for sympathy. Peter had forgotten how hard it had been, stirring more than just good humor out of Jessie.

Nothing. The rooms looked clean and good. A quiet, calm life.

Back at the Porsche, Peter opened the door and climbed behind the wheel.

Jessie smiled and waved good-bye from the door.

The Trans pressed against his hip as he buckled himself in.

CHAPTER 15

YOU COULDN'T SEE most of the old prison from the main approach road. Construction on San Andreas had begun in 1854. The complex had been emptied and decommissioned just two years ago, the stretch of magnificent Bay Area beachfront having long since become worth more to the state as raw land.

Now, tall, mobile demolition units were pulling or knocking down most of the fortresslike walls, swinging aside huge chunks of concrete and tangles of chain link and barbed wire. To the east, toppled concrete guard towers lay stacked in trios like old cheese logs, cracked and gray, facades of bricks clinging like red mold. Piles of brick and stone and concrete rubble rose in hundred-foot mounds behind construction fencing. Muddy truck-rutted gravel roads crisscrossed a wide stretch of no-man's-land still colored by jagged pentangles of lawn.

There remained intact the famous North Gate, hallowed in film and TV, with its huge brick arch. Several slogans had glamorized that dreadful span over the years, including the infamous "Pain Is Your Last Constitutional Right. Welcome to San Andreas." There had also been, "Don't Give Up Hope. Just

Give Up." All the old admonitions had been replaced by a rippling, shiny plastic banner reading HAMPTON'S SAN ANDREAS PARK BUSINESS LEASES AVAILABLE.

The new glassed-in security booth was manned by corporate guards wearing plain black uniforms. They checked his name against the appointment book. "You're going to see the Trans boys," the portly, pleasant-faced chief of security mused as he hefted an e-pad. "They've had folks in and out all day. Busy, busy. Photo ID?"

Peter produced his driver's license and the guard used his pad to scan it from the wallet. He then returned the wallet and vanished back into the booth.

Peter had nearly gone to prison once. An obscenity trial in Los Angeles in 1973 had ended in a hung jury. Even had he been convicted, Peter would not have ended up in San Andreas. This was the box that had held the twisted hard candies of crime. "Scum de la scum," Peter murmured nervously just as the guard emerged from the booth.

"Pardon me?" the guard asked.

"Did you work here before?" Peter asked.

"Not me," the guard said. "Knew some guys who did. Scary. Me, I'm a Libertarian." He gave Peter a small wireless card. "You're cleared, Mr. Russell. This is your electronic pass. If you go outside your zone, the card beeps and you show up on our screen here. Then we have to come looking for you. If you lose the pass, you cause all sorts of bother. You're going to the old DP building." He handed Peter a crisp paper map and drew him the way with a marker. "Right to the heart of San Andreas. Very exclusive." The guard smiled, showing beautifully even false teeth.

The gate, an ordinary wooden beam, lifted. Peter entered with just the slightest grind of gears.

CHAPTER 

"YOU LOOK SO *serious*," Weinstein said as he and Peter walked down the long polished concrete floor between the tiers, three stories on each side. Peter was frowning up at the cells. The bars had been removed and workers were now bustling along the walkways, carrying desks and chairs or stringing cables.

"It's a serious-looking place," Peter explained. He did not much like the decor, but Weinstein seemed pleased. Exhausted, but pleased; even a little manic.

Weinstein stared back at Peter through red-rimmed eyes. "We only have a few cubicles in this block, for overflow, you know," he said. "We took the pit right out of the peach. Got into this deal early and scored the DP block."

"DP?" Peter asked.

"Death Penalty. Dead man walking. The complex right around the gas chamber."

"Whoa," Peter said.

"Out of death comes life, and out of incarceration comes real estate.

Both lead to profit. And the ladies adore it. I cannot tell you how many times in the last month . . ." He waggled his hand from his wrist.

"Why would you rather be here than, say, Sausalito?"

"Therein lies a story," Weinstein said. "My office is right ahead. It's pretty close to the old chamber. We have all rights to the chamber, you know."

Peter did not like the way the walls seemed to close in. Trick of perspective, he decided—or deliberate design. Prisons had been made to punish after all.

Weinstein went on breathlessly. "The chamber has a table in it with straps and tubes, not a chair. Lethal injection. They stopped using gas a long time ago."

They walked through an open gate of thick bars painted a nasty shade of lime green. "This way." Weinstein pointed left, down another, shorter block, where work had progressed to the point that the cells now had glass inserts and Dutch doors. He waved his ID card over a security plate and a latch clicked. He pulled the door open. "Welcome to the office of the champion funding guru. That would be me. Thanks of course to you and to Mr. Benoliel."

The cell was equipped with a desk, a file cabinet, a PC, and a small refrigerator. The walls had been painted a fashionable but neutral gray and sported a white board and a small corkboard covered with file and business cards. Retrofit ducts and cable conduits snaked around the ceiling and floor.

"Telecoms melted down a few years ago. Remember?" Weinstein asked with a twitching wink. He opened the refrigerator and offered Peter a Pepsi. Peter popped the top and sat in the chair before the desk, which filled half the cell. The office. "WorldCom and some offshoots of Enron and a couple of other biggies were going to transform San Andreas into a huge business park, with condominiums and shops lining the waterfront. Five hundred acres of prime waterfront, can you believe it? Best views in Marin. Anyway, they were in the deal to the tune of five billion dollars when it became obvious that the old prison better suited their CEO needs." Weinstein grinned ferociously and leaned back in the office chair. "The feds shut down the whole development. But the prison was theirs to dispose of, and it came with a sweetheart tax offer from Marin, so someone made a quick decision. What's the difference between Dilbert cubicles and sad harmonicas in the Big House?"

"Not much," Peter said.

Weinstein nodded decisively. "A few surviving startups bid for space. Google wanted it, but we got in first." He lifted his Pepsi and toasted Peter.

"My apologies. It took me far too long to realize that you're the director of *Rising Shiner* and *The Private Lives of Helen and Troy.*"

Peter smiled. "Old history."

"I love those films. John Waters, eat your heart out. I go to psychotronic festivals whenever I can, which isn't often, lately. What I'm saying is, to the younger generation, you're a legend."

"I didn't know that," Peter said. Nor did he believe it.

"Well, we can play it that way in the trades. Out of the onetime slammer comes a promo campaign headed by Peter Russell, the edgiest sexploitation director ever." Weinstein's face grew serious. "And, to be honest, Russ Meyer turned us down. But then he suggested you, one Russell to another."

"Nice of Russ to give me a plug," Peter said. He glanced over his shoulder at the door. The office was remarkably small.

"It was fate." Weinstein's eyes shifted. "Cells for the condemned," he said with a barely perceptible shudder. "I try to get out whenever I can. A different route, each time, just in case." Weinstein pushed back from the desk. His chair bumped the concrete wall. "Needs a few canaries, don't you think?"

Peter chuckled, but there was little real humor in the air.

"Let's go meet our Nicola Tesla," Weinstein said. "If you two hit it off, we're in clover. By the way, do you have your Trans?"

Peter removed the unit from his coat pocket.

Weinstein put it in a desk drawer. "We don't take them any closer to the transponder than this. Sparks, sort of. Not just energy, either. *Information.*" Weinstein pushed forward another grin, this time excessively wry. "Fascinating effects."

PETER DREW INTO himself as he automatically followed his host down the relentless corridors. Talk of Russ Meyer had taken him back.

Weinstein led him into a circular cell block, older, fashioned of large ocher bricks. The cells here were larger. They passed row after row of offices occupied by eager young men and women staring at monitors.

Peter pulled up from his reverie in time to walk through a steel door, into the largest cell he had seen so far: at least nine feet by ten, concrete walls painted pale green and blue, a stylish curved desk covered with printouts and a laptop. No posters or pictures. The abode of a high-tech monk.

Weinstein introduced him to a large, bearlike man in a golf shirt and black jeans, rising from behind the desk. "Peter Russell, meet Arpad Kreisler."

The bear held out his hand and squeezed hard enough to hurt, but his face was childlike in its eager friendliness. "Pleasure to meet you," Kreisler said with a trace of some Middle European accent. He stood over six feet tall, with large, square features, and broad, stooped shoulders. Stringy black hair hung into deep-set black eyes. The way he stood revealed a casual but awkward strength, and a strangely coltish grace for a man of his imposing size. "Stanley tells me you saved our butts."

Peter looked pleasant and decided he would say as little as possible. He had no idea where he stood here. Seconds passed before he realized they expected a response. "Thanks, but I didn't do much, actually. Mrs. Benoliel did the persuading. Sorry to zone out," he added as an afterthought. "I haven't been sleeping well."

"None of us has been getting much sleep," Kreisler said, his eyes momentarily losing focus. "Too much work. But we get the hang. We are adjusting."

Peter sensed tension, but could not determine what sort: startup tension, brilliance pushed to the limit, or just working too hard and needing a year off. *Nothing amiss,* he tried to convince himself, ignoring the other voice that insisted he should leave, and sooner rather than later.

"Wonderful opportunity, working with such as you," Kreisler said. "Has Stanley told you what we are doing? What Trans does for the communication of the world?"

"I left most of that for you, Arpad," Weinstein said. "You're the heart and the brains."

"Also kidney and spleen," Kreisler said, deadpan. "I used to work for Xerox, they hire me right out of Ukraine, then for Microsoft Research, you know? I am the best." He screwed his finger into his head and winced. "But a little cracked."

Weinstein chuckled. "Definitely."

"So I do not handle money or go out in public," Kreisler said, raising his eyebrows to read Peter's reaction.

Peter managed a smile. "Maybe you shouldn't tell me too much," he warned. "I haven't signed a, what is it, an NDA or anything."

Kreisler's grin was wicked. "Not a problem," he said. "We are a hundred years ahead. We could show you everything and do the math right in front of you, and still you would have nothing."

"Brave New World," Weinstein said.

"We have yet to tell the world how brave it is," Kreisler said. "Perhaps you do that for us."

Peter pulled himself up. "Look, Stanley, Arpad—it is Arpad, isn't it?"

Kreisler nodded like a child expecting a scolding. "We haven't talked money, to be sure—"

"Not at all. I haven't made a movie in twenty years. My skills are more

Mystery Science Theater than MTV. With Joseph's money, you could hire anybody you want. So why me?"

"Actually, no," Weinstein said. "We've already spent most of it."

"Bills," Kreisler said, his lip curling and voice deepening in disgust.

"We're looking for someone different," Weinstein said. "Honestly. Not retro, but unexpected. Why not sell sexy technology the way you used to sell sex, the old-fashioned way, holding back a little? We have ever so much to hold back, and ever so much to offer. Your techniques are a natural. Compared to Hollywood today, you are innocent. So are we. But we're also the real thing. A true whiz-bang."

"Perhaps you are like wide ties and bell-bottoms," Kreisler suggested. "You are taken from the closet every thirty years, back in fashion."

"Gee, Arpad," Weinstein said, wagging his finger in warning.

Peter listened in concerned silence. They would not take no for an answer. There was more here than met the eye. Arpad seemed friendly enough, but Peter was getting cold feet—and not just because of the prison atmosphere. He was afraid of falling flat on his face all over again. He could not afford another failure. And for that reason, he was about to screw himself out of a job, if he didn't pull back and think things through. "Maybe," he murmured.

"You are not too expensive?" Kreisler asked.

Peter laughed. "I doubt it," he said. "I need the money and I could certainly use the work. I just want to be truthful."

Kreisler looked touched. "Five years ago, six of our people—one my wife, beautiful lady—walk away with fifty million dollars. They do us a favor—we are not even a blip when tech stocks and telecoms melt. Two trillion dollars go south, what me worry? But they delay us by years. Not so good after all. Truth is something we honor. I think you are our man, Mr. Russell."

"Help me, Obi-Wan Kenobi," Weinstein said, cupping his hands around his ears.

"I tell you more," Kreisler said, his voice dropping even lower. "When Stanley says he meets you, I am thrilled. I use your books to learn to read English when I am young, in Kiev. American TV-show paperbacks. I am a fan. I tell Stanley you are famous. Honor to meet you."

"What did I know?" Weinstein confessed.

Peter crinkled his eyes. Despite himself, he was touched.

"Stanley has told you the basics already, no?" Kreisler asked. "We are here to solve imminent crisis."

"Amen, save the world and make money doing it," Weinstein said.

Kreisler smiled indulgently. "Three billion people will own wireless phones and computers by year 2030. Houses, cars, refrigerators, televisions, wristwatches, eyeglasses, earrings, all will talk to information centers and receive news, guidance, entertainment, and upgrades for essential services. Companies will sell whole-body sensors that transmit data to doctors and hospitals around the world. No one will ever need to be alone and in danger again. That is what we have been promised. But the truth is much otherwise. In less than twenty years, world will run out of bandwidth. Radio, TV, cell phones, wireless, all will halt screeching growth." He smiled. "But world's problem is solvable. I have solved it."

Kreisler rose and started to move his arms, slowly at first, then describing large arcs. "No need for waves, for radiation. I discover new source of bandwidth, forbidden information channels, not truly radiation at all, unknown until now. Channels in what I call Bell continuum, after John Bell. He is famous physicist. Trans is like the way photons and electrons and atoms, everything tiny, sing to each other all day, every day, tell each other where and who they are, to balance the books and obey the laws and keep everything real. We send our messages along similar channels. That means you can use Trans anywhere. No degradation to huge distance."

Peter's eyes were playing tricks again. Whenever he blinked, he could still see the outlines of the office, the former cell. The new furniture was not there, however: just a bunk, a wall-mounted steel toilet and sink, and a small set of shelves—a prison cell, nothing more. The cell was unoccupied and still, except for an ankle-deep layer of dust.

Between blinks, the dust moved.

"In fact, for Trans," Kreisler continued, "distance means nothing. Plus, so far as we can measure, our data travels instantly." His voice had risen to dramatic heights. Now it sank to an intimate whisper. "From this time forward, nothing is the same."

"Damned right," Weinstein said. Whatever stress they were under, Peter could tell that, for them, Trans was much more than money. It was their meat and drink and religion besides.

"Faster than light?" Peter asked, rubbing his hands on his pants. He was going over the edge once again, hiding behind hallucinations, just to avoid that most dreaded F-word—failure.

"We agree, it may be a philosophical problem," Kreisler said. "But that is what we measure. Evidence is everything, no?"

With his eyes closed, Peter saw the cell as if it were drawn in glowing blue ink on black paper. If he kept his eyes closed for more than a second—which fortunately the circumstances did not permit—the colors started to shift to the hues of bruised flesh.

He worked hard to keep listening.

"Like cell phones, Trans units always tie into network. They are always on. What is more remarkable, as they work, they actually change surrounding space, perhaps permanently. They alter information permittivity. Do you know permittivity?"

"No," Peter said, then remembered his electrical training from three years in the army. He struggled to fight back, to seem competent and calm. "Is that like capacitance?" His chest was starting to bind. He wanted to shove his fingers under his ribs, but instead took short breaths. Soon the sweat would start. *I am so screwed.*

"Yes, but we use term as metaphor," Kreisler said. "A capacitor stores up charge. Space stores up information, but over time, it fades, dissipates. When Trans accesses the forbidden channels, she increases space's permittivity. Information does not fade, but builds up until it jumps like a spark. Sometimes this happens in nature already. As if space has weather, and currents of permittivity sweep past. As Trans units change space, they become more efficient. Eventually, over less than a year, our transponder will carry many, many more signals than now. Billions of units, large and small, will make our communications revolution last forever. Trans for everyone on Earth, no problem. And they will use no more energy than flies buzzing. Perhaps, in time, we even carry power. Trans can do that, you know. Power without physical power lines. An entirely new industry. And we hold all the patents."

There were footprints in the dust beside the lower bunk, the marks of big, old-fashioned shoes with flat soles. Peter could not help himself. He bowed his head and rubbed his eyes, just to take a better look, whatever the consequences. The footprints moved, sliding about slowly on the concrete. They kicked up low, dark puffs. Peter pulled away his hands. The footprints were not Kreisler's or Weinstein's.

Different shoes, a different time.

"Changing space. Faster than light. That isn't impossible—maybe dangerous?" Peter asked abruptly, hoping he wasn't sounding like a complete idiot.

"We never feel it," Kreisler said. "Trans reaches below our world, lower than networks used by atoms or subatomic particles, to where it is very quiet. Down there is a deeper silence than we can know, a great emptiness. Huge bandwidth, perhaps infinite capacity. It can handle all our noise, all our talk, anything we have to say, throughout all eternity. Even should we expand to populate entire galaxy, we can never hope to fill it." He approached the white board with marker in hand. "Are you mathematician, Mr. Russell?"

Peter thought he had heard that silence, soothing and peaceful. "Not so's you'd notice," he answered after a pause. His eyes stung. Weinstein was catching on that something was wrong, but seemed determined not to queer their deal.

Kreisler laid the marker down with a look of amused tolerance. "You can take our word for it?"

"Why not?" Peter said. Despite the delusions, the footprints, his attempts at self-sabotage, he knew this was his last chance to snatch the ring and win a prize. And there was something in Kreisler's attitude that drew him in.

"Do you have an attorney to handle your side of the deal?" Weinstein asked.

"I have an agent," Peter said, just managing to avoid a hiccup. Weinstein was watching him like a hawk. "Sorry, but I still don't have a clear picture of what you want. Commercials? Previews for trade shows? A documentary?"

"All perhaps, in time," Kreisler said, encouraged. "First we start with low-budget promotional video. Something to present to companies with whom we wish to partner. Perhaps later we edit to a tantalizing commercial, thirty-second spot. We emphasize universal need, practicality, how solid are the patents." He smiled. "We have never designed such a rollout. We would like to hear concepts."

"We'll be starting with just one short media component and in time work it up to an entire campaign," Weinstein said, still focused on Peter. "As Arpad says. Drum up partners and investors. Cash is going to be slim for a month or so. You'll have your finder's fee ... We'll write you the finder's-fee check before you leave here today. Pretty substantial. Five grand."

"Ten," Peter corrected.

"Right." Weinstein did not miss a beat. "Can you coast on that for a while? During the conceptual phase. Once we get our bearings on our relationship and firm up the contract, we can put things on a more professional footing."

Peter did not like that sort of arrangement, but he had no choice. He hated desperation, and hated begging worse. "I can cruise on the check for a while," he said. "But I will need a cash advance. I'm pretty short." He did not say, *I helped pay for a friend's cremation.*

The tension seemed thick, and then Kreisler began to snicker. He broke into a guffaw, and Weinstein joined him.

Terrific, Peter thought. *Red-eyed, acting half drunk or crazy, then hitting them up for a loan. I've become local color. The true smell of old Hollywood.*

"We have some petty cash," Weinstein said when their laughter slowed. He lifted his hands and explained to Kreisler, "His friend died last week. He's also up here to attend the wake. It's been a rough time."

"Sorry," Peter said.

"Not at all. *We* are sorry," Kreisler said. "Loss of friend, that is worst."

Weinstein opened his wallet and gave him three hundred dollars. "All I've got except grocery money."

Kreisler pulled out his own wallet.

"More than enough. Thanks." Peter folded the crisp new twenties. "I'll drive home and get to work. When should we talk again?"

"Soon. Trans will be good for reaching you, no?"

"Of course," Peter said.

"And for our next meeting, in a week or so, we'll spring for airline tickets. Coach, I'm afraid."

Kreisler said good-bye, returning to his desk and piles of papers. Weinstein walked Peter out of the cell and the block of offices.

"Kreisler likes you," he said. "That's good. He can be thorny. It is so damned difficult to teach great people how to do great things." Weinstein tapped his cranium and put on a conspiratorial look. "Want to see something truly cool?"

He led Peter deeper into the building, down a long corridor lined with windows covered with thick wire. They passed other Trans employees, sitting in converted cells, gathering around tables in former guard stations made into meeting rooms, sharing open boxes of pizza. A low buzz of talk and activity. Weinstein exchanged greetings with a few young men and women hustling from place to place. All had bags under their eyes.

"It's part of our rental block, centrally located to all our spaces, available, and, well . . . empty," Weinstein said. "Absolutely glowering with history. Could be wonderful material for a promo. Besides, we didn't know what else to do with it. It's not as if we're going to open it to tourists, right?"

Peter's eyes stung with the effort of not blinking. He followed Weinstein around another turn. They passed an old steel door marked MEDICAL EXAMINER ONLY. The next door, spaced along the outside of a gentle curve, carried a placard saying OBSERVERS. A third door immediately adjacent, also along the curve, was marked GOVERNOR/WARDEN. All three were padlocked.

"We keep server farms in these rooms," Weinstein said. "Earn extra money running corporate Web sites and advertising ventures."

"Spam?" Peter asked.

"Spam," Weinstein confirmed without any trace of embarrassment.

They approached a portable privacy curtain on wheels. Weinstein shoved the curtain aside, knocking loose a plume of dust. Through a heavy iron gate, chained and padlocked open, they entered a short hall. In passing, Weinstein jangled the chain with a swipe of his hand. More dust. "Great place for a Halloween prank, don't you think?"

Peter slowed and then stopped as the hall abruptly opened into a high-vaulted space. He looked across and up and slowly spun full circle, surveying an octagonal turret over seventy feet across and eighty feet tall, topped by a high cupola. Dark iron beams supported the peaked copper roof. Between the beams, small windows set all around permitted a haze of light to suffuse the upper air.

Motes flashed in the distant rays.

"They used to call this the chancel," Weinstein said, his voice sliding into uncharacteristic reverence. He stepped to one side. "Like around an altar. Are you Catholic?"

Peter reluctantly drew his eyes down from the tiny spill of daylight. Pressing close to the opposite wall, resting on a concrete foundation, almost lost in shadow, stood a hexagonal chamber with its own smaller peaked roof, like a bizarre, diminutive chapel. An iron rail formed a half-circle around the chamber. The floor beyond the rail was divided by grated black iron drains, a sinister ornamental border. The chamber walls were plates of riveted forged steel enameled a sickly green. Three thick glass windows set in bolted frames afforded a view of the black interior. Someone had mounted a bumper sticker on the middle window. It read: HONK IF YOU LOVE JESUS. Peter saw nothing else inside the chamber but a few blinking lights: red, white, and green.

To Peter's left and facing the chamber, three long single-pane picture windows dominated the concrete inner wall. All were curtained on the inside. The curtains were drawn. Peter deduced that the doors along the convex outside wall opened to rooms behind these windows. He imagined special visitors walking into the rooms, concentrating their view until they saw only the chamber. Focusing on the death to come.

"Voilà," Weinstein said. "What kind of spin can we get from this? Out with the barbarian past, in with the bright, gleaming future. Out of death comes talk. Something like that. You're the artist."

Peter looked up, stuck his hands deep into his pockets, turned around again. He did not know what to say.

"They used to treat this whole place like a church," Weinstein said, eyes still bright. "Except the priests wore Sam Brown belts and thirty-eights and the penitents wore orange suits and shackles. Processions. Step by solemn step. Everything but organ music. Now it's ours. Well, we rent it anyway."

Peter tried to imagine this awful place as one's last stop on Earth, a prisoner's last view of this world; antique, lightly corroded, filled with crude, scientific efficiency. "Tear it down," he said, swallowing a lump.

"Beg your pardon?"

"I'd bring in the wrecking ball. Break it to pieces."

"You don't think we can use it?"

Peter made a sick face. He knew a little about capital punishment, had read up on it while brainstorming ideas for horror films. Watched Susan Hayward being led to this very chamber, or one just like it, reconstructed on a Hollywood set. *I Want to Live.* Paying state employees to turn human beings into limp meat.

For a moment, he forgot not to blink. As he closed his eyes, seeking blessed relief from the dryness, the pain, the chamber, he saw:

Nothing.

Just the dim, descending sunlight, reddened by the blood still pulsing in his eyelids.

But below the calm, like magma below a dormant volcano ...

Stop it, damn it. He blinked several times. *Nothing. Nothing yet.* He took a deep breath. Seeing the death chamber had to force everything into a brutal perspective. *You're still alive. Get on with it.*

"Well, fuck, what *do* you do with a place like this?" Weinstein asked. "Give it the high-tech finger, I say. So we put our heart in there, the heart of Trans, the most advanced piece of electronic equipment on Earth, Arpad's transponder. We didn't even have to upgrade the power supply. And you know, they never did use the electric chair. Just hanging, gas, and lethal injection." Weinstein swung about and tapped the chamber's thick window. "You can almost see them in there, can't you?"

Peter glanced away.

"Strapping them down." Weinstein's eyes widened with speculation, and his throat bobbed. "Letting the pellets drop—isn't that what they did, way back then? Gas spewing up from tanks of acid. Cyanide. Or being strapped to the table, letting the doc pinch up your artery, insert the needle. Did it sting? Did they use alcohol first, to clean the skin? What was the point? The patient didn't have to worry about infection, right?" He was really into it now.

With some embarrassment, Peter observed that Weinstein had a small but obvious bulge in his pants.

Weinstein pointed up at the iron arches. "I don't think they ever hung anybody."

"Not in here," Peter said, feeling ill. "They built scaffolds outside."

BACK IN WEINSTEIN'S office, the young man wrote him his advance check, returned Peter's Trans unit with a magician's flourish, and said they would be speaking again soon.

They had a deal.

Outside, Peter blinked regularly as Weinstein escorted him to the guard booth. He could not make out the faint black-and-blue world beneath the daylight. They shook hands firmly and Peter returned his pass to the guard.

"We must be brave," Weinstein proclaimed.

"Right," Peter said.

"Trans is just like walking on the moon. That's what Arpad says." Weinstein shook his head in almost frenetic admiration. "You should write that down. Sheer genius."

CHAPTER 

WITH MONEY IN his pocket and the Porsche full of gas, he sped south on 5, intent on getting to Los Angeles as fast as he could. The bland straight miles on the freeway and the steady controlled rasp of the Porsche's air-cooled engine worked like solitude and music, or should have, but Peter was certain he was losing his mind. The more he racked up the miles, the less he knew whether he was coming or going, seeking or fleeing.

He talked the situation over with himself, glancing at his eyes in the rearview mirror, before he grew tired of rehashing the facts or his perception of the facts.

It had all begun with Sandaji in Pasadena—or earlier, at Salammbo.

It had all begun with Phil.

The truck-rutted asphalt of the freeway played rhythmic hell with his tires. *Sandaji, Salammbo. Sandaji, Salammbo.*

Lydia's cast-off emotions, as if even living people could manufacture ghosts.

The eel shadows so eager to get into Phil's bedroom.

The eroded figure and the phantom children at the beach.

Peter tried to hum a tune. Suddenly, he needed music. The radio had been broken for years, but only now did he miss the chatter and noise of the busy outside world, talk shows, pop music, religious sermons. The air was full of information, and all you needed was a receiver, but his radio was broken.

Until now.

"I do not know what the hell I am trying to think, here," he shouted, and rolled down the window just to feel the Central Valley air blow past. The interior of the Porsche became a resonant, pulsing bellows. "I am not a radio. I am not tuning in to another world."

He took a break at a rest stop and got out of the car, stretched his legs, watching people walk their dogs on the designated grassy field. He restlessly tried to avoid staring at anything for very long.

What if some of the things you see every day aren't really there? What if they just look normal? You seldom compare notes with anybody, do you? You don't bring along a video camera and record every minute of your daily life to see what you might have seen that wasn't there after all.

He dipped his head. He was doing it again. "Oh, crap," he murmured under his breath. "None of it makes sense. I'm losing it. I'm afraid to get back into the saddle."

An elderly woman came into hearing distance and he clamped his teeth. White-haired, wearing a flower-print dress and antique white nurse pumps, she had pink hearing aids tucked up in both ears like little plastic mushrooms. A Pomeranian on a short, taut leash tugged her forward.

"Nice day," she said, nodding pleasantly. The dog's tongue hung out as it pop-eyed frantically at the bushes, eager to move on. The old woman awarded Peter a grandmotherly expression, mouth shaping a pleased simper, head nodding slightly as she looked at a point just beyond his left arm. The Pomeranian husked and strained. The old woman lifted her gaze back to Peter, expression full of matronly congratulations. "Lovely," she said, and then, with a jerk on the leash that made the dog gag, moved on.

Peter stopped and made a one-eighty. The woman was solid, real. The Pomeranian was fluffy and orange and ridiculous. He stood for a moment, and the despair burst. A chuckle came out gentle, not harsh, from deep in his chest. Life was too weird. A way with the ladies. Phil would have seen it immediately. He could almost hear Phil in his head, *You remind her of someone. An old beau, maybe. The best orgasm she ever had, sixty years ago, you bastard you.*

And as for the rest of the morning:

Nothing unusual; just concrete walkways, lawn, small trees, brick buildings, a volunteer coffee booth manned by two fit-looking gents about his age but looking older and happier, people walking, dogs walking, kids running.

A rest stop. Real and solid. Nothing more.

He felt like squaring his shoulders but instead just took a deep, easy breath. He had a job. He had work, finally—decent work that could put him back on top.

Maybe it had been self-sabotage, maybe not. But whatever, maybe it was over.

CHAPTER 

THE PORSCHE STOWED in the garage—it had made the long trip in high old style, he was proud of it, would have liked to stuff its noble nose into a big old bag of oats—the house in good shape, no burglaries, everything quiet, calm; Phil scattered to the ocean, back to the carbon cycle, the best anyone could do for him now; Peter's mind sleepily going over schemes for how to promote a new kind of telecom product—and wasn't that rich, he was so out of it he could be trendy again, like string-bean ties—and the porch smelling of late-summer jasmine; the blackboard by the Soleri bell empty of new messages, his answering machine silent and empty of calls; nothing to stop him after the long long drive from simply peeling off his clothes and climbing into bed, no shower on the way, he did not stink so bad—still smelled of Jessie's soap, in fact—so tired. A warm spot in his heart for good old Phil, dammit, he had done his duty to his friend, there would be missing him and maybe more tears later but that part of his life had to be over. Shirt off, pants halfway down, he stopped by the full-length mirror. His chest-hairs were gray and he wore loose boxers now rather than BVDs because BVDs made his balls ache, he had a tight little paunch that wouldn't go away, but life was not over, far from it. He was tired. He had done well, dammit. He had a job.

He crawled into the unmade bed, then reached down to peel off his socks. Still flexible. He could reach his ankles. He could still please a woman in bed four or five different ways—more if they were inclined to be creative—and that was good.

It would come. All that was good would return, a second summer for Peter Russell.

He pulled up the sheet, all he needed on this warm night. A breeze blew outside, fresh and welcome; the wind chimes in back tinkled. Bed felt so good. He was well into a dream about set construction and actors when someone knocked on the front door, then donged the Soleri bell. He was a light sleeper. He had to be, the house was old and easy to break into. He hated thieves.

He pulled on a robe and went to answer, feet slapping bare against the parquet and then the tile. He stared through the glass at Carla Wyss, rubbed his eyes, and opened the door.

Carla returned his stare and then looked down at her feet, her knees, like a little lost girl. "The bastard," she said. "It's over."

"What's over?"

"I'm an idiot. I'm too old."

"You're not too old," Peter assured her, yawning. He opened the door wider. "What happened?"

"What always happens. This time, even stupid old me knew it was coming, and I was ready. I clobbered him. I scratched his cheek. I screamed. I became such a *bitch*, Peter." The tears began, dampening her cheeks as she stood pigeon-toed on the tile floor in her leather miniskirt and white blouse and lace net nylons and high-heel black pumps. "Am I a bitch?"

"Only when you need to be," Peter said, still standing there, waiting. He would not send her away. She had been a lover, she was still a friend, and he did not know what she needed, much less what she wanted.

"You are the only man who was ever decent to me," Carla said, her lip quivering. "I treated you so badly."

"That's not how I remember it," Peter said.

She faced him. "It doesn't matter. It just doesn't matter anymore, but am I, like, a complete hag?"

"You're gorgeous. You know it," Peter said.

"I feel like a bag of trash left out by the curb," she said. "I try not to be a down chick," she added after a swallowed sob, "and the world just hammers and *hammers*." Spoken softly and reasonably. Hands by her sides. Color gone from her face.

That made him jump. He did not like colorless faces.

"Tea," Peter announced.

"What?"

"You need some hot tea."

Her sad, stern look melted and she wiped her cheeks with her finger. *No mascara streaks, thank you, Lord.* "Oh, yes," she said. "And chocolate. Do you have chocolate?"

"Godivas good enough?"

She looked up, delighted, more like a little girl than ever. "Really? You have Godivas?"

"Tea, the best chocolate, and sympathy."

"Oh, Peter." She tried to grin wickedly. "I am a chocolate vampire, and you are my victim. You are the one." Then the tears started all over again. Peter put his arm around her shoulders and led her into the kitchen.

"I keep them locked up," he said. "The maid sneaks them."

IT WAS OBVIOUS Carla did not want sex, and Peter quickly discovered that despite initial yearnings, he was far too tired to care. He was just glad for company. She took a BlackBerry from her purse—essential equipment for actors hoping for agent calls or e-mails—and turned off the phone part, removed her clothes in the bathroom, put on one of his old shirts—something that he usually found extremely stimulating in a woman—and lay down beside him with an expression that drew the last of the blood from his erection. She looked utterly and fatally lost.

Peter snuggled against her.

"No sex," she reminded him.

"Of course."

"But hug me," she said. He did.

"I never learn," she said a few minutes later, just as he was starting to nod off. The red letters of the clock said it was four in the morning. He could tell even with her back to him that she had her eyes wide open.

"Can we talk later?" Peter asked. "I've had a very long day."

"Uh-huh," she said.

HE CAME WIDE-AWAKE at nine and lay beside Carla's dark, snoring form. She had rolled herself up like a sheet sausage, stealing most of the covers. In boxers and T-shirt, Peter slipped out of bed and strolled into the kitchen, bending and straining one arm to scratch between his shoulder blades. He put a kettle on the stove and inspected the refrigerator. There were five eggs. He smelled the open package of bacon, plastic streaked white with cold grease; still good. Milk not fresh but drinkable. The cream in its smaller carton had become a cheesy mass. Two apples, jam, some bread that would toast up nicely once he scraped off a little mold. Good enough for a surprise breakfast, he thought.

He stared at the stove, bits of carbon sintered into the stainless steel but otherwise clean. A clean bachelor stove. Something chimed lightly and far away, not the Soleri bell. He puzzled over what it could be, then remembered the Trans in his coat pocket.

What with finding the coat—draped over the purple chair—and fumbling out the unit, he flipped the case open by the seventh ring. "Peter here." He was half-expecting Michelle or perhaps Weinstein.

"Hey, Peter, it's Hank! Thought I'd give you a call, or whatever. This Trans thing sounds great. You're as clear as a bell."

"Yeah, you, too," Peter said, glad to hear another male voice. "How's Prague?"

"Wet. Whole city is up to its ass in filthy water. Six productions have been flooded out, including ours. But we're back to work tomorrow. I strung big lights in the hotel dining room and hooked them to the company generator. We sang songs and drank coffee and beer all night. It was like the Sahara in there, the lights were so hot. Hotel porters came in to dry out. Everyone cheered right up."

"Sounds great," Peter said. He added some gray to his tone. "Phil's wake went okay. Lydia was there."

"Ah," Hank said.

"I spread Phil's ashes on the beach at Point Reyes."

"He would have liked that."

"Yeah. Still might have some under my fingernails. Want me to save you a speck?"

Hank laughed nervously. "I'd prefer Phil as a diamond, you know, all squeezed down. They do that."

"Yeah, well, he was a gem, all right."

"When I was a kid," Hank said, "I heard the word *cremation* and thought it meant they turned you into cream."

Peter groaned. "That's awful," he said. "Carla is here now. She ran into another one of her agents."

"Did you give her Godivas?"

"And tea. She's asleep. I'm fixing her breakfast. It's good to hear your voice. Good to know someone's working."

"When the water level drops, I'll be working. Right now, I'm sitting in a hotel room reading a stack of *Asterix* I borrowed from an Italian stand-in."

Phil had once owned every single issue of *Asterix*, in French and in English. They might still be in boxes in the house, Peter thought. "I might have a job myself," he said. "Doing commercials and promos for Trans."

"That's great! Money or credit?"

"Money, they say. I'm so out, I'm back in."

"Hey, when you're not hot, you're cool. Everyone here has a Trans," Hank said. "They must have saturated LA, because I swear, the entire crew is carrying them around. I fit right in. Even Bishop has one. He calls his wife every day, tells her to send him dry socks."

"Sounds like an adventure. I envy you."

"Yeah, well, envy me after I run my cables through a puddle and fry the DP. He's a right bastard, a real chiaroscuro type. He's running all of us hard around corners. I won't have any tread left in a week."

Peter could pick up the expressions a crew invented during a shoot. Films were little wars and every crew had its catch-phrases and scars and campaign medals.

"But hey, Prague's great. No ghosts, though. We're all very disappointed."

"Give it time," Peter said, not so lightly.

"Right—"

Then, abruptly, a burst of harsh cricket chirps ended the call.

"Hank?"

No answer. The connection was gone.

Peter heard the deeper silence and pulled the unit back from his head. "Nothing's perfect," he muttered, and listened to Carla moving around in the bedroom. He folded the unit and placed it on the dining table.

"Breakfast for sleeping beauty," he shouted to her. "Coffee with no cream, bacon, and scrambled eggs."

Carla came out still wearing his old Pendleton. "Man, did I dream," she said.

"Sit, eat," Peter invited. She surveyed the table with sad, wise eyes.

"You are the best," she said.

"Tell me something I don't know," Peter said.

SHE MOVED AND sat slowly, as if walking through mud. Peter recognized the symptoms well enough.

"Why so low?" he asked, sitting across the table to give her room to make her own decisions, in her own time.

"I am such a fuckup," she said, placing both hands on the table. She was still astonishingly beautiful, though not in a credit-card commercial way.

"Shh," Peter said. "You're taking the sacred name of sex in vain."

She shook her head like a toy whose action was winding down. "I am forty-two years old. Never married. No career. I sleep around sometimes and from what I've learned, there isn't a man in town who won't fuck me, and not one willing to stick around for more than a week."

"I did."

"I was younger then, and I was working for you," Carla said, facing him with a soft frown. Her eyebrows swept gently but with determination over dark blue eyes to a high but not too assertive forehead. Those brows still feathered at their ends like a girl's, untouched by makeup. Peter watched her face with professional appreciation, automatically checking how he would light it, where he would set up diffusers and umbrella, where he would place the baby spots to accent. Beneath the Pendleton, she wore no underwear; that was good. No red lines and dimples from bra hooks to smooth. And it was morning; her tummy would still be flat from lying vertically for so many hours. By mid-afternoon, one had to change the lighting and adjust angles carefully to minimize the sagging effects of gravity.

"It's so awful, Peter," Carla said, and abruptly lifted her hands to cover her face, not to cry, but to hide. "I don't want to have ever been in this business."

"It was good for a time," Peter said.

"It's a dead end."

"Not for some."

"For you and for me, it is."

"Oh," Peter said. "Well."

"I wasn't good enough, long enough," Carla said.

"You just need to find a better class of fellow. Play hard to get. You're a knockout."

This brought her hands down. "I'm honest," she said. "I trust men and I like them. Is there something wrong with that? I had a wonderful father, and that spoiled me."

Peter had not heard this angle before. He smiled.

"I just never know what to expect from men," Carla finished.

"I never treated you badly," Peter said. Before she could disagree, he added, "Eggs are getting cold."

Carla took a bite. Some of the sadness and anger went away with the taste of food. She sipped from her cup and made a face. "Mr. Coffee," she said. "Maxwell House."

"Folgers. I'm not a rich guy, Carla."

"I prefer Kona coffee or espresso."

"So do I."

They sat in silence for a moment while she finished her eggs and started on the bacon strips. The thing about Carla, Peter knew, was that her sadness, even when it was deep, never lasted for more than a few hours. She was naturally sunny.

"I had some weird dreams last night," Carla said, raising her eyes to the kitchen window, mouth full.

"Oh?"

She finished chewing. "I dreamed somebody like you was horny and had been dreaming about girls and sex and when you woke up, they just hung off of you, like old, naked balloons."

Peter made a disgusted face. "That is truly . . ." He could not find the word.

"That isn't all. The books in your shelves were shedding limp white sacks. I looked around and there were like these sacks hanging off them, like condoms, or you know, like when a spoon pulls up the skin on hot milk."

"Gaah," Peter said, and got up to put the dishes in the sink. Carla had never shown a creative or surreal talent before. He found the images disturbing; he could imagine them very clearly.

He scrubbed a pan for a while, feeling her eyes on his back.

"It was so real," Carla said. Her thoughtful look returned. "You were getting up to go to the bathroom. I rolled over in bed and watched. You dragged these deflating women after you, and something dark swooped down and ate them, just like that. Picked them off of you. You didn't even notice. God, I remember it so clearly now. Wasn't that a weird dream?"

Peter had gotten up twice to go to the bathroom. Lying next to Carla without moving had not been easy, but he could not remember dreaming about sex.

It's why you don't remember most dreams. They get eaten, like Lydia's cast-off emotions.

Peter jumped as if stung by a wasp.

Carla jerked in sympathy. "What's wrong?" she asked.

"Nothing," Peter said and turned to look down at the scrapings in the sink, trimmed edges of crisp egg white. He poked it all down the drain and reached to switch on the disposal.

"Damn, I've turned you off," Carla said when the grinding ended. "Isn't that just my luck."

Peter rinsed his hands. He was not turned off. Of all things, behind the numb expectancy of more weirdness to come, he was even hornier than he had been before.

Carla sidled up behind him.

"May I?" she said, and took his shoulders and turned him around. "I need a good guy, just to balance things. Let's get *sacred*, Peter."

As they made love, Peter could not help thinking that what he had, whatever he had, was contagious. It didn't matter. Everything was so frantic and sharp through his entire body, he felt as if he were sixteen again and could go all day long. He had been without a woman for six months. Peter Russell, without a woman. For six months. He had not gone without sex for that long since he had lost his virginity.

That was it, really; that explained it all.

CHAPTER 

THE WIND CHIMES sang below the bedroom window, waking him from a doze. He looked at the red letters on the bedside clock. It was two in the afternoon. He felt totally refreshed.

Everything began from this point. Sex had always made him feel that way. Looking down on a naked woman had always filled him with a sense of wonder; privilege and lust and something that stood a little further aside, telling him of his value. Peter measured himself by the joy of his women.

He rolled over.

Carla sat up in bed. She sighed and smiled. Her smile revealed a little more tooth and gum on the right side, and that made her extraordinarily beautiful. "Is it true, a woman once asked you to come over to her house and teach some teenage boys about oral sex?" she asked.

"Yeah."

"Amazing."

"That was in the sixties," Peter said.

"Still, it's pretty gutsy. Did she have, like, permission slips from the parents?"

Peter pushed his pillow up beside hers. "I don't know," he said. "She thought it was her civic duty. Teaching young men to keep their women happy would help them stay married."

Carla watched him. "I need someone to keep me happy, and it will never be you. Though you do cheer me up."

"Thank you. I think. You cheer me, too."

"I was afraid, from the look in your face, when I told you—"

Peter twisted and pressed a finger lightly against her lips. Carla did tend to spoil good moments with chatter. A minor flaw, but he was enjoying this new beginning too much.

She nibbled the tip of his finger. "I bet you taught them well. But, how did you, I mean—show them?"

"Flash cards," Peter said, making a broad sweeping gesture. "Anatomical charts. I wore a cap and gown." He swung a stiff arm, pulled down an imaginary map, and pointed out the highlights. "Labia, vulva, clitoris, fetching water by the high road, swinging donkey by his ears, bringing honey home for tea." He pantomimed with nimble fingers, then reached to demonstrate. Carla looked shocked and squirmed out of reach with a giggle.

Peter raised his head. "It was years before every porno film in Christendom showed young people how to give head."

"Did the boys get married and stay married?"

"I don't know," he said.

"I feel so much better," Carla said. "Thank you so much. And now I have to go." She got out of bed and picked her clothes from the top of the hamper, where she had left them the morning before. She regarded him intently as she slipped on her black fishnet hose. "Hush," she said.

"What?"

"You're thinking too loud."

"Your legs are too long."

She put on her blouse, then her skirt, zipping it up the front, rotating it, and finishing the zip. Arching one knee, she pushed her feet into the black high-heel pumps, then angled her elbow, giving him a coy three-quarters glance and running fingers through her long black hair.

Peter smiled.

"Well?" she said.

"Come back to bed," he said.

"You couldn't, and I shouldn't," Carla said, smiling sweetly. She blew him a kiss. "Say good-bye in here," she instructed primly as she walked through the bedroom door.

In the living room, sun poured through the big window onto the back of the couch and made a yellow wedge across the floor. Carla stood by the front door. He went to her in his robe and leaned forward to kiss her with equal primness.

"I would still like my glossy," she told him, all business now. "I'm out of copies."

"Boyfriends?" Peter asked.

She made a face. "Agents and filchers. Some were boyfriends. Isn't that perverse, taking souvenirs?"

"I guess," Peter said.

Carla unlocked the door and opened it. Peter heard another woman's footsteps. "Sorry," Carla said, stepping back.

Helen came through the door and swept the room with her eyes, swept up Peter in his robe, swept Carla up and down the whole length of her. She smiled and did not look in the least upset.

"It's been a long time, hasn't it, Peter?" Helen said as Carla murmured something and backed through the door. "Don't run away mad in the heat of the day!" Helen called out after her. Then, closing the door, she took a breath and added, "Just *run away.*"

HELEN SEEMED TO be enjoying his discomfort. She sat on the couch with her arms slung back and contemplated Peter, with his hands stuck deep in the pockets of his robe, standing in the middle of the living room.

"Still no beer?" she asked.

"Still," Peter said. "Where's Lindsey?"

"In school, dope," she said. "But tonight's the night. I very much need your services. I'll be bringing Lindsey over about nine. This could be the one, Peter."

"New guy?"

"I've been seeing him off and on for a year. We've cleared away some blockages, he's needy … Tonight, he might even carry a little velvet box."

"Congratulations. Good luck," Peter said.

"You'll be here?"

"Helen, I haven't seen my daughter in months. I'd love to have her stay over."

"Because sometimes I never know."

"I'll be here."

"You won't be off at Salammbo running errands for Michelle and Joseph?"

Helen was convinced there was something between Peter and Michelle, that he was betraying his aging boss. She had met Michelle once, three years ago, and had been instantly suspicious. But then, Helen had been suspicious of every woman in Peter's sightlines.

Yet she had been the one to cheat and walk out in the darkest hour of their lives. Not without excuses, of course. Madness and grief had taken their toll.

"Not tonight. I have work to do here. Will she need dinner?"

"I'll feed her first."

"I'll be here," Peter said, gritting his teeth.

"A little old for you, don't you think?" Helen asked, pointing her nose at the door. "Pretty, though. What's her name? Is she a model?"

"No, yes she is, Carla Wyss, and yes. She can't find work, not the kind she wants."

"Nor the men, I'll bet," Helen said. "But you'll do in a pinch."

Peter needed to stay on good terms with Helen. She seldom showed outright anger, but she could withhold that which was not hers to withhold—sometimes for months. He had long ago learned that where he was concerned, Helen preferred her negative opinions, and confirming those opinions in any small way humored her.

He gave her a deliberately sappy, little-boy smile. "I yam what I yam," he said.

Helen surprised him. She looked down at the tile floor and said, "You're being helpful. I'm sorry. I have no right. I am just so nervous."

"It's nothing. Bring Lindsey by. Nine tonight, right?"

"She's going through a rough time. No surprise. I can't always cut it. She needs a father," Helen said, still looking at the tile.

They both turned at the sound of a delivery truck pulling up the driveway. Helen's car was blocked for the moment. She watched Peter sign for a package from Marin. That reminded him. He pulled Weinstein's check from his wallet and dangled it in front of her.

"Real work," he said. She made a surprised, approving face.

"I'm impressed," she said.

"I'll write it over to you," Peter said. "Take out the next two months' for Lindsey. Bring me back the rest."

"It might take a week to clear. I don't have enough in my account to cover it."

"I'll survive." He signed the check over to her. Then, feeling generous, he held up a finger for her to wait a sec and retrieved a Trans from the box in the hall. *"Pour vous,"* he said. "Free talk, from anywhere, to anywhere on Earth."

"What's the gimmick?" Helen asked.

"It only lasts a year. Then, if you're nice to me, maybe you'll get another."

Helen looked at the unit, but did not take it from his hand. "Very pretty," she said. "But I don't like strings."

"No strings. Big promotional rollout. Only the best people are getting them."

She twitched her lip, took the unit, and slipped it into her purse. Walking through the door and across the porch, she called over her shoulder, "Congratulations on the job. But remember. Lindsey. Your daughter. Nine P.M."

Peter watched her go. Helen's car now carried a bumper sticker proclaiming that in choosing between men and dogs, she preferred dogs. Peter refused to believe that he had done that to her; he was pretty certain that despite everything, as far as male company went, he was still the best thing that had ever happened to her.

And, of course, he was the father of her children.

Child.

He ripped open the package and stared at the contents: thick contract on top, letters from Arpad and Stanley, a clipped batch of sketches—of the prison offices, the gas chamber, smiling men and women using Trans. Someone had scribbled professionally drawn banners in silver marker across three renderings of the gas chamber, making a sequence. The banners read: A FEW YEARS AGO, TELECOMS WERE EXECUTED BY WALL STREET. / NOW, THEY'RE BACK FROM THE DEAD AND READY TO WORK FOR YOU! / TRANS

Peter scanned the sequence several times, aghast.

Stanley's note said, *"We have engaged Throughput, a great agency in Palo Alto. They'll work with you on video design, layout and such, content and script to be mutually decided. We're very excited."*

Arpad had written, *"I am handing it all over to Stanley and you. Glitches with the system absorb my time. These sketches are just some ideas. Bad ones, I think."*

"No shit," Peter said. On every project, there came a time when you were painfully deflowered. He wondered how much Throughput was going to be paid to bugger him.

Well, maybe he could turn that around. Anything he came up with had to be better. Arpad seemed sensible, even creative; he knew bad from good. Suddenly and perversely, Peter felt reenergized. This was just like the movie business: piling up the manure until a flower popped out.

He was back in the game.

CHAPTER 

HE TOOK A brass key black with age and unlocked the door to his basement office. The floor and part of a wall at the back of the basement oozed moisture sometimes after a hard rain and he had covered them with plastic. The duct tape holding the plastic to the concrete had failed and the sheet curled sadly. Water had stained a box filled with old newspapers. Back then, Peter had been a pack rat, keeping everything—magazines, newspapers, hoping to search and clip them and put quotes and quips and philosophy into a long-planned collection. That had stopped two years ago.

He hadn't entered his office in a year.

A big metal war-surplus desk filled the corner of the office. On it perched an old IBM computer and an Olivetti portable typewriter, stacks of paper covered with more plastic sheets. Behind the desk rose a warped wooden bookcase filled with paperbacks, some of them bulging with moisture. The room smelled damp. He opened a window high on the north wall to let in some air.

Against the south wall, his huge drafting table still held a pasteup for a photo comic he had been working on. Dialog labels had come loose and slipped to the metal catch-strip on the front of the table. They made amusing juxtapositions: *Hey, this one's on fire// With all the passion// a boiled onion.*

You look like// screaming metal on the highway.

Don't worry, bub// drop your H's.

Peter stared down at the old work. Ancient history. He knew he had a pad of television-style storyboard paper around somewhere, out-of-date for sure but still usable. He pawed through musty tablets and blocks of watercolor paper, found the tablet he was looking for, and then cleared the drafting table, scooping the loose dialog labels into a little bag. He slipped the unfinished page into a tall metal blueprint file cabinet in the corner. He switched on the overhead light and the light over the drafting table.

At sixteen, he had fled from Buffalo, New York, away from the horrors of home and high school, to San Francisco. There, he had witnessed the seamy heyday of Haight-Ashbury. The wonder and druggy awfulness—and the sex—had impressed him mightily, teaching basic survival skills that had served him well ever since.

Running out of money, and with his father refusing to take collect phone calls that in any case he was reluctant to make, Peter had dropped his already bogus student deferment and showed up at the Selective Service Office one drizzling November day in 1966. He had been shipped to boot camp at Camp Lejeune, North Carolina. With typical army economy, he had then been returned to California to spend two and a half years at Fort Hunter Liggett. A relatively intelligent sergeant who had shared Peter's taste for comics had enrolled him in the School of History and Journalism, a small program designed to create writers who would counter the cultural poison of hippie protesters.

Peter had found himself surrounded for the most part by the spoiled sons of middle-class eastern Democrats, mostly from New York. Far from considering hippies to be poison, Peter had spent all of his leave time in Berkeley and Oakland. There, he had avoided drugs heavier than beer and pot and had lived with a succession of confused, artistic-minded women in their late twenties. The woman who had sold him his first camera—a used Nikon body with two beat-up lenses—had tutored him in both health food and cunnilingus. The camera had belonged to her fiancé, a photojournalist killed in Mexico. Peter had paid her twenty dollars for it.

He still had that camera somewhere.

In an old apartment in Oakland, in front of a large bay window, she had posed on a couch, an unlikely beauty—lithe, classy, a pale patrician face, large, deep black eyes, frizzy auburn hair, a body somewhere between Klimt and bulimia. Peter's photos had made her look haunting and luscious.

He had discovered a knack. Soon, he had packed away a hundred pages from his first novel and started submitting photo layouts. The woman, impressed by Peter's artistry, his ability to turn "a thin old broad into a classic wet dream," as she had put it, had brought in a trio of female friends curious about "artful photography." She had encouraged Peter to practice both photography and lovemaking on them all.

Amazing woman. Amazing time.

She had died in a traffic accident in 1969. That year, out of the army, out of work, and now out of a house, he had wandered into a clandestine movie studio in a Tenderloin warehouse, a windy cavern of darkness and dust interrupted by movie lights. Actors naked beneath open robes, wearing bath slippers and smoking hand-rolled reefers, had wandered through dirty passages between flats shoved together to make crummy sets.

It had been day two of a cheap nudie. For the first time, while the photographer sat wasted and despondent in a corner, Peter had peered through the viewfinder of a sixteen millimeter Arriflex. He had offered to load film, claiming that he had shot movies in the army. He hadn't. The producer—a small, thin dude who wore a Stetson and called himself Brock Werst—had broken off from a fit of monotonous cursing and coughing and suggested, with not a hint of irony, that maybe Peter could become a grip, maybe he could become a focus puller, maybe he could become a cameraman, how about director of photography.

The next day, the director had been a no-show. Peter had taken on that task, as well. Coming down from a cocaine binge, stanching a perennial bloody nose, Werst had handed over the ten-page script as well.

That night, sitting in a tiny hotel room on Shattuck Avenue, Peter had ballooned the script into thirty pages and sketched storyboards on a Walter T. Foster art pad. He had reported to the warehouse the next day wearing a white baseball cap on which he had scrawled, in Magic Marker, "Direct This" above the brim and "Shove Film" across the back. The actors had loved it, and Werst had laughed and proclaimed, "Shit, you're the man."

The picture had been released—escaped, some claimed—as directed by Regent King. His next film, shot the following week, had been credited to King Regent.

Those had been bad times for erotic cinema, legally speaking, and things would only get worse, but there was money to be made, pretty women to take to bed, exciting times moving actors around under hot lights, and of course, that perennial flower in Hollywood, dreams of bigger things.

Peter had made twenty-one films between 1969 and 1983, fifteen of them under his own name. During the same period, he had sold over a hundred photo layouts, beginning with basement men's magazines like *GRR* and *Tuff.* Then had come a spread in *Rogue.* In 1972, two layouts in *Oui* had followed. Those sales, and three films paid for in cash and released in one month, had helped buy him his used Porsche and the Glendale hills house.

Big-busted and leggy women had arrived in Peter's life, more than even he could imagine dealing with, attracted to power, any power, and desperate for anything resembling charm. But compared with Peter's dreams, it had all seemed small potatoes.

Then had come his three months with Sascha and, coincidentally, felony obscenity charges in LA County Superior Court. That had forced Peter to realize that his wave was breaking. He was little more than a grunion snatched off the local beach to serve as an example to deepwater sharks. Hard core was beginning to dominate the skin-flick industry, bringing with it sharp but futile jabs of legal repression and a pall of mob activity.

Eventually, Peter had sold five cartoons to *Playboy.* But every novel and story he had submitted—written on sets during downtime and at home—had been rejected. Finally, with too much energy and too many bills to pay, he had taken on a novelization, writing a book based on a popular TV show, *Canine Planet.*

"On Canine Planet, dogs rule and men are slaves . . ."

That, at least, had come out under his own name.

He dusted off the drafting stool and sat on it with a sigh. The storyboard sat blank and silly before him, with its rows of old-fashioned TV-screen templates.

He tried to conjure up some way to begin a spot about Trans: a film, a video, anything. Thought of Carla's dream. Sketched frames of people dragging word-balloon voices behind them, leaving trails of talk.

Doing the human thing. To talk is human. To listen is divine. To do it on the cheap is just good business.

He smiled, shook out his hand, and quickly sketched a Phil cartoon of a nebbishy guy with a big silly smile clutching a stack of word balloons and handing them out to people, boarding taxis, subways, on bicycles, men and women chatting away with big smiles, swapping word balloons. He and Phil could trade styles when they wanted to, and now a Phil guy seemed the better choice.

Talk is what we do. Reach out. Touch them with your voice before it's too late. Talk to your mother, your father, your friends . . .

Before they're gone.

That stopped him. He stared down at the Phil guy: long nose, big sloppy grin, slyly handing out word balloons. Free talk.

Peter spent ten minutes dotting a circle on the border of the paper, then looked up at the basement window, listening to birds in the backyard. An hour went by. With a short, grunting hum, he stepped off the stool and lay down the pencil.

He did not know where to begin. It had been decades. These ideas were nothing like the films he used to make. If they wanted the old Russell, edgy-cheesy, he was failing miserably. That man was long gone.

Peter shook his head and climbed the stairs. In the kitchen, the answering machine was flashing a big red 2. In the basement, he had not heard the phone ring. He pulled up a stool, a little out of breath, and pushed the playback button.

"Mr. Russell, this is Detective Scragg, LAPD. Something got me thinking about you and Mrs. Russell. We haven't talked in a while. I've been going through some paperwork here and I thought I'd find out how's it going. Nothing new, I've just been thinking over details, have some more questions. We should touch base. I'm calling from—"

Peter closed his eyes and pushed the stop button. The next message was also from Scragg. They had last spoken six months earlier, and there had been nothing new at that time. A dead-end case. Peter did not want to think any more negative thoughts. He erased both messages, then backed away, as if the old kitchen phone might be tainted. He picked up the Trans and punched in a standard phone number. He hoped the number was still good.

He hadn't spoken to Karl Pfeil in years.

CHAPTER 21

PFEIL STOOD SIX-FEET-THREE-INCHES tall in—literally—his stocking feet. His long blond hair swayed forward over his eyes as he leaned across the swoop of glass-topped desk to clasp Peter's hand.

"Eight years! I looked it up. We haven't talked in eight years," Karl said. "How the time shrieks by."

The walls of Karl's long, windowless office were covered with framed posters, photos, and three big plasma screens, two turned off, one still exhibiting rough animatics—computer graphics loops of lizardlike characters walking.

"You've done great," Peter said with genuine admiration.

"Don't look," Karl warned cheerfully, and punched a button on the desk to turn off the screen. "Jim Cameron's new movie. Well, maybe. Top secret. What brings you to Santa Monica?"

"I'm old," Peter said.

Karl made a face. "Bullshit."

"I've been out of the business so long, I don't know a lens from a pixel. I need professional advice."

Karl sat and leaned his elbows on his desk. "If I can return any favors . . ."

As a green kid, Karl had worked on Peter's final picture, *Q.T., the Sextraterrestrial,* putting together two stop-motion sequences. Karl had animated—for almost no money—an anatomically correct monster alien rampaging through a college campus, chasing coeds who had taken one too many tabs of LSD.

Now Karl was in charge of one of the best computer graphics studios on the West Coast.

"I've got a commission," Peter said.

Karl looked tan and buff and wore a silk shirt and linen pants, his geeky hair and face now part of a stylish personal signature. Peter's chest suddenly felt cold.

"I presume I'm going to shoot HD video," he continued, his tongue gluey. "I've never used a Betacam, or whatever it is now. I'd like to see some of the equipment, just to know what to rent."

Karl shrugged. "Hell, with what's in Circuit City right now, you might as well buy. Only cost you a couple of grand for something pretty terrific."

Peter shook his head. "This is professional, Karl."

"That's what I'm *saying,* Peter. Something the size of your hand, locked onto a hundred-dollar tripod, will give you great results. What kind of budget?"

"Hasn't been set, but it's promoting a telecom startup."

Karl worked to keep a straight face. "Are they actually going for psychotronic?" he asked with a speculative squint.

"Probably," Peter said.

"Ah. Then they'll want a film look, bad color correction. Scratches and blotches. Just like the old days. I've got a terrific Arri Super 16 gathering dust in my attic. Yours for the asking."

Peter nodded his thanks and walked around the room, studying the posters. "I saw your last picture. Beautiful work."

"Not much of a challenge," Karl confessed. "We turned Robin Williams into a talking elephant. Did you know he's a fan of yours?"

Peter laughed.

"No, really," Karl insisted. "He quoted me some lines from *Q.T.*"

"I didn't know that," Peter said.

Karl pushed back his chair and stood. "Come on. I'll show you something. CGI is about to put all your pretty ladies out of business."

KARL GAVE PETER a tour. They walked down a hallway lined with more posters and passed a fifty-seat viewing theater. Karl opened a heavy white metal door and they stepped into a quiet, shaded room filled with long rows of cubicles.

"Our genies," Karl said.

Weinstein had been right—there was little difference between a cubicle and a prison cell. Inside each cubicle was a desk holding a twenty-one-inch monitor, a trackball, and a keyboard. Shelves were filled with books and manuals and plastic toys. A young woman in jeans and a T-shirt sat manipulating blocks of color around a plain-vanilla human figure. She grabbed a limb and positioned it to her liking, then swiveled on her chair and leaned back to smile toothily at Karl.

Karl benevolently returned her smile, boss to wage slave. "Tracy, this is Peter, an old friend."

"Good to meet you," Tracy said. Her eyes were glazed. She yawned and stretched. "Sorry. I've been working here since four in the morning."

"Take a break."

"I'm fine," Tracy said, returning with fated slowness to her screen. She made the animated figure grimace.

"Tracy is twenty-two," Karl said as they walked to the end of the corridor between the cubicles. "Just out of MIT and one of the best in our building."

"MIT?" Peter asked. "Not USC?"

"She debugs our Slicer and NextMove software," Karl said. He took Peter up a flight of stairs into a long loft space filled with more posters, figures of dinosaurs and dragons, and a full-sized chrome-plated skeletal robot. *"Ah am pumping iron,"* the robot intoned as they walked by. It swiveled its head and swayed its arms menacingly. *"Scrahtch my bahk."*

"Sheila—my wife, I'm married now, believe it?—she rigged that for my birthday," Karl said. He plopped down in a red leather chair and switched on a forty-inch flat-screen monitor. "This is top secret. Not even Sheila knows. Just some of the boys. You're going to love it." He clipped on a receptionist's microphone and earplug.

Jean Harlow glowed into being on the monitor, in black and white, seen from the shoulders up, her hair a dazzling silver cascade. A radiant, crystallized glow outlined her head.

"Helllooo, Jean," Karl said. "Where *have* you been all my life?"

Harlow turned to face him. "Is that you, Karl?" she asked, and rewarded him with a bored smile.

"None other. I'd like you to meet Peter."

"Is he *rich?*" she asked.

"Very."

Harlow peered directly into Peter's eyes. Peter laughed nervously as she winked and threw him a kiss. "Why don't you and I go dancing and leave Karl to his monsters? I've been cooped up in this box *all day.*"

"My God," Peter said. "She looks real. Is there a . . . ?"

"Model in the other room?" Karl finished, and scoffed. "Do you think I'm made of money?" He tapped his nose. "Jean, could you get Jane for us?"

Harlow tossed her blond hair and assumed a could-care-less moue. She stepped aside and Jane Russell moved into view. Karl spun the mouse wheel to pull back. Russell stood on a soundstage with a wind machine and a cloudy-sunset backdrop. She was wearing the blouse and bra made famous by *The Outlaw.*

"Jane, honey, how about a little cleavage?"

The figure shrugged, said, "Boys will be boys," and started to bend forward. Hands on her hips and elbows out, she gave a little wiggle. The resulting pendulum motion was very convincing.

"They're all anatomically correct, and very willing," Karl said. "We have Marilyn, Bettie—"

"Davis?" Peter asked.

"No, Page, joker. And about a dozen others. They run off the same engine, and not even I can tell what they'll say next."

"Wonderful," Peter said, but he did not sound convinced. In fact, he was starting to feel uncomfortable.

Karl brought Bettie Page on-screen with her trademark straight-cut black bangs. Dressed in a leopard-skin skirt, Page was in the act of pinning fishnet hose on a clothesline crowded with dainties. Behind her was a pink couch. She raised her head to deliver a summer-promise smile. "Why, it's Karl," she said. "Who's your friend?" She sashayed forward until her face filled the frame. "Could you boys help me move some furniture?"

"Not tonight, Bettie. Nice, huh?" Karl said to Peter in an aside. "Next up . . . Sascha Lauten. Our prize. I have to admit, your photos inspired us, Peter. The best-covered model we have, actually—if what you did can be called coverage."

Sascha appeared on-screen before Peter could protest. And it *was* Sascha, right down to the way she folded her arms—Karl had always been a master at capturing subtleties. She wore a filmy scarf and nothing else. Peter felt his face pink.

"Good to see you, Sascha," Karl said.

"Good to be seen, and by *such* talented eyes."

"Peter Russell wants to say hi."

"Is that really you, Peter? What a surprise!" She sat demurely on an office-style chair, pulling down the edge of the scarf. Sascha had been his best-looking model—gorgeous, buxom, and classy, with a come-hither look that seemed not only natural but accidental. In Peter's photos, she had appeared surprised and pleased at once that anyone could find her sexy—giving her a naïve vulnerability that belied her ample charms.

"Let's skip Sascha," Peter said, but Karl was busy and did not hear him. Sascha's image had frozen and bright red pixels were marching like ants across the bottom of the screen.

"Damn," Karl said, clicking up a set of command buttons and picking through some digital remedies. "Tracy refuses to debug this software. Leaves us at a disadvantage."

Peter could not take his eyes from Sascha's face. "White man steal soul," he said, his mouth dry. Even in still-frame, she looked healthy and natural. And she was no older on this screen than she had been when Peter had last taken pictures of her. "I mean it, Karl. Please."

Karl looked up. "Jeez, you look awful," he said. "Are you feeling okay?"

"I don't want to see her like this," Peter said.

"Sorry," Karl said, dumbfounded. "Let me clear the buffer." He tapped the keyboard. Suddenly, the image jerked and became ragged at the edges. The eyes went milky white, then dropped out of sight completely, leaving black hollows. Peter watched Sascha de-rez. Her colors dropped out as if bleached. The copy stared at Peter—directly into his eyes—with those blank hollows, and said through jagged lips, in a reedy skirl, "You shouldn't leave me alone in here. I'm a very needy girl. *Where have you been, Peter? Why did you leave me all alone?*"

Peter felt a shooting pain in his rear molars and down his arm. He reached up to his shoulder and stooped forward.

"Sorry, she's caught in a loop." Karl tapped madly on the keyboard. He made another sweep of the mouse and reached for the monitor to just shut it off. Before he could do so, the image jerked, reversed its last movements, and juddered to another freeze. He held his finger above the monitor button, curious as to what might happen next. "Whoops," Karl said. "Bad girl. Well, she's down. Shit." Karl punched off the monitor. "My apologies. Good night, ladies!"

Peter backed away from the monitor station, still stooped. "Could we get some water?"

BACK IN THE front office, Karl gave Peter a bottle of Evian and some aspirin and sat on the edge of the desk as Peter massaged his arm.

"You look shook, Peter, if you don't mind me making an observation. Does your arm hurt?"

"I'm fine," Peter said.

"My dad had angina pains in his head and arms. He had to—"

"It's just indigestion," Peter said, slugging back the pills with a long draft of the flat-tasting bottled water. He usually hated Evian but the liquid felt good in his throat.

"Have you had an EKG?"

"Last month," Peter lied. "I just ate too much for lunch and it's pushing back."

After a moment, Karl looked crestfallen. "You don't approve of our ladies," he said.

"They're lovely," Peter said. Too lovely. Images, memories of the dead—except for Bettie Page and Sascha, still alive but now disturbingly like wraiths, bits of information forced to dance through an endless loop of wet dreams … Male lust tuned to the nth degree. He felt a shudder creep up his back. It was too much like a nightmare distortion of his life's work, his movies, his photographs.

Another important meeting headed for salvage.

"You make me feel like a fifth wheel, that's all," Peter said. "Just thinking about what it takes, with masters like you around, makes me jumpy."

"Sure," Karl said, unconvinced. "Well, the ladies aren't commercial. They're just a hobby. Geeks will be geeks. We don't even have image licenses." Karl gave Peter a searching look, as if regretting the entire afternoon. "We could get in trouble if someone found out, you know?"

"Don't worry."

Karl walked around the desk and put his hand on Peter's shoulder. "Hey, they want you, man. Not some MTV version of Ridley Scott. They want what you did so well, and there's no reason you can't do it again, right?"

Peter nodded, gripping the plastic bottle.

Karl could not hide his relief as he accompanied Peter down to the parking garage. Standing by the Porsche, Karl said, "If you need equipment, anything … let me know. We have sweetheart deals all around town. I'd love to help."

"Thanks."

Peter opened the car door. Karl was almost twitching to get back to work.

"Man, it is great to have you visit," he said as Peter slid into the seat. "Just like old times. Hey, do you remember that class you taught?"

Peter looked up. "Class?"

"Lessons in oral sex. Cunnilingus."

Peter said, "I don't remember you being there."

Karl grinned sheepishly. "I was sixteen, a total nerd virgin. We looked up to you like a god. Jeez, you knew it all. Well, it worked. Sheila and I have been married for sixteen years. Thanks, man. I owe you."

But Peter could tell. The next time, Karl would not take his call.

CHAPTER 22

HE PULLED OFF and parked near the Santa Monica Pier. It was six o'clock; he had three hours until Helen showed up at the house.

Peter rolled down the window and took a deep breath.

The sun was dropping slow and rich over the water, with that special light the coast manages to wear like a silk dress in the evening.

Maybe he should go get an EKG. He had responsibilities after all, and he had been making excuses too long. Besides, this had been an exceptionally hard week. Idly, he removed his black address book from his coat's breast pocket, turned the pages, searching for old colleagues, those less well placed than Karl, less busy; an old boy's network for the grumpy, date stale, and unpredictable.

Then, closing his eyes, he folded the book and felt a fresh wave of despair. *Face it.*

Face what? What was he supposed to face? His failure? He hadn't started yet; he hadn't had time to fail. Face up to a lack of confidence? Even in his so-called heyday, Peter had never felt confident beginning film projects.

He could not shake the de-rezzed images of Sascha. On the screen like that for all the world to see, forced to do whatever the world wanted, *forever and ever.* What if every photo Peter had ever taken, every frame of film he had ever shot, had stolen a bit of an actor's soul? Would that explain why so many actors and models seemed to fade, to get more and more eccentric and desperate over time?

To become so *needy?*

Were they ever pushed to the point where they had nothing more to give, nothing left to be sucked away, *and the camera knew?*

Disgusted at his own imagination—there were thoughts that did not deserve thinking—he buckled up. He was done for the evening. He would get home a little early, fix supper, wait for Helen and Lindsey. Seeing Lindsey again would help.

Peter needed all the help he could get right now.

CHAPTER 23

A HUGE TRAFFIC jam had packed the 5 and spilled out onto the 10. Peter sat in his low, low seat behind a massive SUV—a Porsche SUV, he noted with a slight curl of his lip, built like a stack of shaved hockey pucks. Was nothing sacred?

He could not see ahead to know whether to push right and get off at the next exit. When he edged right to reconnoiter, he saw the surface streets were already jammed and that traffic was, if anything, moving more slowly there than on the freeway.

It took an hour for the never-ending conga line of red taillights to ooze like cold molasses to the interchange. Peter glanced at his watch—an old, scarred, gold-plated Bulova he had had since high school—and saw it was eight-thirty.

"Damn it," he said, clenching his fists on the wheel. Helen would be at the house before he got there. He would not have food for Lindsey's breakfast or ice cream for a late night snack. He was once again a loser, fulfilling Helen's heartfelt expectations.

Suddenly, he hated Los Angeles, the freeways, his ineptitude for not foreseeing such a delay. He had lived here most of his life but had not in fact braved Friday-night traffic for years, his social life being what it was. *Blame LA. Blame everything and everyone.*

After ten long minutes of angry speculation, the Porsche finally crept around the slowdown's dreadful cause. Traffic was snaking to the right. Purple flares created a proscenium around a stage of spun and crumpled wrecks, like gaslights for a theater in hell. Firefighters and police waved red-muzzled flashlights to get traffic to move along, move along. Two of the wrecks, still smoking, had been doused with white foam.

Despite his vow not to look, Peter stared, thought for one plunging moment Helen's car might be among the ruins, he might see them trapped or on stretchers. Two covered stretchers were being lifted into a big square white van. Cars had halted to let an ambulance push out from the shoulder of the highway.

The wreckage fell behind and still the traffic did not let up. He endlessly shifted and pushed in the clutch and brought the revs up for first gear and let the clutch out and turned the wheel minute fractions of an inch, watching the temperature needle move closer to the red—it did that in prolonged slow driving. He crept along the last mile until he could get into second gear on the off-ramp.

Five minutes later, he pulled onto Pacific and breathed a sigh of relief, watching the temp gauge drop back to normal. Traffic here was light. He might make it.

Climbing into the hills, with less than a mile left to the house, the oil pressure pegged on zero. The Porsche made a desperate little grinding noise and coughed a chuff of blue smoke. The engine mercifully died. By dint of quick action slipping the car out of gear, he was barely able to coast to the curb.

The time was now 9:05.

Peter lifted the rear lid and looked at the engine, but he knew already that the problem was nothing he could fix, not here and not now. A tow and expensive days in the shop would be necessary. The Porsche had not given him this kind of trouble since an engine rebuild five years ago.

Gently, as if lowering a dead pet into a grave, he dropped the lid and latched it, then dialed Helen's cell number on the Trans. Her network was busy. He tried the apartment number. All he got was a sharp run of wheedling chirps. He had left his own cell phone back at the house. After three more tries, face grim, he rolled up the car window and locked the doors and began the long walk.

At 9:37, out of breath but with, fortunately, no chest pain—and wasn't that proof it was only indigestion?—he walked up the asphalt slope of the driveway and past the black hollow of the garage. The crickets were busy and the air was lovely and soft and cool and the house was dark and quiet and looked empty.

They have come and gone, Peter thought. He had not even left the porch light on. The sadness as he walked under the twining loops of jasmine was deep and hard, a determined letting down of something that had more in it than just Helen and Lindsey; a sadness that was totally bottom line, the sum of an indulgent life too deep in arrears ever to make good.

Bankrupt Peter Russell.

He removed his key and was about to fit it into the brass lock when he saw the French door was already open. Helen had come and gone and had left the door unlocked behind her, hoping perhaps he would be robbed, and wouldn't that teach him a lesson?

And what would the robbers take—books? Vinyl records? An old TV and stereo worth maybe a hundred dollars—that might go. But the even older magazines? Basement file cabinets full of moldering, feelthy pictures a lot less suggestive than what you could catch any night on cable TV?

Peter pushed the door open with a small squeal of the upper hinge and stood for a moment. He surveyed the darkened living room, the sun-warmed silence after a day of broken clouds, the faint mustiness of corners filled with dust that always eluded him during halfhearted attempts at cleaning. Empty life, empty house.

Peter's shoulders sagged. He walked down the dark hall, not bothering to turn on the lights. In his bedroom, stumbling over a pair of running shoes, he relented and turned the knurl on the pullout wall lamp. Light flashed across the room. Normal light, normal night.

He had arranged the Enzenbacher chess set on his dresser, below the mirror, all the pieces neatly lined up, game ready. In the mirror, from where he stood, Alice's copy of the chess set showed in reverse. He took a step forward and looked down at the real board. On the side of the silver pieces, good guys and ghosts, the king's pawn had been advanced two squares. Phil's favorite opening move. Had he jostled the piece after setting them up? He distinctly remembered leaving them all straight.

Stillness, stillness, and then the creak of a roof beam settling, an almost laughable pause, followed by the sharp crack of furniture or a wall stud somewhere, sounds he had heard for decades, often at this time of night. Chunks of wood pushed up against other wood, just happening to enjoy tandem moments of relaxation from the heat.

From the twin's bedroom his ears caught a rustling as of disturbed linens.

His heart thumped a mighty thump and his throat itched as he heard, from down the hall, "Daddy?"

Suddenly everything changed, and he was happier than he had been in years, all his debts lifted and failings blown off through the roof to the stars and clouds.

Helen had come and left Lindsey behind, tucking her into bed.

"I'm here, sweetie," he called, walking down the hall, pushing the door open, and stepping softly into the girls' bedroom. She had chosen the right-hand bed, where she lay with her face poking out from under the covers, a small moon in the blackness above a pale smear of gray that was the coverlet, a band of lighter gray that was the counterpane, straight and tidy. Two thin arms lay folded on the counterpane. She looked smaller and younger, lying in the bed in the dark, and she sounded younger, too, perhaps afraid of the dark, waiting for him to come home.

That would give him some leverage with Helen, leaving their daughter alone in the house with the front door unlocked. Was any date hot enough to be worth taking that kind of risk?

And then she would come back at him for his not being there in the first place, when she needed him, betraying her once again . . .

Peter stowed all that and knelt beside his daughter.

"Where have you been?" she asked.

"Stuck in traffic," he said, smoothing back the dark hair above her forehead. Her skin was soft and cool. "It was a monstrous big beast that grabbed me. Nothing else could have kept me away."

"Traffic," she echoed in just his tone of voice. "A beast." She rolled to one side, facing him. He wished he could see her more clearly, but just touching her sent a thrill up his arm and into his body. It was the babies that mattered, the sex that made them was nothing—it was the babies that made one feel so excellent and unworthy. He wanted to lay his head down on his daughter's lap and beg forgiveness, spill his sorrows, but he was a daddy. None of that.

He would be here for her when she awoke in the morning. He would walk down to the market and get milk and cereal; no, he would just wait and they would walk down together.

"Mother left you here," he said.

"Yes."

"Well, that's okay. You're here and that's what matters. I've missed you."

"I've missed you," she said. "It's been too long."

"Now you just sleep."

She nodded a big up-and-down nod. He reluctantly got to his feet and watched her for a long, lovely moment, all the loneliness gone. Full again, to the top.

Then he turned and looked to the left, at the broadly sketched suggestion of an empty bed in the lighter shadows on that side of the room. He seldom came into this room now, but somehow, with one bed filled, the empty one was tolerable.

It was a condition of life everywhere that parents sometimes lost their babies; knowing that did not stop the pain, but with Lindsey here, he was all right. He could believe that life would go on.

"Sleep cozy," he whispered, and closed the door to a crack.

PETER SAT IN the kitchen, wishing that he had just a single beer, for this moment. Just a wish.

No beer, no liquor, no drugs—not that he had ever done much in the way of illicit drugs. Working as he did, under the sort of federal and state scrutiny it was all too easy to imagine, drugs had never seemed a smart move and had never appealed to him anyway.

No, it was alcohol that had seemed a safe haven and then had turned around and slowly, blearily blotted out six months of his life. Phil had found him in this very house, alone, passed out in his pajamas in the bathtub. Days before, Helen had taken Lindsey and moved out. Phil had been both sympathetic and disgusted. *"Jesus, Peter, you still have a wife and kid."*

"I had a wife. I had another kid."

"Well, shit. You still have a daughter, and that's all that matters."

Other than the Scotch in Phil's motor home—utterly excusable—Peter had not taken another drink in eighteen months. He put a kettle on the burner to make tea. Spooned a small mound of Earl Grey into the wire filter sitting low in the cup. Poured the hot water.

Christ, he missed those times, all of them in the house. It had all gone wrong in so many ways, his fault, Helen's fault . . . neither of them to blame.

He thought about returning to the bedroom to look at his daughter, decided not to bother her. Just sip the tea and linger on the moment, feel like somebody other than a wastrel—such a word. A loser. A man who could not jump-start his life. But at least, and most important of all, a father.

For now.

Helen had gained custody by having her lawyer tell the judge what Peter had done for a living. Not that Peter would have contested. After all, look what he did for a living.

He actually smiled around the first sip of tea. A ridiculous life, but it *was* his life. And it *was* ridiculous. After the marriage, he had locked up all his photo files in the basement, and Helen had considered it done with.

In the late nineties, to supplement his earnings from the Benoliels, and to fill the spare time, Peter had fallen back on writing movie and TV novelizations, as fast as one or two a month. He had planned a mystery novel and they had talked about his writing full-time. Helen had gone back to construction, this time working in an office, and for a while, together, they had brought in more than enough money. They had started a nest egg, a college fund. A writing career had seemed possible.

They had been a family. He had been happy, though restless. Always restless.

What he would not give to go back for one hour.

The boiling hurt was no more than a simmer now, cooler than the kettle as its whistle subsided.

"Tomorrow I'll call the tow service," he said. "I'll get my life back in shape. No more stalls. No more weirdness. No more self-destruction."

Peter finished his cup and thought about going to bed. Maybe he would descend to the basement office first and look at his notes, now that his head was clear and he was feeling good. It was the depression that had kept him down, kept him from thinking clearly and being inventive. With that lifted, surely he could move forward, if only a few steps.

Happy.

Jesus, he was actually *happy.*

He marched barefoot down the steps into the basement and opened the door. Just as he switched on the lights, the phone rang upstairs. He jumped up the steps two by two to get to the phone before it woke Lindsey. Out of breath and face flushed with irritation, he lifted the receiver in the kitchen. "Hello."

"Peter, this is Helen."

"Sorry I wasn't here to meet you," he said quickly. "She's—"

Helen interrupted, "I was going to call earlier. The bastard stood me up. To hell with them all, right, Peter? To hell with men. That's the story of my life. I'm not the raving, enchanting beauty I once was, am I?"

"Well, I'm glad you—"

Helen broke in again, her tone still bitter, but she was trying to hold it back. "Lindsey was sorry not to see you, but I'm a nervous wreck, and I'm certainly in no mood to drive. She's watching TV. She's mad at me. Well, maybe I'll bring her over this weekend. Maybe we can all go for a drive. Have a picnic. That would be nice. Are you available?

"Peter?

"Peter?

"Damn it, it's *not* my fault, Peter."

She hung up.

Peter had left the receiver dangling by its cord. He was walking stiffly and deliberately down the hall to the girls' bedroom. The weirdness had not gone away. It had lain in wait for him to drop his guard.

Lindsey always slept in the left-hand bed. How could he have forgotten?

Daniella had always slept on the right.

CHAPTER 24

SOMETHING STOPPED HIM in the hall. He did not dare to turn on the light to see what it was. He could feel it watching him, part of the general darkness. It almost had a shape, almost had a smell—a dry coil of eels, a nest of long smooth lizards, all joined together and smelling of charcoal and damp earth.

Many shaped into one.

It was very old and yet it had been born in this house, or reborn. It was hungry but patient. He did not dare move or go back into the bedroom for fear of rousing it and exposing his daughter—his *dead* daughter, he reminded himself—to whatever danger it represented.

Sweat broke out all over his body. He felt something in his hand and realized he had picked up the two-foot-long piece of steel rebar he kept in the corner of the kitchen, hidden by the stove, ready to hand in case of burglars. What did he expect to have to defend himself against? Not burglars, not this time.

What could he protect his daughter against now?

They swarmed and fed. They ate the image of Lydia. Predators.

No.

Scavengers. Scavengers go after the dead and all they leave behind.

Peter's thinking was sharp and chilly. He took a soundless step forward and felt the darkness at the end of the hall contract reflexively. The charcoal scent became more like mud, like damp, moldy wallboard. Whatever was waiting in the far corner was imitating the odors found in an old house, as camouflage. Peter could tell the difference, like seeing the colors of a jaguar trying to hide in the jungle.

He cleared his constricted throat. "I know you're down there," he said. "Go away. Get out of here." He could almost see the coils tighten, the scavenger press back into the corner. *How can a shadow twitch? How can a shadow know I'm here?* It was not happy that Peter was watching for it, addressing it. For once, Peter felt some power. The rebar would do no good, but so long as he was here, the predator could not attack.

Could not go after his daughter.

His dead daughter.

Somewhere in the house, another—or the same—stud or beam let out a sharp crack, like a gun going off. A pause, and then the furniture replied.

As if a door had slammed, everything changed. The hall was suddenly empty; no coiled thing waited in the darkness. The smell of mud and charcoal and mold returned to the dry, familiar smell of an old house nestled on a dead-end street in the Glendale hills. Peter dabbed at his face with the back of his hand. Anger and fear flashed in his head like lightning. His fingers reached out and touched the light switch, then, with a jerk, he pushed the switch up. It rose in apparent slow motion, thudded into the on position, and light moved out in an oily wave from the milky glass ceiling fixture, washing up against the corners, flooding the walls, and splashing out to fill the hall. Brightness lay over everything like a thick coat of paint, but he was not reassured; paint could cover things up, but they might still be there. So he waited for a while until he could smell only the house and had stopped sweating.

The girls' bedroom door was still nearly closed.

Peter opened it and walked in.

"Honey? Sweetie?"

Both beds, revealed by the spill of light from the hallway, were prim and neatly made. The matching Harry Potter coverlets and neatly folded counterpanes had not been disturbed. They were just as Helen had left them two years ago, with a few wrinkles made by Peter's dusting every now and then.

His hand let the rebar drop. It landed on end, then toppled onto the patchwork rug between the beds with a heavy, ringing thump. He took a shuddering breath and squatted. “I’m here,” he told the room. “Please, Daniella, give me another chance.”

Of course, there was no answer.

The world had become real again.

CHAPTER 25

SOMETIMES, THE ONLY thing that saves us is a fantasy, a memory, something stolen from the library of the past and long past its due date, but we keep it anyway, grateful and not in the least guilty.

Peter took a morning shower and dressed and thought, when he thought much at all, *I'm okay. I'm all right.*

What could have, should have shattered him did nothing of the kind. He was not seeing things and he was not crazy. He would not give himself that kind of artistic credit; for a fact, in all the months he had wished he could once again clearly visualize Daniella in his memory, or in his dreams—see her without looking at her pictures—he had failed.

It was not imagination that had brought his daughter back to him. Daniella was in the house. She was in some sort of trouble and she had come to him. With him around, she would be all right; he provided protection. It was all vague—vague, nebulous, and unconvincing—but it was enough to keep Peter moving through the morning. He called the tow company and then his favorite Porsche garage. He would walk down to the car during the daylight; nothing would go wrong during the daytime. Perhaps day here was night on that other side of the world and everything there slept or hid out. It was beginning to make sense. Perhaps Phil's death, or Lydia's phone call, had started it all, pushed him over the line.

As a teenager, he had loved *The Twilight Zone*, reveled in the thrill of half believing there was something more than this ordinary life. Well, now here it was. He had proof to tip his own balance scales. Skeptical Peter Russell had swung back to credulity, but this time he had real, if entirely subjective, evidence; he was no longer desperately reaching for straws but forced to acknowledge the tree trunks floating by.

Peter went about his necessary business in a thick daze, waiting for evening and another chance to spend a few moments with Daniella. To protect her as he had not protected her before.

He walked down the hill and saw the Porsche, undisturbed where he had parked it—a small miracle in itself—and noted the striped police tape and crayoned impound date and number on the back window.

In the late-morning sun, he leaned against the roof of the Porsche, waiting for the tow truck. Today was very like the day he had received Lydia's call, waking him to a larger reality. He visualized sunshine pouring through the house, even into the hall corners, keeping the scavengers at bay.

Keeping his daughter safely hidden.

The tow truck arrived on time, and Peter spent a few minutes thumbing through the battered, greasy 356C manual to remember how and where to arrange the hooks.

CHAPTER

AFTER AN EARLY supper, Peter took one of the smaller rattan chairs from the backyard and placed it at the end of the hall. He sat there with his length of rebar, waiting.

He had left the door to the twins' bedroom cracked open, but not too far. Perhaps those on the other side were as skittish as deer, like fawns afraid to break cover. He would trust their instincts. He would trust his daughter to know what was best.

"Whenever you're ready, sweetheart," he murmured. "I'm here for you."

Around ten o'clock, he fell asleep in the chair. He awoke at dawn, stiff but refreshed. He was not alarmed or unhappy; had anything happened, he knew he would have awakened, would have jerked to complete alertness had anyone—or anything—arrived.

The house had been quiet.

He could not expect miracles every night.

Peter stretched and showered, then descended into the basement and began sketching, automatically it seemed. Floodgates opened. The ideas looked pretty good to him.

At eleven he took the phone call from the repair shop. Tried to wrap himself around a two-thousand, four-hundred dollar estimate and a long list of parts and necessary services.

Peter could not abandon anything in distress, not now. He had to preserve his past, any part of it. Peter told the mechanic to go ahead, get her fixed, he had money coming in and would pay them next week. He had used the same shop for twenty years, they had done his last engine rebuild, they knew him well. He had never welshed on a bill. One good relationship left in his life, thank God.

By four o'clock, he had thirty sheets of breakdown paper and twenty pages of script. Just like old times. Preserving the past had reawakened another, younger Peter Russell, more flexible and confident. With satisfaction, he stacked and tamped the sheets and slipped them into a black folio binder. Really, was being haunted any different from dropping into another world while he was writing? Briefly living in another space or time? Perhaps art and writing were like seeing another kind of reality.

"Sure," he said with a chuckle. "*Canine Planet.* Dogs driving motorbikes and hunting women in fur bikinis."

There, see, he told himself. You have perspective. You can tell silly ideas from those that make sense.

My daughter coming back makes sense.

My dead daughter.

He worked through most of the night, slept briefly, and resumed on Sunday morning, producing dozens of drawings, sheets of script, scribbled scenarios. A flood of ideas.

Only for a moment did he feel lost and desperately fragile.

This is too good. It can't go on.

CHAPTER 27

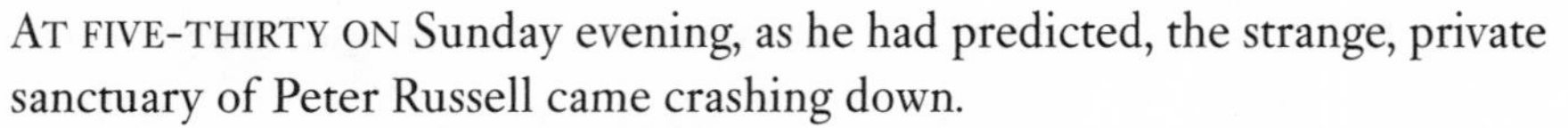

AT FIVE-THIRTY ON Sunday evening, as he had predicted, the strange, private sanctuary of Peter Russell came crashing down.

He had been here before, full of desperate hope that the past could be reclaimed, or at least a shred of it. One night eighteen months ago he had drunk himself into a near-stupor and persuaded Phil to drive him into Sherman Oaks to visit a psychic. The evening had cost him five hundred dollars and had ended up a complete disaster.

Phil had brought him back to this house, a basket case, weeping uncontrollably. He had brewed Peter coffee and sat up with him all night and into the morning.

Peter could not let that happen again.

As the sky darkened and the phones and Trans did not ring, as Sunday passed with no call from Helen, Peter sat in the backyard slouched in the solitary rattan chair—the other was still in the hall—with his hands folded on his stomach. The sky declined from robin's-egg blue through a series of dusty shades to brown-tinted darkness.

Wind chimes tinkled behind the house, not ten feet away.

All the rationales had worn thin. "What did you see?" he asked himself in leaden tones. "Maybe you didn't see her. You made up what you wanted to see."

But he had mistaken her for Lindsey. Lindsey was a close approximation, but not exact. Lindsey and Daniella had not been identical twins. After their births—within three minutes of each other—the doctors had told him, and later, Helen, coming out of her general for the Caesarean, about a third type of twin, neither fraternal nor identical; the upshot was that both he and Helen (and Phil and a lot of their friends) had always been able to tell Lindsey from Daniella, even as babies, even when they had been dressed alike.

Wasn't it possible, then, that a wraith of Lindsey had appeared—a leftover image of Lindsey's emotions from years past, from just after the funeral?

Peter nodded at the grim logic of that. Even if he was sane, he had yet to see a full-fledged ghost, a haunt, someone dead. But what about the sandblasted old man and the children near Point Reyes?

Yet in Peter's memory, the dim face he saw so clearly above the shadowed counterpane in the girls' bedroom was indisputably Daniella. His expectations of Lindsey had colored what he had seen.

Even a wraith of Lindsey would never have slept in Daniella's bed.

His misery and confusion deepened.

AT SEVEN O'CLOCK, he climbed the short flight of steps to the porch and walked through the rear door into the kitchen. He listened for a moment to the pops and cracks of settling timbers, all soft. No starting pistols announcing a leave-taking of his senses or the world changing into something new.

He was not hungry, so he walked to his bedroom and searched the shelves for *The Doors of Perception.* He found Huxley's book, a slender volume, blue board covers and black cloth spine, minus its dust wrapper. The pages were well thumbed—he had bought it from an alternative bookstore in Laguna Beach back in 1969 and had read it once, but the previous owner had read it almost to tatters. He sat on the corner of the bed and leafed through the pages until he found the reference to philosopher Henri Bergson's valve that kept the brain from being flooded by the minutiae of the real. The valve that kept us free of metaphysical persiflage, kept us sane and focused on what was really important in life. Focused on what could actually kill you, not just distract you.

Huxley had died on the same day as JFK's assassination, November 22, 1963, leaving behind a slip of paper on which he had scrawled just three letters: *LSD.* Perhaps Huxley had taken LSD just to keep exploring. To jam that old Bergson valve wide open even after death.

That theory didn't feel right, however. What was happening to Peter was less like the opening of a valve and more like a loose seal on a spigot: the drip, drip, drip of bad mental chemistry, mundane and sad. His uncle on his mother's side had suffered from schizophrenia. Peter had never had any symptoms ... until now. But he had gone off the deep end before. Trying to find out. Trying to learn how to bring something back.

He lowered the book and stared at the wall, at the eight-by-ten pictures of the girls hanging there in simple brass frames. Daniella, in the last year of her life, flashing him a cheesy smile with her index finger screwing a little dimple into her plump cheek. Lindsey, on the same day, more serious, with wide blue eyes and lips drawn into a firmly noncommittal line.

Peter told himself, "No, you are not crazy, and you are not making up excuses. You're a bereaved daddy, and that's hard to live with, but you're seeing real things. You're trying to figure out what they are and what makes the most sense."

He then asked with a wry grimace, "So why is it just *you* seeing things, me bucko?"

Huxley's book lay open on the bed, not very helpful after all.

The house phone rang in the kitchen. He walked across the hall and picked up the receiver from the cradle, tugging its long winding cord to hold it to his ear. "Russell here."

"Mr. Russell, this is Detective Scragg. Robbery Homicide. I called earlier. We haven't talked for quite a while. I hope this is a good time, or at least not a bad time."

Peter turned. The kitchen was dark; the only light came from the porch through the window over the sink. A wood-slatted Venetian blind over the window cast bars of shadow on the cabinets and counter.

The voice on the other end continued. "I just wanted to set up an appointment to meet with you again. Discuss some things, if you don't mind."

"It's Sunday evening," Peter said.

"Yeah, well, weekends don't really exist for me. I'm going over open cases, cold cases. I do that. Someday I'll learn, but not yet. Mrs. Russell won't take my calls."

"Right." Peter didn't feel like telling Scragg about the divorce.

"I don't blame her, but there's some things I need to go over with you, not new stuff, just to refresh my memory. Wind up the case ticker again."

Peter did not know what a case ticker was. "What can I do?"

"You know, this is the second anniversary."

Peter looked at the calendar on the wall. His fingers tightened on the phone.

"I just wanted to go back and ask some of the questions I might have asked before, and I might not have. New perspective. Cops change and grow. Maybe I'll see something differently this time."

Two years since her death. Suddenly, Peter could visualize his daughter so clearly, walking across the porch, laughing with Helen as they folded laundry, sulking after a fight with Lindsey. Trying to make her real again in his head. That was it, right? Make her so real, as if she had never gone away. He hurt with the effort.

"Nothing new?" Peter asked.

"No, sir. Nothing new," Scragg said. "Nothing concrete, anyway."

Peter turned slowly in the dark kitchen, winding the cord around his arm. "If I can help . . ."

"I'm sure you can, Mr. Russell. Sorry if I'm imposing. What I wanted to ask about was, did we miss interviewing anyone, talking to people, anybody, even those we couldn't possibly suspect—anyone interested in masks . . . I'm reaching here."

Peter closed his eyes. The killer had painted a raccoonlike mask around Daniella's eyes and nose, using mixed dust and blood. He felt his own blood slow throughout his body, turning into cool, sluggish rivers everywhere but behind his eyes.

His eyes.

"We've searched high and low for something similar, and we've found nothing, Mr. Russell. But we're sure this person has killed before. Can you think of a hobbyist, a collector maybe, some sort of artist, someone who knows you, who might have singled you out for special attention . . . I mean, who has killed before, but hidden his crimes. He would need a safe place to store bodies, perhaps lots of bodies—"

Peter kept trying to see his daughter as she had been when alive, defense against the images so horribly replayed for him. He stopped listening to Scragg's voice. He could not focus on that particular fountain of unbearable truths.

He opened his eyes and reversed his turning, unwinding the phone cord.

The twilit shadow of a ten-year-old girl stood in the doorway that led from the kitchen back to the hall. It was Daniella, not Lindsey, with longer hair, smaller and slighter, younger—of that he was certain. Her outline was distinct, her form fully dimensional. A spot of pale yellow light seemed to rest on her midsection. She watched him, basking in his attention.

Scragg continued to talk, a distant murmur of sympathetic but cruel reality.

Daniella raised one hand as if to point. Peter stared, the heat behind his eyes like a blast of tropical air. His seeing made her more real.

Scragg's voice perversely grabbed his attention again.

"—someone she knew, someone she recognized," Scragg said. "Can you think of anybody we did not interview?"

"I'll ask her," Peter said.

"I beg your pardon?"

"She's here, she's back," Peter murmured in awe.

It was not just the reappearance of his daughter, it was what she had become—translucent, gossamer, as beautiful as a piece of crystal. Peter could not combine what he was hearing with what he was seeing. The detective spoke of death, of suspects and murder, but Daniella was here, demanding his attention.

She smiled.

He frowned and shook his head, resolved to focus. If he did not, he might lose the one impossibility that was far more important to him. "I can't talk now."

"Mr. Russell—"

Peter hung up.

This image was not just Daniella seen from the outside, not just a ghost of the exterior; as the seconds passed, he could see deeper, through the wisps of what might have been an afterthought of clothing; deeper still, below the skin, into lightly sketched outlines of bones and organs, kept in place by some slavery to mortal form, but no longer functional, certainly. No longer necessary. As with the outside, so the inside. She looked like a medical school model made of glass—or more correctly, like a human diatom, translucent and nacreous.

"Ghosts have bones," Peter murmured.

She looked to her left, mildly concerned about something waiting down the hallway, and then returned her gaze to Peter.

"Hello, Daniella," he said. "Is *it* still there?" he asked gently, as if discussing a spider or some other small vermin that had distressed her. *Wait a minute. I'll get a jar and put it outside.*

She agreed with a girlish nod, it was still there, whatever *it* might be. Peter wondered if she could disagree with anything he said. Maybe ghosts were like puppets, forced to do or believe what you suggested.

In his mind, he tried various statements, *I love you. Where are you, sweetie? What happened to you?* and wondered if she could pick up what he was thinking. He had been talking to Daniella in his head for years, saying all the things there had not been time enough to say while she was alive.

He finally settled on, "Tell me if you're real."

She rewarded him with a step forward. Apparently, whatever was in the hall did not worry her too much—if she *could* be worried. *Past all mortal cares, right? But on to other cares, postmortal?*

What in hell could that mean?

Peter felt as if he had just drunk six cups of strong coffee. His pulse raced. He was not sweating, however; he was not in distress, just excited almost beyond words, excited out of his wits. Overjoyed.

"I love you so much," he said. "Thank you for giving me another chance. Thank you."

Little motes of light floated up from the floor and found their place in her. The closer she came, the more solid she seemed. He could almost reach out and touch her, embrace her.

No.

"You're real," Daniella said. Her voice was a reed instrument through yards of thick gauze, a bad connection from across impossible seas. She raised her hand and spread her fingers as if to lay them flat on his chest. Once more Peter noticed the glow, like light falling on her midriff, as if she contained a small luminous cloud, a sunset within a ghost.

"What do you want, sweetie?" Peter asked.

"Look," she demanded, and made another step. This time, as she moved, he could see the discontinuity—a jerk, as if a video were being rapidly advanced. Behind her face he discerned the outlines of veins and arteries, teeth behind the lips, skull beneath the skin. *No wonder we think the dead come back shrunken and decayed. But she's made of crystal. She's beautiful, not ugly and broken.*

Daniella was now within his reach. With a moan, Peter leaned forward. He felt resistance, like pulling together the equal poles of two bar magnets. His skin tingled. She lay against his chest, sighed—the echo of a sigh—closed her eyes, and wrapped translucent arms around him.

From every point she touched flowed a welcome weariness, deeper than repose, the seeping desuetude of death: sadness and distance and loss, loss of motive, utility, connection. His muscles grew limp. Too late, he realized this was not good. This would not work.

Peter gasped for air.

"Daddy," she said, and spread up and around him.

CHAPTER 

IN MEXICO THE dead are not mocked but laid and sweetened by candy skulls.

Ancient tribes, enlisting shamans trained in sympathies and magic, placated their dead. They surrounded and confused them with ritual, gently separated them from life and the living, and tried to make sure they did not return, or that if they did return, they had no power. Their darkness was deeper than ours, their nights longer; they truly lived in the shadow of the Earth, and on some nights, haunted nights, the sun itself was reluctant to show his face again.

For the living, it is love. For the dead not yet departed, it is a clinging, sapping necessity. The old ways speak of dangerous needs that cannot be met or assuaged. Wise mothers protected their babies against *mal occhio*, the unreasoning affection and desire of both the desperate living and the envious dead.

He should have prepared and protected his baby.

Mal occhio

Evil eyes

Time has slipped; he has slipped and fallen.

He saw her so clearly. She was there.

He almost makes sense out of it. The dead can never return to their old homes in the same way. They need release, forgetting. Freedom.

(The sunset within the ghost . . .)

The weeping will never stop.

Peter just wants his daughter back.

CHAPTER 29

HE LAY ON the sloping driveway outside the house, staring at a crusted patch of old oil flecked with clay litter. His pulse rattled in his ears, blood pumping like gasoline through a stalled engine. He did not remember coming out here and falling, but his knuckles and knees were skinned. There was no pain; pain would have been welcome.

His face was wet with emotion, but he could not remember why at first and wondered if it had finally come, if the angina or whatever had finally split his tissues.

He rolled over and stared at the graying sky. Dusk or dawn? The sky was getting brighter. It must be dawn. Had he been out on the driveway all night?

The phone rang in the house. Not the Trans; the old wall phone. Communication. Talk from distant lands. He counted seven rings before it stopped. Got stiffly to his knees on the drive, faced the house like a penitent about to inch toward a shrine. Slowly, memories returned. He was saying his daughter's name over and over. He looked down. His shirt and pants were covered with a thin layer of dust, not driveway dirt. Grayish white. On his fingers:

house dust, as if he had crawled under a bed. He stood and sniffed his fingers. Unmistakably, the scent he had associated with Daniella from infancy clung to him, sweet and primal. "God help me." He leaned against the wall of the garage. His pulse steadied, his breath eased, vitality returned. He felt a dangerous kind of good, that sense of relief and well-being after a skipped heartbeat. He wanted more. He wanted to return to the house and see if Daniella was still there. This time, he knew that if they touched he would not wake up. And that would be okay. That would be just fine with him.

The phone rang again.

Still dizzy, Peter walked toward the house. A little stumble on the low curb beside the driveway. He crossed the patio, stubbed his toe, lurched, and brushed the Soleri bell. The key broke loose from its tape and fell onto the bricks with a blunt *ting.* He stared down at it, letting the phone ring.

The key was covered with dust.

Peter bent, picked it up, sniffed it, and put it in his pants pocket.

CHAPTER 

HE LIFTED THE receiver on the tenth ring.

"I feel awful," Helen said without waiting for him to speak. "It wasn't your fault. I don't blame you for being angry."

Then, when he still didn't answer, she said, "Peter, damn it, are you there?"

"I'm not angry," Peter said.

"Why don't you answer your phone? I know you're angry."

"I'm not feeling well," Peter said. He could see himself in the glass of the kitchen cabinet—and frankly, he thought he looked a little luminous.

"We want to make it up to you," Helen said.

"I'd love to see you both," Peter said. He had questions, so many questions to ask so many people.

"I really think we should go on a picnic."

Softly, as if reaching for a life preserver, he asked, "Can Lindsey stay here overnight?"

"Of course," Helen said a little sharply, her aggression not yet abated. She felt guilty but justified. Doing this would make her feel better. Well, he'd take what he could get, whatever would lure him away from that blank and dangerous place that had held him for so many hours.

"Why are you calling this early?" Peter asked her.

"What? Silly, it's ten o'clock."

He looked outside. The sun was bright. "The clock wound down."

"Your electric clock?"

"Power out, I mean."

"Is everything all right?"

"I think so."

Over the phone, he heard a dryer buzzing. "Sorry. Just a sec." Helen's voice dropped away and she called out, "Lindsey, come say hello to your father."

A brief pause and a *clunk*. Lindsey took the phone. The first thing she said was, "Hi, Dad, we need to talk."

"Sure," Peter said.

"Mom's getting the laundry in the other room," Lindsey said, dropping her voice. "We need to talk and I can't tell you why."

"I know," Peter said. "I miss you, Lindsey."

"Something's changing, Dad," she whispered. Then, louder, "Here's Mom."

CHAPTER 

RAVENOUS, PETER MADE himself a late breakfast of oatmeal. As he ate, he could feel the nutrients push along his bloodstream, warm and sensuous as dollops of hot gravy wrapped in mashed potatoes. After touching the dead, even oatmeal could be sinful.

In the back of the cabinet he found an ancient jar of Tang and made himself three glasses, breaking up the fossilized orange clumps in tap water, stirring and stirring with the clinking spoon, then lining them up and drinking down all three. The sugar was like electricity. He could feel everything with a sharpness that was both exhilarating and worrisome.

Lindsey needed to talk with him.

Peter put down his spoon, suddenly ill. A few minutes passed before he knew that what he had eaten was not going to come back up—ghost of breakfast. He could not eat any more. He looked at the phone, at the answering machine on the tile counter below, with its light steady, no messages. And no wonder. He had switched the answer mode to off. He did not remember doing that.

He reached out and turned it on again.

Peter wondered if Daniella would leave him messages like a ghost on an episode of *The Twilight Zone*, dialing out of the graveyard over a storm-dropped telephone line. Of course, Daniella was not in a graveyard. Helen had had her remains cremated. There was an urn in a columbarium. *No. Don't go there.*

I've never been *there. I did not do for her what I did for Phil: return her to the sea. Helen forbade me from taking my daughter back to nature.*

Scragg. Detective Scragg. After all this time, still checking out the case. Looking at the calendar, two years. Just a coincidence. How devoted, how dedicated. People we have not thought about. Suspects all.

He leaned over the breakfast-nook table, hands grabbing the metal rim, and just stared at the shiny marble-print linoleum top, at nothing, nothing whatsoever.

Bit his lip, then his cheek.

She had been missing and dead for three weeks when a jogger found her buried in high, dry grass, under a pile of leaves.

Former nudie movie director Peter Russell's ten-year-old daughter has been found in a shallow grave in Griffith Park.

Whoever had kidnapped and killed her had just scraped at a patch of grass and earth and dumped her there. She had been stabbed many times, a frenzy. Their only solace, thin solace—Peter's, Helen's—was that Daniella had not been raped.

Ghosts did not reflect the violence done to them in life, the sickness, the murder.

Time seemed to have slowed, so rapidly were all these thoughts spilling out of his deeps.

No, that's not it at all. She died of leukemia. She was sick for months, not murdered. Don't be an ass.

She died in a car wreck,

a bus accident.

She died falling off a rock on a school outing,

broke her neck; she was beautiful, lying there in the coffin with all the flowers.

Who in this awful, awful world would want to slaughter such a lovely little girl, and then leave her outside to rot?

SOMETIMES, RARELY, THE missing kids return alive, and the TV cameras return as well. When the kids return, dead, who will believe? *Peter Russell's daughter comes back from the other side. Nation rejoices. After the break, a happy father.*

Those terrible three weeks of not knowing, Helen shrieking in the bathroom, scratching her arms bloody. Lindsey hiding in her room or under the stairs down to the basement, at eleven too young to really understand death; and who at any age could ever understand or accept the death of a loved one?

Next, on Oprah*—mourning or forgetting? Pain or insanity?*

Weeks into months.

When the police could do nothing, find nothing, Peter had gone out himself. Bought books on solving crimes. Returned to the scene over and over again, standing in October sun or December rain, coming home with muddy shoes, running on in an optimistic fury about what he would do the next day, what he would investigate.

Lying next to Helen at night, reading from the textbooks, until she grabbed up the blanket and went to sleep in the living room.

Finally, that short last step into madness, going to the psychic. And all along, drinking like a fish just to *hope* to feel normal for five or ten minutes out of the unendurable day.

Working on autopilot. Flying blind.

Who did this to you, sweetie? And why?

Weeping quietly, his shoulders shaking, rubbing his sternum with a stiff finger, he sucked in a breath. "Humpty Dumpty time, Peter Russell," he said.

CHAPTER 32

PETER WALKED UP the hill from the small grocery store, carrying two paper bags full of milk and salad makings and lunch meat and bread and a six-pack of ginger ale. He saw a red Mercedes 500SL parked on the sloping drive before his house and paused, then hefted the paper bags and continued.

The Mercedes' California license plate read TRANS4U2.

Stanley Weinstein was pacing in short arcs on the porch, stopping to thwong the Soleri bell with a finger. He jumped as Peter said hello. "Didn't hear you coming. What a great house. Classic rambler. Hope I'm not interrupting something interesting."

Weinstein was a bundle of nerves, but not nervous energy. The bags under his eyes had darkened since their meeting in Marin.

"No problem," Peter said, unlocking the front door. "Come on in. I'll put these away. Want a ginger ale?"

"Don't you have white wine? Whiskey?"

Peter shook his head. "Won't keep it in the house," he said. "Besides, you're driving, right?"

"Responsible fellow," Weinstein said, following him inside. He flipped the cardboard lid on the box in the hallway. "You still have a few units, I see."

"A few," Peter admitted. "I don't get out in public much. Gave them to several friends, however."

"All's well, then," Weinstein said, a not completely appropriate response, Peter thought. As if the young man was only half listening. "I'm meeting with more moneyed interests in Santa Monica tonight. Lots of cash on the sidelines. Raising money is kind of like show business, don't you think? See and be seen."

"Show business is all about raising money," Peter agreed, taking the bags into the kitchen.

"Truth is," Weinstein continued, "I also wanted to see how your work is going. There have been Questions."

"What kind of questions?" Peter asked, washing the lettuce in a battered colander in the sink.

"Wiser heads say I've taken a bit of a risk. Some of our newer investors wonder if you're the best choice. I'm here to bring back ammunition—conceptual samples. Have you looked at the work done by our design firm?"

Peter came out of the kitchen into the living room, wiping his hands on a towel. "It's awful," he said.

Weinstein snorted. "We paid a fair amount for their assessment. They're among the folks who wonder about you, to tell the truth."

"Well, let's always tell the truth," Peter said, feeling his cheeks pink. *Watch your mouth. Delicate time. No more self-sabotage.*

"No offense," Weinstein said. "But we need to move forward."

"Other difficulties?" Peter asked.

"Other than keeping everyone on the same page, none," Weinstein said, but would not meet Peter's eyes. "Geniuses are not my first choice for business partners. They keep going off on tangents. They get lost in theory. Let's consider this, let's consider that. You know the drill. The *dental* drill."

"I haven't got much to show, yet. Arpad sent me a note with the design team sketches, and he doesn't like them, either."

Weinstein now faced him with what was apparently meant to be an accusing glare. "Well, yes, Arpad. Truly our Tesla, is he not? And with about as much business sense. If I'm going to fight for you, I need some genuine Peter Russell material. Inspirational."

"If?" Peter asked.

Weinstein pulled his head to one side to take a kink out of his neck. For a moment, his eyes looked wild. "We've got a week to prove ourselves, and not one hour more. If I can keep *Arpad* from getting morose, if I can keep our investors from turning into a pack of hyenas ... Please. Anything."

Peter decided that Weinstein was little worse than most of the producers he had worked for. The lower the budget, the more they complained. But he had usually delivered, and he would try now. "Handing out word balloons," he offered, draping the towel over his arm like a waiter.

Weinstein cocked an eyebrow. "Beg pardon?"

Peter made as if he were uncorking a bottle of champagne, pantomimed pouring it into his fist. "People on the street, blowing up word balloons and giving them to each other. They take them home and the word balloons pop ... out come messages. 'We're only human. Talk is what we do.' "

"Sounds self-defeating," Weinstein said. "Not in the least sexy or edgy."

"I'm working on that," Peter said. "Fan dancing. Men and women, naked, holding word balloons in front of their privates, waltzing around a street."

Weinstein snickered. "Well," he said, noncommittal. "Well." He walked along the big front window, hand to chin.

"Amateur actors," Peter said. "Old and young, not all hip pretty kids. Slightly baggy nudes, but they're all having fun. Maybe their skin suits are a little too obvious. Shoot super eight. Or you can buy me a used Arriflex Super 16, more control, we can pull it down in the lab. About thirty grand. Cheaper than renting if we're going to do several commercials or promos back-to-back."

Peter would not ask Karl Pfeil for a loan, not now.

"What about digital video?" Weinstein asked, wincing a little.

"Not the look you said you wanted. But maybe things have changed."

"No, no," Weinstein said, backing down. He pursed his lips. "We can rent."

Peter sensed acquiescence. "Give me a budget and I'll put together a team. I can do wonders for fifty grand. If we rent. And that's exclusive of my own fee. Twenty grand per promo, fifty grand for a commercial. If we work fast, I can get you some short stuff in two weeks." Peter secretly took a deep breath.

Weinstein resumed pacing. "You cannot believe the pressure. Six of our key people resigned yesterday. It's got us seeing double."

"Maybe they shouldn't be working in a prison," Peter suggested.

Weinstein shot him a look that Peter could not read, then turned away. "Your agent," he said.

"I work with a lawyer," Peter said. They hadn't spoken in over seven years.

"Fine," Weinstein said. "Get me the papers. You don't like the other ideas, huh?"

"They were going to use the gas chamber," Peter said.

"I suggested that," Weinstein said. "Psychotronic, right?"

"Suicidal," Peter said, feeling an odd strength roll back into him. "You're selling talk, not video games. But if you want to sell Trans to jaded teenage boys . . ."

Weinstein considered this, his face blank. "All right," he said, and held out his hand, waggling his fingers like a beggar. "A sample, anything. I'm desperate."

Peter took up a sketchpad and a Magic Marker and drew a large cartoon of four of Phil's nebbishy guys, clutching their word balloons down low. "Don't walk the walk without the talk," he said, sharing the words across the balloons. Then, over it all, he scrawled, "When talk is cheap, life is good. And that's the naked truth." He handed the page to Weinstein, who glanced at it and grimaced.

"Flabby nudes? The naked truth? Do you know the kind of people I'm facing, Peter? They are locked into hyper-cool. They compete with each other to buy superexpensive sports cars, just for bragging rights. Their women fit the perfect waist-to-hip ratio, like they order them from a catalog. They can smell blood in the water from a mile away. They can *taste* failure, like eels taste sickness and death."

Where is that coming from? Peter asked himself.

Weinstein's cheeks tightened to form deep dimples around his lips, beyond anger and into desperation. "If I let our investors meet Arpad now, the way he is, I'm sunk. We're all sunk. He's going through a crisis."

"What sort of crisis?" Peter asked.

Weinstein shrugged that off. "I need assurance, cool, stability, savoir faire. I don't think dull wit and flabby nudes are going to cut it."

"Then why did you ask me?" Peter said, his voice breaking. "You know my reputation. That's all I've ever been good for." He had had enough.

"Because I thought you might still have something to add," Weinstein said.

Peter made as if to tear the sheet of paper in half, but Weinstein snatched it from his hands. "Fuck it. A meeting tonight, bigger money than even Mr. Benoliel can dream of. And this." Weinstein swiftly and neatly rolled the paper. "Got a rubber band?" he asked.

HALF AN HOUR after he saw Weinstein out the door, Peter sat in the kitchen, vibrating with anger and wondering if he knew what in the hell he was doing, with Weinstein or with anyone else in his life. He tried to sip ginger ale, but his hand was shaking so badly it spilled. The phone rang.

He looked at it for a moment, sick of talk, any talk, then set down the glass and picked up the receiver. "Hello."

It was Michelle. "Joseph is doing poorly," she said. "He wants to meet with you. He won't tell me why. Can you be here?"

Peter drew himself together. "Of course," he said. "My car's in the shop. I'll go pick it up and be right over."

The garage sent a Jeep. The Porsche was all fixed and ready to roll. But he would have to be back before it was dark.

If he dared.

CHAPTER 33

"THANK GOD YOU made it," Michelle said as he climbed the steps.

She was seated with legs crossed on a wicker peacock chair on the long shaded veranda. It was three o'clock and she held a martini in one hand.

"What's up?" Peter asked.

She shrugged. "He won't tell me. Emotionally, he's been going downhill for a week now," she said, and added, through prim lips, "Sometimes I wonder if I even know the man." Then she bucked up and set the glass on a round, glass-top table. "Between you and me and the alcohol."

"Of course," Peter said. Beside the glass, he saw that she had arranged a pile of silvery pushpins to form a clownish, grinning face, like a jack-o'-lantern.

"I should quit," she said, lifting the glass again. "I don't drink much, but I should quit completely. It's false, isn't it, the way it takes the stress off? Because the stress is still there."

"You just don't feel it as much," Peter said.

"You quit a long time ago," Michelle said, looking up at him with heavily made-up and inquisitive green eyes. He had not seen her use so much makeup before: rouge-pinked cheeks, false eyelashes, mascara. It bordered on the grotesque.

"It would have killed me," Peter said.

"You're strong." She changed expressions, brightened. One moment she was somber, the next, friendly and curious. "How did the interview go?"

"I've got a job," Peter said, smiling. "Thanks to you."

"I try," Michelle said distantly. "Joseph might be pleased to hear about that. He likes you, you know."

"I know," Peter said. "I wouldn't want to disappoint him, or you."

"How in hell could you disappoint us?" Michelle asked, astonished.

"I may be losing it again," Peter said. "It's as if I'm trying to sabotage everything."

"Like last time?" Michelle asked, leaning forward.

"Worse than last time. I'm seeing things."

She reached out and brushed the back of his hand. One of her long nails briefly scratched the skin there, leaving a white mark. "What makes you think you're losing it? Joseph sees things all the time." She smiled as if that might be a joke—or might not. "He won't confide in me. It's as if I can feel the storm clouds, but . . . I don't know where they're coming from. He talks in his sleep, sometimes. We all get old, I guess."

Peter looked across the broad green lawn, embarrassed. "Well, it's worse for me."

Cloud shadows chased over the estate.

"Tell me about it," Michelle said. She leaned forward, resting her elbows on her knees, and gave him a sidelong look. "I care, Peter. I listened before, I can listen now."

"I wouldn't know where to begin."

"Start with yesterday," Michelle said. "As good a place as any."

"What I'm seeing or not seeing, that isn't the worst of it," Peter said. "It's the pattern. It's caring and losing and then breaking down. Don't ever have kids, Michelle."

"I won't," Michelle vowed.

"No matter how much of a selfish bastard you think you are, kids come along and they dismantle you, they rebuild you. You put everything you are into them, all your hopes and fears. It's as if you have to reach out and protect everybody—the whole family, the whole world. I used to lie in bed afraid that I'd lose one or both of my children, afraid of what that would do to me, to me and Helen."

"Well, that must be common enough," Michelle observed.

"Yes, but I still didn't keep track, didn't listen to my own fears. I lost my focus. I was off on a trip ... doing research for a book. A stupid little book that wasn't going to go anywhere, no matter how much research I did. And a bit of the dark world came and took her."

Helen calling on the phone, Daniella was missing. Flying back on a commuter plane from San Francisco. Getting into Burbank Airport, Helen picking him up curbside, rushing home ... to sit and wait, talk to police officers, digging for photographs, writing down descriptions for the Amber Alert, slowly working their way up after four days to Detective Scragg.

Just four days, and then they were talking to Robbery Homicide.

"Dark world?" Michelle repeated, incredulous. "Devils and demons? She was murdered, Peter."

"It's a metaphor. Kipling," Peter said. This was getting him nowhere.

"I'd still like to know what you're seeing. Maybe it can help me understand Joseph."

Peter squinted across the lawn. "I don't get you," he said. "It doesn't mean a thing, because it can't be real, right?"

She shrugged. "Sometimes he sleepwalks. Screams in the middle of the night. The doctor says it might be a reaction to his blood-pressure medicine. It's worse at night, but now it happens in the daytime, too. When you aren't here. When you're here, he's on his best behavior." Michelle rubbed her hands and stared at her knuckles. "He talks about you like a son." Her face went blank. "So I guess that makes me your mother, and that makes me responsible for both of you. See? I can feel responsible, too."

"He hasn't told me any of this."

"Well, he wouldn't, would he? It's up to me, when you're gone, to bear up under that particular brunt." She sat back in the chair, eyes like flint. "I don't think anybody here is going nuts. You or Joseph. But there *is* a mystery. Two big strapping males start worrying about their sanity and spending big money on gurus in Pasadena." Now she stood. In her short-sleeve white blouse and pleated slacks, she looked like a Howard Hughes protégée, about to portray Amelia Earhart. She might have been a ghost herself, an actress visitor from Salammbo's past, from the 1930s. "Go to him."

"Of course." He got up from the chair and headed for the door.

"I still can't get my Trans to work inside the house, past the veranda," Michelle called after him. "Ask Weinstein about that."

"I will," Peter said.

* * *

JOSEPH WAS SEATED in front of the open French windows in the upstairs room. He wore a sweatshirt and what looked like ski pants. "Happy hunting?" Joseph asked as he heard the door close. He did not turn to look.

"Pretty decent," Peter said. "They're giving me a job. I owe it to you and Michelle."

"Michelle did the legwork, as she is most talented in that department," Joseph said. "Come sit. Don't make me bend my neck. I'm stiff all over today."

"Why not get out and get some exercise?" Peter asked.

"Because I'm . . ."

For a moment, Peter thought he could anticipate what Joseph was going to say: *losing my mind.* But Joseph pulled his words back and amended them to, "That Sandaji woman's assistant has been pestering me ever since your visit."

"For more money?"

"No. Apparently you impressed her maidservant or whatever she's called."

"Jean Baslan," Peter remembered. "I doubt she was impressed."

"Well, somebody was. Sandaji would never call directly, not even me, her benefactor."

"Wary of filthy lucre?" Peter offered.

"She enjoys her money. But she spends too much time dealing with troubled people and she probably likes her privacy. How's that for insight, Peter?" Joseph afforded him a wan smile.

"Pretty good," Peter said.

"My producer instincts. Now cheer me up. Tell me about your job."

Peter outlined the generalities of the commission, and told him about the awful pitch scribbled by the consultants in Palo Alto and the dicey meeting with Weinstein at the Glendale house. He felt not the slightest inclination to tell Joseph about his ghosts. Here, in the clean old room with its dark, expensive furniture, the view of the endless lawn, back at Salammbo, life felt normal. He could be half convinced it was all an inside job. Psychological. Falling back into an old, old rut. Well, he had survived that before, he could do it again . . . and so on, as he rolled out the story of his visit to San Andreas.

"Jesus," Joseph said when Peter finished. He made a face. "They actually have their switchboard thing in the gas chamber?"

"They're proud of it, in a weird way. I'm trying to convince them that stunt is a little too juvenile for the open market. A certain amount of respect is called for when you go big time."

"Spoken like a true king of exploitation," Joseph said. "Are they heedless nerds?"

"They seem to have social skills," Peter said. "Arpad Kreisler . . . he's pretty interesting."

"Head on his shoulders?"

Peter nodded.

"A new beginning," Joseph said.

"Maybe."

"Well, we might not need you here much longer," Joseph said. "That would set you free to watch over my investment." He swallowed. "Michelle's investment."

"I can still help out here when I'm needed," Peter said, suddenly uneasy, as if about to wake up from a nice dream. "Gratis. You've both been good to me."

Joseph motioned for Peter to move his chair and sit directly in front of him, in the pool of sun coming through the window.

"Are you sure you're all right?" Joseph asked.

"Pretty sure," Peter said. He would confess his worries to Michelle, but not Joseph; that's how it was.

Joseph checked him over through narrowed eyes, and for a second, Peter wondered what was going on. Joseph's look as much as said, *What do you know?* "Well," Joseph drawled, pulling back this scrutiny, "one last errand, and then I'd like you to put all this behind you. Go through that gate, and don't come back."

Peter was surprised into a moment of silence.

"It's not about you," Joseph continued. "My past is about to return and sit on my lap, and it's not pretty. I've made some fairly big mistakes, one in particular. I should have known ... producer's instinct. But *cojones* ruled."

"You're sounding a little scary, Mr. Benoliel."

"As I said, this doesn't concern you," Joseph said mildly, as if speaking to a favored child. "Do this for me. Go back to Sandaji. She apparently has some questions, her handmaid was vague about what sort. Maybe she needs your masculine services. Even Mother Teresa must have had her moments."

"I doubt that very much," Peter said, drawing his brows together.

"You have time to go see them, for me?"

"I think so," Peter said.

"This evening?"

"Okay."

"And what will you do if they clue you in to some cosmic mystery, some further answer to my original question?"

"Tell you all about it. If you don't lock the gates."

"I'll never lock the gates on you, Peter. But it's time for you to move on. Still, if they clue you ..." He nodded and set his jaw. "Call and tell me. And if something happens to me ... watch out for Michelle."

"Of course I will," Peter said. "But nothing's—"

"I mean it," Joseph said. "Promise me you'll humor an old man. You'll watch out for her."

Peter nodded, at a loss what to do now. Joseph waved him off and stared blankly out the window. "Tie up the loose ends. And thanks, Peter."

"My pleasure," Peter said. As he opened the door, Joseph—as he often did—issued a dramatic set of parting words. "Don't believe what you read in the papers."

"Right," Peter said.

MICHELLE LOOKED BACK at Peter as they walked down the long front steps below the veranda. "Joseph and I haven't had sex in years, Peter. I'm okay with that. There's been far too much sex in my life. But this other stuff—this brooding—that worries me."

"Thanks for sharing," Peter said.

"What, afraid of the fate that lies in store for all old men?"

Peter sniffed.

"I assume you're leaving soon to go to that Sandaji woman. Can you drive me over to Jesus Wept?"

"Sure. Or we could walk."

She looked up. "It's going to rain. That woman's creepy, don't you think?"

"I don't know," Peter said, detecting a hint of covetousness he had not heard from Michelle before. *Is everyone a little off these days? Phil was the starting pistol. Then Sandaji. Then me. Now Joseph and Michelle. We're all in Wonderland.*

"Anyway, drive us over and leave from there. I'll walk back. I want your opinion."

Peter wondered how much time Michelle spent at the other house. This was the first occasion she had invited him to see what she was doing. How she occupied her time when Joseph was being moody ...

Despite his tastes in women—he thought without apology that twenty-five to thirty was the age range of perfection—he had never had much faith in May-December relationships.

Peter opened the Porsche's door for Michelle.

"I've always loved this car," she said, slipping into the low seat with otter-like grace and pulling in her legs. "I hate our Arnage. It's a boat." Her lip curled. "I feel embarrassed driving it."

"Sell it," Peter advised. "You could buy ten or twenty of these, and I could use the parts."

Michelle smiled. A whistling freshet lifted her hair. An offshore deck of mottled clouds was moving inland. Sprinkles fell by the time they swung around the low hills and U-turned by the huge bronze statue of El Cid that dotted the long exclamation mark of oleander hedge. They approached the Mission-style mansion down a sloping drive.

"Did you know there's enough poison in that oleander to kill a small town?" Michelle asked. "Make a note for your next mystery."

"I haven't written a mystery in years," Peter said. That had been Phil's forte. Involved, complicated mysteries with what seemed to the average reader a large number of loose ends. They had not sold well.

"I could help," Michelle offered. The look she gave him just as they pulled up by the row of five garage doors was at once speculative and blank. She tossed back her hair in a way that Peter knew from experience meant a woman was considering making a pass. The blankness, he suspected, was a combination of not wanting to show her hand too early and possibly of not being certain or happy about her plans. Something drove her forward anyway. "You should do what you need to do," she told him. "I've known you for years, Peter. Old friends. And now I do mean *old.* Time is running short."

It really was Wonderland. For the first time with Michelle, Peter felt acutely uncomfortable. He had long ago learned how to turn down passes both overt and covert from women of all walks in life without arousing too much resentment. Still, the fact that he was thumbing through his mental three-by-five card file of polite rejections was disturbing. He had always thought Michelle was too smart and too classy to advance this little card onto the table.

Joseph would smell it on them both, even if it never went beyond a simple pass—he would know it right away, producer's instincts.

Still, where women were concerned, Peter had always been dangerously curious. He followed Michelle up the two tiers of steps to the huge, wrought-iron-studded door. Michelle swung it open with a shove of one fine, long-fingered hand; it was not locked.

"Welcome to my beast," she said. They entered the mansion. Their footsteps, crossing the black slate floor, sharpened in the sonic retrospect of the entry, transformed into a suggestion of razors. "I just can't figure out what to do with this place. The more I spend and the harder I try, the uglier she gets."

Enough light filtered in from high windows over the front door to light their way, but the circular foyer was still gloomy and unwelcoming. Staircases descended in heavy swoops to each side. Iron railings on the stairs and along the balustrade were a marvel of dark, eye-snagging difficulty.

Michelle swung her arm up to the balcony. "See what I mean?" she said. "I could hang klieg lights up there and she would still depress me. But you should have seen what she was like before. The fire made such a mess of her. I've torn down walls, opened up rooms, painted, fixed floors . . . Like most old ladies, you can lift and tuck, but you can't hide bad bones. Still, I've always thought she has potential. Don't you?"

Peter tried to conceal his unease.

Michelle walked to the center of the foyer. Her voice seemed to fan out and come from all around. "Joseph once told me something terrible happened here, but he won't say what."

"Murder most foul," Peter suggested.

"Yes, well, more likely an orgy went wrong. Lost innocence, drugs, Coke bottles. Fatty Arbuckle stuff." She smiled. "But it's not in the history books or the newspapers, so who knows? Maybe *you* can pry it out of him." Then she made a moue. "On second thought, forget it. He's not up to sad stories."

Joseph hasn't told her about ending my employment, Peter thought.

"You know the tunnel between the houses? With the tracks and little cars?"

"I've never been down there."

"I think we're going to fix it up. Clean it out and make it run again." Michelle gave him another blank look. For the first time, Peter felt that she was lying, and he could not begin to guess why.

"Come into the kitchen," Michelle suggested. "It's the best place."

"I'd better not," Peter said. His curiosity had evaporated. "I've got to run my errand."

"Be that way," Michelle said lightly enough, returning to stand close. "Did you bring your Trans?"

He hadn't. "I think they're having network problems," he said. The truth was, he had simply forgotten it on the way out of the house.

"Well, maybe that explains it," Michelle said. "I haven't told Joseph, but the units don't work inside *either* of the houses. Wouldn't want him to think we've bet his money on a lame horse. Are you all right?"

"Just cold. I'd better get moving," Peter said.

Michelle wrapped her arms around herself. "It is chilly. And she does show better when the sun is shining."

Outside, she became Joseph's Michelle again, comradely and straight. She patted his arm. "Don't let that woman bum you," she advised, standing by the driver's door as he buckled himself in. "Sandaji's turned Joseph into a pill, I'm sure of it. Trying to get more money, I bet. I just don't like her."

Peter said he would do his best to protect Joseph from predatory gurus. He tried to smile but his face just wouldn't cooperate, so he gave her a wry grimace and a wink. Then he backed up and left Michelle standing on the long, cracked concrete drive, before the huge old house with its high Alamo-style peak and second-floor rows of narrow, deep-set black windows.

Not like eyes. Like the gaps between stained teeth.

CHAPTER 34

JEAN BASLAN OPENED the door. Without a word, she let him in and motioned for him to wait in the living room. He carefully sat on an antique Morris chair and folded his hands. He heard her short hard heels clicking across the dining room and down the hall.

Peter turned his head at a small sound behind him. An extremely elderly man stood by a square pillar supporting one half of the archway into the living room. He wore a blue cardigan buttoned at the belt, loose, baggy pants, and a white shirt, and above his high forehead, a brush of gray hair jutted. Round glasses covered rheumy gray eyes. Narrow shoulders slumped like folded wings and long arms hung with elbows bent slightly, hands gripped as if practicing a golf swing.

With a small, shy smile, he stepped gingerly around a spray of dried flowers in a large ceramic vase and sidled along the edge of the coffee table.

"Sandaji will join us shortly," he said, his voice soft and deep. "My name is Edward Schelling."

"Pleased to meet you," Peter said, standing and offering his hand.

Schelling shook his head apologetically: no touching. "Brittle bones," he said. "Compared to you, I'm like a piece of glass." He let himself down onto the couch with a release of locked joints, and slumped alarmingly to one side before sitting upright again. He managed all this with great dignity.

"It's been many years since Sandaji last spoke to me," he said. "Something of a privilege now, that we should be afforded an audience."

"Costs some people plenty," Peter said.

Schelling raised his brushy white eyebrows in agreement. "For being such a spiritual woman, security in this life is very important to Sandaji. Still, let us not be catty." He paused and leaned his head back to inspect the woodwork on the ceiling. "Do you remember being told that she is not a psychic?"

"I remember." Peter needed to understand what was happening here. Was he still representing Joseph, or had that relationship been tossed aside? "You're an old friend?"

"I am not an acolyte, if that's your question," Schelling replied. He lifted his shoulders briefly, then let them sag back. They might have been connected by springs, or weighed down by time. "We were married once, in another life. Sorry, I'm not being clear. In this life, but before she was Sandaji."

Peter silently opened his mouth, *Ah.*

"She will not be staying here much longer. The house and what is in it have become too much for her. Still, it will be a major inconvenience to move. This is an important time of the year. Many visitors."

"Sorry to hear that," Peter said.

"May I ask you an odd question?"

Peter lifted the corners of his lips.

"Are *you* psychic?"

Peter drew back. "No."

"Have you recently experienced suspicions, odd feelings ... sensations? Or induced the same in others?"

"I'm sorry, Mr. ..." Peter had forgotten his name.

"Schelling." The old man's eyes were very bright. He reminded Peter in some ways of a superannuated Dashiell Hammett, or perhaps Faulkner.

"I'm not sure why you're asking," Peter said.

Both men turned their heads. Sandaji walked with slow dignity into the entry, as if seeking distance and time to inspect Peter. Schelling's neck crackled. He pulled back his shoulders with more conviction and stood. Peter followed suit.

She wore a green velvet gown with a dark bronze belt, as if trying out for the role of Ophelia in a geriatric version of *Hamlet*, and she looked thinner, older; the beautiful radiance from that first meeting had diminished. Still, even with the force of her presence so reduced, it took Peter several seconds to notice Jean Baslan standing to one side, hands tightly clasped.

Having performed her inspection, Sandaji finished her walk into the living room and offered her hand to Peter. "Is Edward giving you the proper third degree?" she asked, her stance belying her tone: light and conversational. Peter clasped her hand and felt something like reassurance pass between. Uneasy, he rejected it without even thinking. He had dealt with charismatic women before; he had also watched them disrobe and assume undignified postures.

Schelling observed their touch with bleared, sad eyes.

Sandaji stepped around the table to the couch. She took a seat as her former husband stepped aside, his bony knees cracking.

"We're getting along famously," Schelling said. They stared at Peter with lips pressed together, hands clasped in their laps, like children in the principal's office—two shy, wise children, a matched set. Figurines in a bizarre antiques shop.

"Joseph Benoliel asked me to come visit him," Sandaji said. "After my troubling experience here, with you, Mr. Russell, I wondered if it was wise to comply."

"Mr. Russell says he is not psychic, my dear," Schelling explained. "I assume that means he is not responsible for the continuing disturbances."

Sandaji raised her hand in rather abrupt dismissal and focused on Peter, leaning slightly forward while still keeping her back straight.

"For the last two days, I've been seeing ghosts," she said, her beautiful eyes fixed on Peter's. "Memories drifting like smoke, but pervasive. Impressions from outside the house, bits of interior dialog, not words so much as images or smells, rarely sounds. And other sensations I cannot explain at all. My body feels moments of exaltation and sadness, moving within me, from other moments in other lives. As well, phantasms of other bodies—sensations within my organs, my muscles, on my skin. Often, I itch without cause. It can be embarrassing."

Despite his concealed distress, perhaps because of it, Peter could not help laughing. "That *is* weird," he said.

Sandaji joined his laughter for an instant, charmingly, and then with a long flutter of her lashes, straightened her face. "I have seen myself, as I will be or have been in this house. That frightens me, because of stories my great-grandmother told me when I was a little girl. She warned that seeing yourself is tantamount to learning you will soon die."

"Remarkable," Peter said. The hair on his neck was now fully erect.

"Mr. Benoliel offered us another large sum of money to come out to his estate. Apparently, something is troubling him. After I made my decision, I enlisted the aid of Mr. Schelling. Has he told you that he is, in fact, psychic?"

"We're not on such intimate terms yet," Peter said. He looked at Schelling. "Are you going out there?" he asked.

"Oh, we have already made our visit. Yesterday," Schelling said.

Peter stared between them, mouth open. "I was just there. Joseph didn't say anything about you."

"I presume he wishes all this to be kept close to home," Sandaji said. "But by sending you, I presume he has also given permission for us to speak. He places some confidence in you. He has been disturbed recently, but he could not tell us why, or by what."

"What did he see?" Peter asked.

Sandaji lifted an eyebrow at this choice of words, but did not answer.

"Sandaji is not alone, nor is Mr. Benoliel, in being *disturbed*," Schelling interrupted. "Today, Jean and I witnessed a child standing right here in this living room. He was clutching a toy fire engine. His clothing was not of the latest fashion, and he was most certainly neither alive, nor physically present."

Peter glanced up at Baslan. She nodded, face pale.

"Usually, even with my abilities tuned to the strongest degree, I see nothing more than wisps, hints, figures in the corner of my eye," Schelling continued. "This time, however, it was as if we had both put on a new pair of glasses. Our little boy was as vivid as you are right now. What I saw made me want to weep. An intimacy, a truth ..." Schelling shook his head, his eyes growing even more watery. "Most remarkable."

Peter swallowed hard. The pause between this sentence and the next seemed unbearably long, and he did not know if he could bear to wait, or stand to hear whatever might come from Schelling's lips.

The elderly man's voice dropped to a soft, rumbling stentor. Now he sounded angry, as if describing an affront to their dignity. He reached into his coat pocket and pulled out something oblong wrapped in tin-foil, and laid it on the table. "We visited Mr. Benoliel, and his wife—we assume it was his wife—gave us this when we left."

His long, thin fingers could not muster sufficient dexterity to unwrap the foil, so Sandaji did it for him. Before she had finished pulling off the last of three layers, Peter saw clearly that it was a Trans—a bright-red unit.

"It's some sort of phone, isn't it?" she asked Peter.

"Yes," Peter said. He tongued the gap between his teeth. "Joseph invested in the company."

"You carried one of these with you when you first visited Sandaji, did you not?" Schelling asked.

"I think so," Peter said. He remembered touching the Trans in his pocket, alongside the roll of hundred-dollar bills. "Yes, I did."

"That could explain quite a lot," Schelling said, blinking slowly. "You confirm my worst suspicions."

Sandaji said, "You're hiding something, Mr. Russell. Are you sure that you, too, haven't been seeing ghosts?"

Schelling did not wait for an answer. He held the Trans to his ear as if listening to a seashell and fastened an even sharper look on Peter. "These devices produce a remarkable effect," he said. "A certain extraordinary *silence.* And then something unexpected ... Like the rising of a curtain before a hidden stage. I, for one, am very frightened by what may be happening to us all."

Peter felt as if his tongue had jammed against the roof of his mouth. *Everyone is hiding something. And some things are no longer hiding from anyone.*

Baslan, now at Peter's elbow, obligingly offered him a bottle of Evian. He opened the sealed cap and took a sip, nodding his thanks. For her part, she continued to regard him as if he were a strange and threatening animal that had been set loose in the house.

CHAPTER 

SANDAJI TOOK SCHELLING by the elbow and helped him through the kitchen to the back door and outside. Peter followed. They stopped by a large oriental stone lantern at the meeting of two perpendicular paths. "A few special people," she said, "have the ability to see deep into roiled waters. Sometimes it's because of what they are, sometimes it's because they have been involved in extraordinary events."

Peter was remembering the sensation he had felt before opening the door to Phil's bedroom. *I do not want to know.*

Jean Baslan closed the porch door, pulling on a blue sweater, and ran down the steps to join them. The rain had stopped for the moment but the sky was still clouded over, threatening. The large backyard was ornamented by clumps of sword grass and papyrus neatly arranged in undulating, brick-walled planters. A Japanese-style teahouse rose above the grass in the back corner of the lot, angled to face the garden; the rice-paper doors were open and lanterns burned inside and along the steps. Order, beauty, calmness; none of which he could share, not now.

"These are special people," Sandaji said as she helped Schelling up the steps of the teahouse. "Some are like saints. Others ... not saints. They have extraordinary skills, and some do not realize what they can do. Edward has met them. He also happens to be one *of* them."

A deck chair had been set on the tatami mat floor. Schelling sat stiffly. "You still haven't answered our questions," he said through a wheeze. Cushions provided seating for Sandaji; Peter remained standing, arms crossed in defense, feeling both dread and embarrassment.

"I wouldn't know what to say."

"We're not enemies, Mr. Russell," Sandaji said.

"I just don't know what's true and what isn't," Peter said.

Schelling lifted his eyebrows and scrutinized Peter's face.

Sandaji looked distressed. "Why don't you trust us, Mr. Russell?"

"Because you take money from lonely people, people in pain," Peter said.

"Hospitals and doctors take money," Sandaji said. "I treat a different kind of illness."

"Well, you wrap it in fake charm and piety. Maybe that's why I don't trust you."

Schelling seemed about to stand in defense of his former wife, but Sandaji placed a restraining hand on his knee before the joint had a chance to pop. "It's a living," she said, eyes dancing. "I believe what I tell people. I truly do relieve their pain and give them peace. And what do *you* do for a living, Mr. Russell?"

"I take pictures of naked ladies," Peter said. "And make movies."

Schelling's jaw fell. He had remarkably straight, corn-colored teeth, all his own, it seemed. "I'll be damned," he said, and looked aside either in indignation or in embarrassment.

"I see," Sandaji said, with as much aplomb—and no more—as if he had said he was a lawyer. "Edward, remember when I posed for your box camera?"

"We are straying from the topic," Schelling said.

"How old were you, my dear?"

"Sixty-two," Schelling answered, throat bobbing.

"A lovely time," Sandaji said. "I was quite the young beauty. And you, my dear," again she patted Schelling's knee, "were very artful, like another Edward I once knew—Edward Weston. Your photographs, Mr. Russell, are for young men who lack female company," Sandaji said, peering up at Peter like a schoolgirl. "Do we not both peddle dreams of happiness?"

Peter could picture himself standing with arms crossed, jaw stuck out like *Il Duce*; a graying genie in a Hawaiian shirt and a beige coat spotted by rain. She could see right through him, and make him know it. "Art for art's sake," he said.

Sandaji laughed. Edward, still looking to one side, began to laugh next. Peter tried to keep a straight face, but the tension and the situation—and Sandaji's charm—drew him in.

He had begun with Michelle; why not tell all to these two, these extraordinary antique figurines? *Because they're no better than palmreaders. You can't ever go there again. It would kill you.*

And yet, here you are.

"Perhaps Mr. Russell is right not to trust us, my dear," Schelling said. "What can we offer him that he needs?"

"Mr. Russell needs to talk, and soon, or he will burst," Sandaji said. "Perhaps we should begin, however."

"Have we not already begun?" Schelling asked, perplexed.

"Not at *your* beginning, my dear. And how long did it take you to reveal that particular tale?"

"Decades," Schelling said, mouth working.

Jean Baslan had gone back to the house, and now returned with a tray, carrying a pot of tea in a knit cozy and four fine china cups.

"It's obvious you understand something about life," Sandaji said to Peter. Baslan noiselessly set the tray on a small sandalwood table. "What do you know about death?"

THE RAIN BEGAN again as drizzle, and soon surrounded the teahouse with a rushing downpour. The roof rumbled and water cascaded from the edge of the tiles and out of the gutters, gathering in furious puddles and stooping the sword grass and papyrus. It had not rained so hard in months.

"I lost my daughter. I buried my best friend. I don't know much at all," Peter finally answered, his strong, thick fingers absorbing the cup's heat.

"Nor do I," Sandaji said. "But Edward does."

Isolated from the world by thin gray walls of falling water, sipping jasmine-scented tea, Peter felt like a little boy. Despite everything, he knelt cross-legged on the pillow in front of Schelling and realized he actually liked both of these people, very much—could possibly even trust them.

What he did not trust and could never trust again was himself, his fallibility, his weakness in the face of absolutes.

"First, Edward, tell Mr. Russell how old you are," Sandaji suggested.

"Today is my birthday," Schelling replied with a wide smile. "I am one hundred and five years old."

Peter was suitably impressed. He could not imagine being so old. For that matter, it was hard to imagine being fifty-eight.

Sandaji beamed at Schelling. "Now tell Mr. Russell about Passchendaele." She jostled his elbow, as if to switch on a tape recorder.

Schelling began his story.

"A man I once knew survived the Great War in France," he said. "He was *me*, of course, in a sense. But I am no longer that trim and idealistic adolescent, so pardon me if I do not use the first-person pronoun. He witnessed horror upon unspeakable horror. He saw thousands die. For weeks, he and his fellow soldiers lay in muddy trenches just yards from the bodies of their friends, who had died hours or days earlier, mowed down in an endless series of aborted advances. As the bodies bloated and were reduced by rats, those still alive gave them comic names, made jokes, placed bets as to when one or another would burst from decay or be blown to pieces by a mortar. It was all done to numb themselves to the horror. For a time, it worked. Humans are astonishingly resilient.

"But after a week, the weather changed ... not the rain, which was constant, but some other weather. This young man noticed the change first. Perhaps he was always a little sensitive. At first, he saw wisps moving across the fields, down the trenches, like whirls of fog. In subsequent hours, at night, he would catch the silhouette, standing in a familiar posture, of a friend long dead. Then the outline of a face hung over him as he slept, empty eyes beseeching. In fits and starts, he saw full figures of his dead comrades return, walking among the living, seeming as real as those still wearing their flesh. They struggled to appear normal, to do the things they had always used to do. Memory is tenacious, Mr. Russell. It is the glue that holds the universe together, and it binds the dead to their friends and family ... for a time.

"Others saw them as well. Assuming perhaps that in this hellish place all the rules had changed—class and etiquette, savagery and kindness, the separation of the living and the dead—a few of the more foolhardy attempted to strike up conversations with their old comrades. At first, the revenants were unresponsive, 'hollow.' They spoke rarely, and when they did, merely echoed, in weird rearrangements, the words spoken to them."

Schelling stared out into the rain. His hand, hanging over the arm of the chair, trembled. "It's no good," he said. "It comes back too clearly.

"Ultimately, being around these heartless specters drained one of the will to live. After a long night trying to elicit a response from one of my former comrades—whose corpse I could clearly see, stuck on barbed wire a hundred feet away—and receiving only sad echoes, I broke down. I made a run over the top, alone. A few quick and observant friends grabbed me by the ankles and dragged me back into the trench. I did not thank them."

Schelling patted Sandaji's shoulder. She was weeping quietly into a handkerchief. "After a few days, the revenants became little more than blurs or outlines, as if suffering through yet another cycle of decay. Perhaps most horrible of all, they now attracted shadows—worms of the spirit and dark, swooping things, like wings without bodies."

Schelling had Peter. He felt unable to resist, or even to move.

"In the trenches, at night, after a day of fierce shelling, we heard the moaning of hundreds of wounded from the German side. And between those cries, we all heard—all of us, in those trenches, perhaps on both sides—an indescribable *skirling*, like birds caught in long steel pipes. In the dark, under the awful brilliance of flares drifting down on parachutes, we saw shadows swarming, harrowing the revenants. There was no escape. That terribleness lasted all night, and nobody dared sleep; it was the most awful night of an unbelievably awful war. Yet it did not last forever. The living endured. And by morning, all was clear.

"That strange season did not return, not for the other young men, not for me, through the entire war. But now, it is back, stronger and stranger than ever. We are all seeing ghosts, and not just on battlefields. Am I speaking truth, Mr. Russell?"

Peter wrapped his temples and crown in his hands. His head hurt from clenching his jaw.

Schelling took encouragement from this response. "All who survived that wretched war returned broken in one way or another, their lives changed, and not for the better. I wanted to believe that what I saw was just a madness of the battlefield. Yet wherever I went thereafter, thirty and forty years later, the faces of the dead swam through my dreams. Rarely, I met them on the street, lost, seeking, watching me with empty, hungry eyes, as if I could help.

"I do not know why I was afforded this third sight, but I sometimes wonder ... Was it because I had witnessed a process no living being should ever see? What becomes of us when we die. And how we die a second time."

Schelling looked down at Peter, his lips pressed tightly together. "Don't confuse death with sleep, Mr. Russell," he said, his stentor growing husky. "Death is more like being born. It's a long, hard giving up of warmth for something you don't know. There's a desperate glamour that surrounds the living, and for a time, the dead think they are still in the game. They cling to any memory of their life—the sharper and stronger, the better. The dead grieve. They grieve for the living, for what they have lost, their places, their possessions, their loved ones, all that defined them in this world. Their mournful need holds them to the Earth. And so they must be shaken loose, like flakes of old skin." Here, he shuddered, not delicately, but so violently and abruptly he upset his teacup. The cup fell to the deck, but miraculously did not shatter. He bent slowly, joints creaking, to stare dolefully down at it.

"If you've seen such things," Schelling said, "I most certainly understand your reluctance to talk about them."

Sandaji returned the cup to his hand, and both contemplated a stone lantern just outside the teahouse. As the dusk deepened, the rain slowed, then stopped, and lights came on automatically in the yard, around the well-groomed bushes, and finally inside the lantern itself.

"Please, tell us whatever you know," Sandaji encouraged. "It could be so very important."

Peter craned his neck to look at the darkening sky, the few stars, and wondered what he was about to do, and what the consequences would be. Michelle's distrust. Joseph's decline.

I saw her. I know I did. I'm not crazy, and it's not just the bad old grief coming back. She's real.

Peter clenched his fists, a menacing, gorillalike gesture that made both Schelling and Sandaji flinch. "It hurts too much to believe."

"What about truth?" Sandaji asked.

Peter snorted. "Truth is a hunter. Truth is what kills you when you give up the lies."

Sandaji said, "An astute observation, but must it be your final answer? When you are ready—" she began.

Peter interrupted. "What do you think the shadows are?"

"I don't know," Schelling said.

"If memories drop away like dead skin," Peter said, "well, there are bugs that eat dead skin, right?"

Sandaji gave him a reproachful look.

"They could be scavengers, like rats, or eels. Or like you said, worms or vultures," Peter said quietly.

"You *have* witnessed," Sandaji said.

"They might also be friends in disguise," Schelling said. "Sacrifice is liberation, Mr. Russell. We're talking about a process and a condition we know almost nothing about, and so if we draw conclusions, they're bound to be erroneous. And if we interfere, it is bound to be disastrous."

It was growing dark. Peter needed to get back to the house, to protect his daughter from the shadows. Back to his insanity. But he could not convince his body to move. He remained seated. Whatever she had become, Daniella was no longer safe—for him.

I don't know how to help her.

Crickets, assured that the rain was over, started singing in the garden.

"Let's say I believe you," Peter said, his voice rough. "Let's say I've seen these things. What caused the change? How can we help them escape, pass on, whatever they need to do?"

Sandaji's expression became sad and radiant, aware of Peter's breakthrough—and the pain it could cause.

"This is difficult to convey," Schelling said. "When we die, we shed all our memories at once—the temporary psychic equivalent of the physical body. But embedded within that immaterial skin, as you call it, is something else, not temporary, different. It departs, but does not always do so immediately. I've seen such only twice, in all my experiences with spiritual matters, but it left a lasting impression: a kind of golden glow, like an inner sunset."

"What is it?" Peter asked.

"Some think that a ghost can still carry its soul, trapped in memories like a bird in a thorny bush. Trauma—war or other violence—may drag out the release. Or because we remember our loved ones too passionately, they cannot let go. This change that we are witnessing, this alteration in the spiritual weather, only adds to their difficulties—and to ours. If we can reverse the change . . ."

Sandaji held up the unwrapped Trans. Peter stared at it in mixed wonder and horror.

"This device is responsible, Mr. Russell," Schelling said. "You carried one into this house, and at that moment, precisely, induced Sandaji's visions. The visions returned when Mrs. Benoliel gave us another. With the experience of almost nine decades of dealing with the spiritual, I am convinced that these instruments of communication are highlighting the dead and their supernatural entourage, perhaps even blocking the pathways of our final liberation. Tell your friends, the ones who built these, whom you are working for, that they must stop. They may be putting us all in worse than mortal danger."

Peter stared at the plastic ovoid. "How?"

"Perhaps you have been told, and simply haven't made the connections."

Forbidden channels . . . Down there is a deeper silence than we can know, a great emptiness. Huge bandwidth, perhaps infinite capacity. It can handle all our noise, all our talk, anything we have to say, throughout all eternity. So Kreisler had told him.

But the forbidden channels were not so empty after all.

Not news of Phil, not the fear of a real, paying job—but getting a Trans.

That was the shot from the starting pistol.

"Such intimate contact with the dead is neither good nor right," Schelling said, his face turning grim at Peter's lengthening silence, his apparent obstinacy. "I have advised Sandaji that it is time to leave this city, to leave the West Coast entirely. It is not healthy."

Perhaps Joseph *was* seeing ghosts; Sandaji and Schelling were, too. If Peter was crazy or sick, it was contagious—but they all had Trans units. "Not just here," he said, his mouth dry. "They've shipped Trans worldwide."

Sandaji's hand clutched his. "Then it's most urgent." She looked even more vulnerable than he felt. "Your daughter. When first you visited, I saw her beside you. Just a face, obviously that of a young girl, a brief hint, but there was a resemblance. You are not beautiful, if I may say so, but she was. That is the way of children."

Tears formed in Peter's eyes. He wiped them quickly with the back of his fist. "Daniella ..." was all he could manage. The observations were tumbling for him now. *The old woman with the silly dog, at the rest stop,* he thought. *She smiled at someone standing right beside me, smiled like a doting grandmother.*

"It was a shock, much more than I was prepared for," Sandaji said. "Before that moment, I had never seen a ghost."

Schelling reached to grip Peter's shoulder. Holding each other, they formed a small circle. "Have courage," the old man said. "We have seen the girl again, but not with you, and not here."

"Where?" Peter asked.

"At Salammbo," Sandaji said. Her look beseeched his understanding. "Both of us witnessed her. Edward and I. And we saw others, so many others. The estate is crowded with the dead. We fear for her, and for you, Mr. Russell. There is a great and old malevolence at Salammbo, and it is growing."

"Did Mr. Benoliel ever do something very, very wrong?" Schelling asked. "Something criminal?"

CHAPTER 

PETER PULLED OFF the 10 onto National Avenue and found himself wandering into the Cheviot Hills. He had been driving aimlessly for the last hour, trying to skirt evening traffic. He parked on a wide street and ratcheted up the emergency brake. Let out his breath. Peered through the windshield, speckled with drops of rain. The skies were clearing after the storm. This was a neighborhood of fine old homes, not too ostentatious but well maintained and beautifully manicured. A place of order and decorum. Peter had always loved this part of Los Angeles, an oasis of neighborhood and sanity on the edge of gray industrial sprawl.

What he was longing for was a place away from his beaten path, where he could put together what he thought he knew and prepare some course of action.

He had planned all along to be home before dark. Now that thought scared him. A pretty little shade, one step behind him wherever he went, waited to hug him, envelop him. He did not want to end up sprawled on the driveway again, a bit of his life neatly sliced away.

He glanced with a shiver at the Porsche's right-hand seat. No dimpling of the upholstery, no wandering specks of dust.

Objective confirmation. Seeing the same things. You know you're not crazy, and you're certainly not just making it up to fail again.

Peter folded his arms and closed his eyes.

Just know what you need to do. If Schelling is right, Daniella is stuck—

He gave a sudden, unexpected hiccup. The effective center of his immediate problem might be Joseph. Peter had no idea what to do now about the Trans units, all over the world, but he *could* drive back to Malibu in the dark and approach Joseph in his upstairs room and ask what in the hell was happening. Ask what Joseph suspected, grill him if necessary about what he had known even before the Trans units had arrived at Salammbo.

Neither Sandaji nor Schelling could describe to Peter the nature of the malevolence they had sensed at Salammbo, only that they wanted nothing to do with it. A man who had seen unimaginable horrors during the First World War, nearing the end of a long and peculiar life ... as frightened as a child.

But the key question was almost unaskable: Why would Daniella appear at Salammbo, to strangers?

Scragg had asked about people who had never been mentioned during the investigation. People beyond suspicion.

Joseph.

Peter was shivering, though the inside of the car was warm. He, too, felt a deep and pervasive fear, what he imagined would be experienced by hunted mice, rabbits; he was a small animal still hoping to escape from greater and carnivorous truths.

But there was no place to hide.

Even if he learned something important at Salammbo, there was still the matter of the units, of Trans itself, blocking the pathways of the dead—and whatever that implied.

"What in the name of all that is holy am I going to do?" he asked out loud. But thus far he had seen nothing holy. Awesome, frightening, dangerous, yes, but holy seemed to have no place in this scheme of things. What Peter wanted most of all, sitting in his old car in the prosperous and orderly neighborhood, was a safe and gentle God to provide answers and guidance. The God of his childhood, gray-bearded and welcoming and full of warm understanding.

Not this spiritual abyss.

Peter's hand reached out to turn the key. He had come to a kind of decision: not Salammbo. Not yet. He needed to be better prepared, stand on firmer ground. He needed to return to the real center of his life, all that he had left.

Lindsey and Helen.

He wound around the neat dark streets, with their old milk-glass streetlights glowing like warm little moons, and finally returned to the freeway. The traffic was hideous after the storm. Lane after lane, road after road, jammed full, horns honking, people getting out of their cars and standing, rolling down windows to share complaints.

Blocked traffic everywhere.

Not a good time to die.

CHAPTER 

LINDSEY RAN UP to the condo door first after Peter rang the doorbell. They stood with the screen between them and exchanged a look that confirmed what Peter had suspected; things had changed in this household—for Lindsey, at least—in much the same way they had changed in his own.

She gave him a scrunched look. "What took you so long?"

"I'm here now, sweetie," he said. "Where's your mother?"

Helen came around the corner from the kitchen and flipped on the outside light. She stood beside Lindsey and eyed Peter suspiciously. "It's ten o'clock."

"Lindsey and I have to talk."

"What about?" Helen asked. "Who invited you?"

"She doesn't know?" Peter asked Lindsey.

Lindsey shook her head.

"Know what?" Helen demanded.

"I need to speak to my daughter," Peter said.

"Mom, can you go someplace for a while?" Lindsey asked.

Peter cringed inwardly.

Helen flashed over. "I control this household, buster. Nobody tells me to leave my own house!"

"I don't barge in like this often," Peter said, trying for an ingratiating smile.

"Mom, it's important. It's nothing like what you're thinking."

Helen stepped back, aghast. "Who here has ever given a damn about what I'm thinking? Sure as hell, you haven't told me something," she said, livid.

"You'd freak," Lindsey said. At this, Helen's eyes popped and she shoved Lindsey inside and slammed the door.

Peter heard them shouting, but it was a thick, burglar-proof door, and he could not make out what was being said. Part of him miserably wanted to walk away, but he stuck his hands firmly in his pants pockets and leaned against the stucco wall.

The shouting inside went on for almost five minutes. He glanced at his watch just as the door opened again. Helen unlatched the screen and let it slide into its roller.

"I am in charge in my own house," she insisted, stepping out and closing the door to a crack behind her. She was subdued, on the edge of tears. "It's the last thing I have. God help me if I lose that, right?" She regarded Peter plaintively, asking for help in the only way she knew how—without asking. Helen had had so much kicked out of her in the last two years; the starch was almost gone, leaving only wrinkles and weariness. He did not know what more to say. He could not reassure when there was no assurance left in him. But he had to try.

Peter straightened. "It's just some stuff we need to hash out, father-daughter. I need to catch up. You know that."

"I know that, all right," Helen said.

"Nothing for you to worry about," Peter added, smiling. The way Helen searched his smile, if there was anything left in it, in him, for her, was painful. "When it's all over, I'll explain."

Fat chance I'll even know how to start.

Lindsey's arm poked out through the door and gestured for him to come in.

"Promise?" Helen asked. She sounded younger than Lindsey.

"Promise," Peter said.

Helen went back into the house. When she returned, she was clutching her purse and a light sweater was half wrapped around her shoulders. "I'll be back in ten minutes," she said, abruptly shoving past Peter. "Is it raining?" she asked, her face bitter and resigned all at once.

"It's stopped," Peter said. "Thanks."

"You two deserve each other," Helen said. "Lock the door. Ten minutes."

"Twenty!" Lindsey called out.

Peter joined Lindsey in the living room. Lindsey offered him a glass of water. "Mom drinks bottled water. I don't mind tap water. Do you?"

"It's okay," Peter said.

"Mom doesn't allow soft drinks or alcohol."

"I don't drink now anyway," Peter said.

"Right," Lindsey said, as if she would reserve judgment on that. "Mom's pretty strung out with this boyfriend stuff."

Peter sat on the couch. With some guilt, he saw that the stuffing was poking from a corner of the armrest; guilt because he could not buy them new furniture. But that was stupid. Helen had never asked. The possible cause of the damage, a young orange cat, sauntered into the living room, stretched out its many-toed feet, and sat on its haunches, appraising him.

"That's Bolliver," she said. "Mom calls him Bolliver Sling-shit. We have to watch where we step in the bathroom. His litter box is in there. He's messy." She stood in front of him and took a deep breath. "How did you and Mom meet?"

Peter looked up from the couch.

"I mean, you're so different."

"She was working on a construction crew," Peter said. "We just hit it off. A year later, we were married."

Helen, unrecognizable now, from this distance, had stood in the sun beside the freeway, wearing a yellow helmet, a ponytail thrusting stubbornly from the back, her professional smile brooking no nonsense from passing drivers; stern brown eyes, dark red hair very curly indeed, muscles instead of fat, nicely shaped, but more utilitarian and healthy than voluptuous. He had driven past, *SLOW,* as specified by her extended orange sign, rolled down the window of the Porsche, and asked her out for lunch at a nearby Hamburger Hamlet.

"You and construction," Lindsey said. "Did you ask her to model?"

"No way," Peter said. "She would have hit me."

"That explains a lot. Yeah." Lindsey's expression told Peter that the time had finally come, and could not be put off. She sat beside him. "This isn't exactly new, you know. What's going on."

"You've seen Daniella."

"Mm-hmm. I felt her over a year ago. I've just never seen her until now."

"Felt her, how?"

"At the house in Glendale, when I visited. She didn't, like, show herself or anything; I just knew. I didn't tell anybody because Mom would have called in a psychiatrist. I didn't need that. I still don't." She had assumed an explanatory, grown-up voice, but Peter saw her hands were trembling.

"And now?"

Lindsey leaned her head back, staring at the ancient popcorn-textured ceiling. "She appeared to me three nights ago, in my room. I had a night-light on. It was late. She was just there. There was something else, too, but I couldn't see it. She didn't scare me, at first."

"At first?"

"Why not tell me what you know?" Lindsey asked. "Because if I'm going to be crazy, you have to be crazy, too, okay? It's only fair."

"I've seen Daniella," Peter confessed. "And other things."

"All right," she said. "My throat is *really* dry. How about yours?"

Peter toasted her and they both took a long swallow of water.

"We have a little group at school, pretty tight, we talk about this stuff. Other people seeing things. And there's this Web site that started yesterday, kids writing about it."

Peter showed his astonishment. "A Web site?"

"Yup. A lot of kids talk about the new phones, like the one you gave Mom. But Mom hasn't used hers. She says it doesn't feel right. I tried it. It's really quiet. I didn't like it, either."

"Your mother hasn't seen Daniella?"

"She sees what she wants to see. She sleeps with eye patches on and stuff all over her face. I think she takes pills. We're not having it real easy here." She fixed Peter with a limpid, *what's-a-woman-to-do* look.

"Have you talked with your sister?" Peter asked.

"First, she's not my sister, not anymore," Lindsey said with a fragile defiance. "She's dead. She's something else." Lindsey looked up over his shoulder, at the front door. "Let's start at the beginning, okay? You first. But hurry. Mom will come back soon. She doesn't trust either of us. She thinks we'll talk about her boyfriends."

"You could be more understanding," Peter suggested.

"Just tell me, please."

Peter described what he had seen at the house, leaving out his attempt to hug Daniella. He asked, "You haven't touched her, have you?"

"No *way*," Lindsey said. "She looked like a *Visible Woman.* I could see her bones, Dad."

Peter stared at his daughter. "You didn't feel sympathy?"

"Well, *yeah,* of course," Lindsey said. "I wouldn't want to be where she is, if that's what you mean."

"No," Peter said. "That isn't what I mean." Her toughness was beginning to be irritating. He had hoped for a little help resolving this problem.

"We love flesh," Lindsey said defiantly. "You said that."

"I did?"

"Or Mom said you did. And the flesh is gone, right? She's nothing but ashes now."

Peter shook his head. "She needs something. She's coming to us for some reason."

"Isn't that what ghosts do? Kind of like homeless people by the freeway? You let her *touch you,* didn't you?"

"Yes."

Her eyes went wide. "Wow. What did that feel like?"

"I blacked out." Peter wiped his forehead. "What did she say to you?"

Lindsey drew herself up. "She used this really *tinny* voice, like it was coming from a cheap boom box turned down low. She said—I think she said—'It's been too long.' She said it a couple of times, like an echo and creepy. I thought I saw something in a corner but it wasn't her. It was something that was, like, *waiting.* I might have screamed, because Mom opened the door and turned on the light, and they were gone."

Peter folded his hands around his face. "You didn't tell your mother."

"Like I said, she'd freak. You're not going to tell her, are you?"

Peter shook his head. "I wouldn't know where to begin."

"When you die, you're supposed to go away and leave people alone, and it's all sad and, like, *sad,* and the rest of us live until it's our turn. Right?"

Peter remembered his own adolescence. An appearance of toughness was sometimes the only armor you had. Still, Lindsey's brisk aloofness irritated him. "She was your sister and my daughter," he said, but cut his words off before he could add, *You shared a womb with her for nine months.* "I don't know what she is now. Still, I care what happens to her."

"What if she *kills* us?" Lindsey asked, eyes burning. "She was in my room, it's *my room,* and she just zapped me. I didn't touch her, but she still sucked up my energy. I pushed back into my bed and just went, *'Go away!'* What if ghosts really are vampires?"

"I don't think that's what happens."

The front door opened and Helen came in hoisting a bag of groceries. Her face was still pale but she appeared resigned to the interruption of her routine. Again, Peter felt a sudden and sharp sympathy.

"I took the opportunity to do some shopping," she said. "I bought Dulce de Leche. Häagen Dazs. Is that all right?"

"I'm going to bed now," Lindsey said, jumping up from the couch and doing a short spin to the hall. "Dad and I had our talk. It went okay, so don't worry." She looked over her shoulder at Peter. "You're going to quit working for that phone company now, aren't you?"

"I WON'T ASK what you talked about," Helen said primly after Lindsey closed her bedroom door. "I'm sorry I was cross. She's just acting strange lately—and so are you."

"You haven't seen anything odd?" Peter asked, following her into the small kitchen.

"If you mean ghosts, no," she answered curtly.

Confused, Peter said, "Lindsey told me you hadn't talked."

Helen squinted. "I deposited your check," she said. "Bank manager gave me some guff, but I kowtowed. It's a lot of money, Peter. I hope the job is going well. I'll get the cash out for you next week." She reached into a kitchen drawer and took out an ice-cream scooper. She then reached to the back of the drawer and removed the Trans. "Lindsey asked me to return this. I guess it works, but I haven't used it."

Peter pocketed the unit, feeling like he had come into the middle of a movie and missed most of the important dialog.

"One scoop or two?"

"Two," he said. His hands trembled and he hid them from her view.

"I'm just feeling an urge to help some man or other be contented for at least a couple of minutes. Is that too much to ask? To make somebody care, be happy, just a little?"

"Not at all," Peter said.

"I wish I could still communicate with Lindsey," she said with brittle caution. "We used to have such an open relationship." She folded two scoops of ice cream into a small bowl, stuck a spoon upright, and handed the bowl to him. "Typical, right? I was the same way with my mom."

"She's okay," Peter said. "She's tough. Just like you."

"She acts tough, but she's just twelve years old," Helen said. "I worry."

They walked into the living room. Helen was working to appear cheerful. She swallowed a bite of ice cream and said, "Um. I just have this feeling there's a conspiracy going on, and I'm being left out."

"No conspiracy," Peter said. "We needed to clear the air before the picnic. About how I haven't knocked down the door to see her." He did not know whom he was protecting now.

"Yeah, well, guilty me, woe is you. The picnic is on for this Saturday. I assume you'll be there?"

"I'll do my damnedest," Peter said.

"No more baby-sitting overnights, not for now. I have no love life." Helen spooned up a larger bite. "My boyfriend—in case you're wondering why I talk about ghosts—is a complete loon. His excuse for ditching me was, he saw his wife walking in the backyard of his house. She's been dead for six years. I really pick 'em, don't I?"

CHAPTER 38

PETER SAT IN the booth at the Denny's, watching people come and go, asking them silently, *And what have* you *been seeing lately?* Two weeks ago, he had been a plumpish bachelor living a skinny existence, a long gray quiet following on a raucous youth, waiting for circumstances to go his way. They had, in a rush; too many circumstances. He swarmed with circumstances.

He stared at the booth across from him, half expecting some elderly lady to congratulate him on his pretty young daughter, and how radiant she looked in this light. *She positively glows.*

But the booth was empty. The restaurant was doing brisk business, solid bodies going to and fro, hither and yon, too many to allow the slow accumulation of Visible Women and Visible Men, like crystal shells full of the departed spirits of bones and organs.

And if he looked at the floor long enough ...

He closed his eyes. Just warmly lit darkness, no footsteps through the accumulated ages of dust and skin flakes. But perhaps they swept this Denny's clean in more ways than one, every night.

If the world was changed forever, no going back, would they hire janitors to clean up after the ghosts? Offer new items on the menu—restoratives, collations, remembrances, plates of wine or of blood?

It was nearly midnight when he finished his fifth cup of coffee. He was wide-awake, determined. A good time, perhaps, to get out to Salammbo and ask Joseph some important questions. They might still be awake.

Sleep no more.

He thought of Helen with eye patches and skin cream, full of pills and oblivious—and tried to connect that image to the first time he had seen her, jaunty, strong, and smiling, sporting a Day-Glo orange vest and patched jeans under the never-ending sun on Pacific Coast Highway.

Friction of life.

He might never sleep again.

He was back in the Porsche when he heard a Trans chime. He pulled out the unit Helen had given him, but it was quiet. He looked around, peered into the backseat, trying to locate the sound.

It was coming from the front.

Peter popped the hood and got out of the car. Nestled in the front storage well, below the gas tank, three Trans units gleamed gold, black, and white under a wedge of streetlight glare. Peter could not imagine how the units had gotten into his trunk. He had not put them there. Senses tuned by shock, he found the chiming unit. He opened it but did not say his name.

Heard a sharp intake of breath—masculine breath—on the other end.

"Peter, is that you? Who's there?"

It was Hank.

"This is Peter," he said with frightened formality.

"Thank Christ. What time is it? Shit, I don't care, I'm sorry. I'm still in Prague. Everybody else is locked in their rooms or gone. The hotel staff ran out last night."

Peter's mind buzzed. Someone had come to his house and moved the Trans units into the Porsche. But when? And why? "It's after midnight. What time is it there, Hank?"

"It's morning. Late, I guess. I wish I was alone, Peter. She's still here. She's been here all night. She's making me sick. You won't believe this."

"Try me," Peter said.

"They've ruined the shoot. They're everywhere. The whole crew is hiding or trying to get out of Prague. Jack Bishop hung himself yesterday, right outside the hotel, from a lamppost. He just climbed up with a rope and dropped. I saw what was after him, Peter. Like a long cloud of soot. He had these shadows clinging to his back and his head like *leeches*."

"This isn't my Trans," Peter said, still trying to think things through. "How did you get my number?"

"Jesus, Peter, we traded all the numbers. I just kept dialing until you answered."

"What's your visitor doing?" Peter asked.

"She's standing by the door and she won't move. She looks so old. I mean, she might have been young once, but now she's just *frayed*, like an old sock, and ... Christ, the room is full of shadows, the corners, the ceiling, the closet."

"Is she a ghost, Hank?"

Prague, city of ghosts. Possibly the worst place on the planet to have a Trans.

"Fuck, yeah, she's a ghost! Haven't you been listening? Oh, shit, now there's another one." His voice, already high, rose a notch in pitch. "God, God, God—this one is worse. I can't even see a face, just wrinkles—"

"Listen to me, Hank. Shut the Trans and smash it. Break it all to hell. Then go out a window or push through ... to the door, whatever it takes. Just get out of there."

"Are you joking? Go *through* them?"

"Just do it," Peter said. "Get on the next airplane. Go to Africa or someplace far away. I have to go now."

"Peter, for the love of God—"

No more debating, no more arguments. He shut the Trans. His hand tingled and he shook it out, dropping the unit to the curb. It bounced.

Sleep no more.

Years ago, when he had taken a vacation with Helen and the girls, he had left a key to the Glendale house with Joseph and Michelle. He had never retrieved it.

One more reason to go out to Salammbo.

He removed the units from the Porsche and dropped them into the street. Something dark had stained the bottom of the trunk. Again, his hand tingled and this time the sensation was painful. He added Helen's Trans, and, one by one, stomped them beneath his feet. It took some effort. Peter danced on them, grunting and flinging out his arms. As the cases finally cracked, like the tough shells of big insects, a pale blue fluid seeped into the gutter.

His hand still tingled.

People leaving the Denny's stared at him in pity.

* * *

PETER STOPPED AT an old pay phone near an Asian grocery, one of the last pay phones in Los Angeles—they were being dismantled everywhere. Everyone was going wireless.

He dropped a small stack of quarters into the slot and dialed Weinstein's alternate office number at San Andreas, ten digits, a backup landline phone. It was late, everyone might have gone home, but he did not care. He had to try.

Weinstein was not the one to answer.

"This is wrong phone. Who in hell is calling?" It was Arpad Kreisler. He sounded upset, angry, and exhausted.

"Mr. Kreisler, it's Peter Russell. I need to ask something."

"It is late. I do not care about marketing now. You ask Weinstein, but he is not here."

"You might be able to answer my questions," Peter said. "I think something is going wrong with Trans. With your network. I don't know how to begin explaining ... I've thought I was crazy—"

"Yes, yes, you are seeing things. So? What can I do for you?"

"It's not just me."

"Of course not. I try to tell them three days ago, Trans network is going bad. Weinstein orders me to shut up, and when I do not, he orders guards to kick me out of San Andreas. I am partner! He cannot do that. He says he will call Homeland Security about my green card."

"But you're there now ..." Peter said.

"Guards at gate quit," Kreisler said. "Gate is open. I am looking for Weinstein. Place is a mess." Then, in a lower tone of voice, almost reverential, Kreisler asked, "What do you see, Mr. Russell?"

"Ghosts," Peter said. "And I'm not alone. I thought I was, but I'm not."

"Of course not," Kreisler said.

"Everyone who has a Trans is seeing things."

"That is not good," Kreisler said, almost a whisper.

"You told us Trans would change space," Peter said. "Something about permittivity, sparking information. I remember that much. Can it go back? Can we shut everything off and make it return to the way it was?"

"Weinstein, he will not let us shut down network. There is so much money involved now. Even so, I try, but I cannot get to the center, the transponder. It is very bad in there."

"I need to know. If I destroy my units, if you turn it off, will it go back to the way it was?"

Kreisler did not answer for a moment. "I have been thinking. I do not know shit. Stuffs of old memory and personality, irregularly coded information, we did not understand about its persistence, even in wildest theory. Embedded in space like carvings, graffiti. But when life is over, it must decay—so the math says—like burning unread books in a library and scattering ashes. I think Trans interferes. Normal decay is blocked. Old library doesn't burn, ashes don't get scattered. And old memories seem to attract bad things."

"Edward Schelling said something like that," Peter said.

"I do not know him," Kreisler said. "Is he physicist?"

"No. A very old, wise man."

Kreisler's voice became simple and determined. "I will find Weinstein. You should see what is going on here . . . indescribable, really."

"Did you have any clue that Trans could go wrong, that this was possible?" Peter asked.

"No, I swear. I am not believer. I am inventor and scientist. Ghosts are figments of long nights and too much work. You know, all that bullshit. Not even on my horizon, what is happening here."

"I've smashed all the Trans units I have," Peter said. "I don't know if that's enough. What will happen if the network doesn't shut down?"

"You tell me," Kreisler said. "You are imaginative writer. What is the worst? Maybe it is permanent, we must live like this—and die like this—forever. But I do my best, that I also swear. Perhaps, Mr. Artist, Mr. Writer fellow, you can come here and help." He laughed, bitter, wrung out, and hung up.

Kreisler's words stung. Peter was not a coward, but he had to think things through. There had to be the right place to begin. He walked across the wet asphalt to the car in the market parking lot and sat for a few minutes. The lights inside the grocery dimmed. A curtain was pulled on the door. The red neon sign on the facade blinked out, but the tubes continued to sputter, flashes of faded brilliance following the cursive circuit of the letters.

Peter watched, hypnotized.

Then he turned the key.

First things first.

Family.

CHAPTER 39

PETER ROLLED DOWN his window and tapped in the number code on the pad outside the big wrought-iron gate. The gate opened with a complaining whine and bounced at the end of its run. He drove forward, stopped, and watched the gate swing shut behind him.

Under spotty, cloud-dappled moonlight, the road through Salammbo stretched in a long V toward El Cid, the long black hedge, and to the left, Flaubert House. He could not see Jesus Wept from this vantage. He looked at his watch. One-thirty in the morning. Sleep no more.

The Porsche seemed incredibly loud on the long stretch of dark road. A warm breeze sighed across the grounds. Only one window in Flaubert House was illuminated; the porch and veranda lights were off. Moon shadows crossed the long stretch of lawn. Peter followed their blurred outlines with a curious sense of disbelief; how could he be sure they were clouds? Perhaps something equally vast was swimming above him, waiting for an opening, a vulnerability ...

He blocked that line of thought. El Cid was bad enough, glowering over the sparkling oleander leaves with an expression of haughty alarm, horse's left hoof poised high over the roadway.

* * *

HE PARKED THE car at the far end of the circular brick drive and switched off the motor. The grounds were exceptionally quiet. He opened the door and put out one leg, then stopped to listen some more, like a cat deciding whether or not to go through an open door. His senses might or might not be tuned to an extraordinary degree; how could you know for sure until you heard something? But the only sound he heard was the scuff of his shoe on brick—that, and a distant whisper of leaves.

The moon hid. Parts of the estate were still illuminated, trees and hills, but where he sat in the car, he could see almost nothing.

He slid out and shut the door as quietly as possible.

The veranda lights came on. They were connected to motion and sound sensors. Broad ovals of brightness played over the limestone and bricks. Joseph and Michelle sometimes hired a security force to patrol the grounds at night, but Peter saw no signs of them. Joseph disliked having too much, and too obvious, security. *"I get claustrophobic. I don't like to have cops and walls shoved in my face,"* he had once told Peter.

Peter walked quickly across the bricks to the steps of Flaubert House. He bounded up the steps into the brighter light and entered a keypad code next to the intercom speaker, buzzing directly into Joseph's bedroom. Waited five minutes. No answer.

Peter pulled his key ring out of his pocket and fumbled to untangle it from a thread. Holding one hand against the heavy oak door, he slipped the thick brass key into the appropriate lock—there were three, all electronically coded. The locks did not move.

Drawing back, Peter looked behind him with a quick jerk. Nobody on the lawn, the circular drive, the road to the main gate. He wondered if it would be best to just get back in his car and try again tomorrow. Michelle might have shut down everything, set the entry codes and key codes to reject, and locked the house up tight. But if that were the case, how could he have gotten through the main gate?

Joseph. What if his problem past had come back? What if something had happened to Michelle, or to both of them?

Experimentally, just testing, Peter raised his hand and pressed the door again, harder. The door opened. He stepped back, his neck shrinking into his shoulders, waiting for a blast of alarms. None sounded. The house security was turned off.

The door swung back toward him with a groan, leaving just a crack. He pushed it again. "Hello, it's Peter!" he shouted into the entryway and the hall beyond. "Hey, the alarm's off!"

He waited a few seconds, then called out, "Joseph, Michelle, it's Peter. If I come in, don't shoot me, okay?" Joseph owned guns; Michelle no doubt had access to them. The house had already been entered. Perhaps the guns had already been used. What would he find if he went inside?

Now he regretted destroying his Trans units and leaving his cell phone behind. Crazy thinking, hauntings, madness. Puts you in a bind when real emergencies come along. Phones in the house required personal four-number codes to dial out. There were panic buttons, of course, but neither Joseph nor Michelle had told him where they were.

"Joseph, it's Peter!"

The entry beyond was a wall of black. As Peter's eyes adjusted, he saw a small red diode glowing like a rat's eye straight ahead—possibly the alarm panel under the stairs. He tried to remember the layout, all the panels and security boxes, and could not; that had never concerned him. As a cat burglar—or a spy—he was a total failure.

He stepped into the entry and did not bother to close the door behind him. "Someone come down here and help me out. Or I'll just turn around and leave, all right?"

He felt like a fool. What could only be worse than babbling such crap would be to babble such crap to the corpses of his friends as they lay sprawled in the shadows, their heads blown off or bashed in. He could not leave without trying to find out what had happened. Then, wiser or not, he could locate a panic button and bring in the police, because this was way beyond starting to look bad. It *was* bad.

The glowing red rat's eye went dark. Peter stopped moving. His breath caught. He found it easy to convince himself he was not alone in the house. Something had passed in front of the diode.

Almost immediately a memory map flashed into his mind and he saw the location of the switches in the entryway, on the right-hand wall, just before one turned to enter a small study. Peter moved right and felt along the wall. His fingers made small brushing sounds against the paint and then bumped into the wainscoting, bruising a knuckle. A short table blocked his way. He stopped and felt around, knocking a vase. The vase spun and wobbled and something brushed his arm—flowers. A fumbling grab stopped the vase from falling, but the flowers and water spilled onto the floor.

At the splash, the red light winked into view, then smeared and dimmed as if a dark translucent veil was sliding between them. By now, Peter thought, his eyes should have adjusted. He edged around the table and found the light switch. His fingers pushed up all five of the switches on the plate, and for good measure, he twirled the round plastic knob of the rheostat.

With shocking slowness, the room filled with light. Light advanced in oily waves from fixtures in the ceiling and a crystal chandelier, down and across the entry and the stairway, sliding over each stair to the marble-tiled floor, which filled as if with brilliant milk.

The light streamed around a shape at the bottom of the stairs, outlining a shaded hesitation of empty air—roughly the size of a hunched grizzly bear.

That, too, filled in and vanished.

Peter blinked to clear sweat from his eyes.

The whole process had taken a fraction of a second—but still, he had seen it and knew that it was wrong, that something dangerous was nearby.

The red diode glowed steadily, part of an open security panel mounted in the wall to the right of the stairs. He closed and bolted the front door.

"I am not crazy, and I am not psychic," Peter said, as if that might be some sort of shield against an incontrovertible fact. He was also most definitely not alone, but he could *not see* what was with him. Whatever, it was huge—at least as large as a bear, if size had any meaning. And like the loops of serpentine shadow in the hall of his Glendale home, it was watching him, waiting. Expecting.

"Get out of here, *shoo,*" he shouted. Then, as if shocked by a small charge of static electricity, his social sense returned. He was in the home of a friend and employer, yelling silly things and acting like a frightened child. With a supreme effort, Peter moved away from the wall.

His shoes scraped and tapped lightly on the tile but no echoes returned, and in Flaubert House that was odd. He had always heard echoes in the entryway—except on the rare occasions when Joseph and Michelle had thrown a party. The huge room seemed full, as if an invisible crowd filled the space around the stairs. He walked swiftly, restraining an urge to stretch out his hands and fend off bodies, people that he could not see. Yet he felt nothing.

He inspected the security panel. A button turned on motion sensors that would activate the house lights wherever there was an intruder. Looking over his shoulder, he pushed it. Then, room by room, he searched the north and south wings, bright ceiling lights in the halls switching on and momentarily turning off again, triggered by his passage.

Ten minutes later, standing in the kitchen, he knew that the bottom floor was not occupied—not by Joseph or Michelle, at least, or any human intruder. Returning to the entryway, he passed the open elevator door and gave it a quick and unhappy glance. Joseph used the elevator to get to the second floor, but Peter never had, preferring the stairs. He did not like elevators to begin with, and this one was small, with just enough room for two. The elevator also had a basement stop, opening onto the tram tunnel between Flaubert

House and Jesus Wept. Joseph had years ago promised to take Peter all the way down for a tour, but then had claimed the tunnel was blocked by stored junk and still stank of smoke.

Just another of Lordy Trenton's excesses, another piece of unused history. Michelle had long ago covered the basement button with tape. "It's like a catacomb down there," she had told Peter.

He climbed the stairs. Upon reaching the landing, he looked over his shoulder. Something was following him. He could feel it watching with curious, invisible eyes, a huge presence of no weight or mass.

His arm hair went stiff as a bristle brush.

"Shoo," Peter said. *You're my death. You'll grab me and shake me like a big channel catfish gulping a lump of carrion. You'll shake and chew and shake some more, until I'm nothing but an empty sack of skin.*

His breath left him in a shuddering moan. Having a vivid imagination was sometimes a real bitch.

The presence had halted at the foot of the stairs. It waited, expectant and serene. It wanted something, that much he could sense—but if it wanted him, here he was, as alone and vulnerable as he would ever be, and nothing was happening.

By main force of will, Peter turned away and peered along the length of the upstairs hall. The first door on the right led to Michelle's bedroom. He had long known that they slept in separate rooms. He had assumed it was the politeness of a younger wife for an old and ill husband.

The door was cracked open. The lights were on.

He knocked lightly. "Michelle?"

No answer.

Peter pushed the door open with the toe of his shoe.

She had chosen one of the smaller upstairs rooms. Somehow, that did not surprise Peter. But the room was a mess, and that did surprise him. Pages of photos had been cut out of magazines and tacked to the walls with a glimmering forest of straight pins, far more pins than necessary. The clippings showed tattoos, hundreds of them, on arms, backs, faces, eyelids, penises, and labial lips. Straight pins outlined the tattoos, straight pins by the hundreds, the thousands; some marched off beyond the borders of the images to delineate prickly labyrinths on the narrow passages of uncovered walls.

Sliced and torn and crumpled magazines covered the floor beside the four-poster bed, a little girl's bed with pink ruffles and duvet and lace-trimmed pillows, barely long enough to hold Michelle's lanky five and a half feet.

He stepped over the piles of magazines and studied the clippings. Michelle had never shown him tattoos; he did not know whether she had any.

Facing the bed was a full-length oval mirror. Peter again skirted the piles of cut-up magazines and looked into the mirror. Lipstick, eyebrow pencil, rouge, and other items of makeup had been used to daub shapes and designs on the glass, stripes and animal patterns, and higher up, grimacing masks.

He stooped before the mirror to line up his own face within a painted mask. The design made him look like a demented badger. An animal clown.

He could not imagine Michelle living here, not the Michelle he knew. Thought he knew.

Masks. Mud and blood.

Lordy Trenton's young wife painted clowns.

Peter turned away from the mirror, his stomach twisting.

The bathroom light was on. The fan whirred faintly. Peter looked inside. The heat lamp and fan timer had ten minutes left to run, out of an hour maximum. The room still felt humid. The shower curtain surrounding the oval tub was beaded with water. The tub was empty except for reddish stains—not blood, but smeared rouge or lipstick. False eyelashes had settled over the drain cover. More than a pair; there were at least six or eight, tangled like a drowned family of spiders.

Peter backed out of the bathroom and turned to the walk-in closet. Shoe boxes had been stacked against one wall inside the closet. Shelves and clothes on hangers covered the other wall.

Beyond any sense of discretion, he took down a shoe box and pulled up the cardboard lid. Inside lay Polaroid snapshots and what looked like digital photo prints: more corpses, freshly dead, no decay, dismayed but fatally relaxed expressions, sprawled on linoleum, lying over a battered couch, slumped into a nondescript corner.

Eyes flat, uncaring.

Judging by the lighting and the angles, these were not official crime-scene photos. Peter pulled down another box, lid askew. One peek inside and his fingers loosened. The box dropped and spilled.

All Polaroids, the photos inside were of a little girl sprawled on a square of plywood. Arms and legs draped over the edges, limp.

He pushed up against the hanging clothes. Pictures spilled over the carpeted closet floor, dozens, dozens.

All of Daniella.

This is it, he thought. He had had enough. Let the thing in the hall come and get him. He did not want to see any more, and if he continued, Peter knew there would be worse things than just pictures of his dead daughter, horrible as they were. After all, he had known she was dead for some time, two years, and that was the principal fact here demonstrated so graphically.

Peter stood in the closet for a few minutes, not moving, staring at the stacked boxes, surprised by his strength. "You'll die when you don't want to," he murmured. "Not a minute sooner."

Someone who used Michelle's room had collected crime-scene photos of his dead daughter. Photos of other murdered people. That was perverse, but it was not beyond belief. Peter had learned about a lot of weird, secret hobbies in his time in Los Angeles. But he could not make the connection. The Joseph he knew—the Michelle he thought he knew—would never do or allow such a thing.

He looked down one last time at the spilled photos. It was indeed his daughter, but without the painted raccoon markings. Not as she had been when the hikers had notified the police. Not on the dry golden grass of a hillside, covered with clods of dirt and leaves.

But as her killer would have seen her.

In the bathroom, the timer clicked off with a short whir.

Peter left the bedroom and stood in the hallway. With real deliberation—it was almost impossible to force one foot in front of the other—he turned right and walked slowly down the corridor to the door that led to Joseph's sitting room, the room with a view over the drive and the estate. Motion sensors again switched on the overhead lights as he walked. The stark white glare from each halogen bulb in its recessed can bounced along the dead walls to the end and rushed back in a tidal echo.

He reached the door and touched the knob. Joseph was inside this room. What condition he was in, Peter could not know; but he could smell the man with senses as sharp as a dog's, instincts tuned by fear.

Things were different between them now.

Peter could almost see it.

Joseph is sitting in his chair, by the window, waiting for me to come in, a blanket over his legs and a gun, a pistol, resting casually on his lap. He will say, "I've killed Michelle. She's down in the tunnel, and now I'm going to kill you, you bastard, for trying to steal my wife. I hate thieves." Joseph will raise the pistol and shoot until the clip is empty. There are plenty of places around here to stash bodies.

Masks and bodies.

Just what Scragg was looking for.

Peter clutched the knob and twisted it. He was not now and never had been a coward. The door opened with the familiar slight squeak. The room beyond the door was mostly dark. Light from the hall illuminated the wet bar. Peter pushed the door beyond its second squeak and entered.

"Don't turn on the light."

For a moment, Peter wondered who was speaking, and then realized it had to be Joseph; it *was* Joseph. But the voice was weak and under strain.

"Shut the door. Watch ... your ... back."

Peter closed the door behind him. Joseph sat in his favorite chair by the moonlit French windows. He was wearing a thigh-length terry-cloth robe and pajamas, both white. The shadow of the window frame covered his face; the moon was high and steady and left a blackness under his chair.

"Joseph, you *bastard*, what in God's name have you done?" Peter said. "Where's Michelle?"

Joseph's hands lay over the ends of the chair arms. They did not move.

"What ... Have you been *asleep?*" Peter demanded.

"I'll never sleep again," Joseph said. "I don't feel well, Peter."

Peter had a difficult time making out his words. "Where's Michelle?" he asked.

"I don't know. Listen."

"Should I call a doctor?"

"Just be quiet and listen."

Peter took a step forward, fists clenched. "You have some real explaining to do. I found—"

"Don't," Joseph said.

Peter stopped. Something in the voice ... He could not see the gun, but it might still be there, hidden in the folds of the robe. Joseph, as always, was in control. "How long have you been sitting here?"

"I don't know. I can't leave just yet. This is for you, Peter. Listen close. It's the only explanation I have. Just after I met Michelle, a woman I knew came back with her punk boyfriend to beat money out of me. I shot both of them right where you're standing."

"My God," Peter said.

"They're down in the tunnel. Michelle helped me bury them under the tracks. She helped me pour concrete over the hole. I thought, *Good woman. Faithful. Does what I ask.* But I guess it broke her spirit. God help me, I triggered something."

Peter leaned on the door, still sick with anger, confused, but strangely no longer afraid. He glanced up; lances and motes of silver danced just below the ceiling.

"I wasn't sure until a few days ago. I might have guessed ... But I didn't want to know." Joseph's voice went reed-thin, below a whisper. "She became an empty vessel. Things had been waiting around here a long time for someone like her. They got in, and they do have their fun."

Peter's throat ached. He reached up to touch it; he could feel his vocal cords vibrating. It wasn't Joseph speaking.

It was Peter.

"I wonder who it was that I loved. Maybe there's a small part of her left," the voice—Joseph's voice in his mouth—continued. "How else could she be so convincing and sweet? She must have put most of them down in the tunnel. A few days ago, they started to come back. I'm sorry, Peter. Hell of a note. I've warned you. Watch out for Michelle. *Take care of her.*"

Peter stood in the growing spell of quiet. His throat relaxed. He tried to breathe. He had not seen Joseph move since entering the room.

The twinkles on the ceiling flared and vanished.

Darkness swirled over his head with a noise like windblown curtains, *hush.*

The cry that went out of him was shameful, quavering. He wet his pants, anyone would have. But he did not open the door and run. Instead, he reached back and flipped the wall switch.

To scare off the shadows. How useless, but the last duty owed to a friend.

Light syruped around the room in resentful waves. The advancing front of luminance crawled up and around Joseph's legs, his pajamas, his torso, and finally his head, juddering there briefly, as if pressing against some gluey obstacle.

Joseph sat revealed. His head hung forward. A white face-cloth had been rolled and propped under his chin. Blood from his lips stained the cloth. Two neat holes pierced the hairy chest between the lapels of the robe. In the skin of his forehead, someone had scratched three words in light, bloodless strokes,

LOVE YOU HONEY

Peter looked down. Whoever had scratched the message had crouched before Joseph, leaving bloody knee prints.

A straight pin glinted beside the slippered left foot.

Peter extended his hand to touch Joseph's wrist. His palm met a blunt bristling. Five more pins poked up from the skin on the back of Joseph's hand.

This was so far beyond Peter's experience that the chemistry flooding his body actually steadied him. His fingers stopped trembling. A fatal curiosity took over; curious cat. Still alive, temporarily beyond fear; all the fear draining down his pants leg, dripping on the floor. *All right, no dignity, what the hell, check his pulse, man.*

Peter pushed back the sleeve of the robe and reached under the wrist with two fingers. No pulse and cold to the touch. He brushed the bluish skin of Joseph's lower arm. Also cold. His friend and former employer had been dead for a long time. Not seconds, not minutes.

Hours.

Peter pulled the toe of his shoe away from the perimeter of gelid blood. Could he believe the confession of a dead man?

A shining lobe of blue plastic poked from the breast pocket of Joseph's robe. Peter gingerly reached into the pocket and pulled out a cell phone—not a Trans. He lifted it as he might some large beetle, expecting its carapace to crack open and wings to suddenly whir.

The phone beeped out a tune in his fingers, "Hernando's Hideaway." He jerked but did not drop it. He could easily guess who was on the other end, on the far deadly side of the universe from the rest of the human race.

He pushed the button.

"Is that you, Peter?" Michelle asked. Her voice was not very clear; she was calling from another phone. She might be in the house.

"Who else?" Peter asked. He sounded hoarse.

"Did you find Joseph?"

"I found him."

"He's dead?"

Peter did not know how to answer that.

"Oh, my God, Peter, he's dead, isn't he? This is so weird. I don't know what to say."

He stared down at the cold corpse of Joseph Adrian Benoliel. "Who are you?" he asked.

"I beg your pardon?"

"Michelle would not do this."

The voice on the other end changed. "Wouldn't she?"

"No, she wouldn't."

"Would you like to speak to Michelle? Want me to rummage around and find her?"

"Who are you?"

"Michelle is so tiny, down inside here, like a little baby, so I helped her. Can you ever forgive me?"

Peter faced the door now, eyes wide. *In the house. Nearby.* "I have to call the police."

"What good would they be? She's been dead and punished for a long time."

"Why did you kill Joseph? Did he make you angry?" Peter asked.

"If I could feel *anger*, I'd be like you," Michelle said.

"Did you kill my daughter?" The old, sane Peter, hiding away from all the horror, could not believe he had just asked that question of Michelle. Her answer was even harder to accept.

"I ride the horse, and sometimes the horse wants to run."

Peter looked around the room, hoping Michelle had left the gun in plain sight; he could use it if he found her. If she came into the room. If he hunted her down on the estate, or anywhere else. "I don't get you," he said.

"My mount. My face. My pretty little mask, Peter."

"Oh." He needed desperately to think things through. "Daniella was just a little girl."

"My horse saw how much you loved that little girl. She cried thinking about it. My horse's father wasn't so loving. To feel those emotions, all tangled, got in my way."

"I still don't understand."

"I know we'll be going to prison, Peter. It will be *wonderful* in prison. So many horses without riders. So many masks to wear."

Fury and a genuine, gut-deep panic made him shake. He could barely hold the phone, barely speak. *She could be anywhere. She's outside the door.*

"Tell me why you killed Daniella."

Michelle sounded petulant, then sighed. "There were only two men my horse loved and trusted. One of them was Joseph, and the other was you. All men are fathers and brothers to my horse. And all men have disappointed her."

"That's a load of crap."

"It's true."

The room seemed to quake around him. He gripped his forehead with one hand and looked down, dizzy with rage. "When I find you, I'll kill you."

"Well, you can't, silly. It's just us, and we don't care. Maybe you'll take your revenge, and empty out. And then perhaps I will ride *you.* And if the police find us, prison will be lovely. So many of us, all in one place, like a family reunion. *Poor Michelle.* Good-bye, Peter."

The call ended. Peter looked in dismay at the cell phone's screen, small and tidy and green. So easy to talk anymore, wherever you were, whatever you might be.

HE DESCENDED THE stairs into the living room. His thinking was cold and steady, like a steel pendulum swinging from one extreme fact to another. He faced a number of immediate decisions: first, whether to call the police. If he gave truthful answers to the police, nobody would believe him—unless they, too, had seen what a Trans could do to the local *dead lines.*

Clever, that. The lines the dead used, not phone lines, but channels of communication nonetheless. Means of escape, diffusion, passage, whatever happened to the memories and experiences and shapes that lingered after death. Arpad had discovered them, a brilliant act, but had then come to the wrong conclusions. Peter thought back once again on that memorable conversation:

"Trans reaches below our world, lower than networks used by atoms or subatomic particles, to where it is very quiet."

Not so quiet after all. Even a little interference made the dead more likely to *spark*, made their sad flakes of memory linger a little longer, perhaps a *lot* longer. Until the shapes of the dead filled the Earth, a feast for shadows, scavengers. Attracting worse things than dust mites or worms or eels: lions, hyenas, bears. Sharks. Huge carrion-eaters seldom seen except during the horrors of war, the madness of vast human upheavals, taking advantage of *a change in the weather.*

The blinking diode, the grizzly-sized invisibility downstairs. A stalker. Something worse even than the awful opportunist that had entered Michelle, that rode her and called her its mount, that played so well at being human.

Intelligence without conscience. Curiosity without check or balance. Playing with them all.

With Daniella.

The Trans units do not work at Salammbo, inside the houses.

The lines here are already jammed.

By what?

Sweet Jesus, I can't know any *of this,* Peter tried to assure himself, but the promise of sanctuary in ignorance rang hollow. He had pieced it together, with Joseph's help—dead Joseph.

Joseph. Daniella. The tug, the compulsion. They cannot speak for themselves; nothing moves the air. They are scraps and little more, attracted to your memories. That is how ghosts suck away your energy, trying to be real. They become real only when you see them and remember.

It all fit. It had to fit. Trans units transfixing that which, by the dictates of any right order, should move on, dissolve, evaporate. Trivial day-to-day chatter unsettling, and then halting outright, the passage of the dead, and exposing another realm, a system of which living things were supposed to be ignorant.

He felt the burden fall heavily on him now, and it led inevitably to his next decision: What would he do about it? What could anyone do now?

Peter had always thought of himself as a small if somewhat talented man, charming to a point and not pushy; not a great spirit or a hero. Ordinary life, sex and friendship and marriage, had after all enticed and then defeated him.

He slowly breathed in, breathed out.

Thieves. That's all they were. Thieves.

He could deal with thieves, couldn't he? He hated thieves.

"Help," he asked softly.

AT THE BOTTOM of the stairs, the first-floor hallways were dark. But as he turned, looking first left, then right, the lights switched on at the far ends simultaneously, then advanced toward the atrium, illuminating walls and paintings, closed doorways, and rich wool carpets, converging on Peter. Invisible things moved along the halls on both sides—things that no longer followed their natural tendency, no longer faded, but instead had been given weight and purpose.

Peter's head began to throb. He could hear his teeth grind and feel his throat stiffen; they wanted to use him, all of them at once. He clutched and slapped at his neck with one hand, then turned to run, but the floor between him and the front door suddenly blurred, then rippled like water. Shadows obscured the marble tiles: swerving serpents, formless waves, swiftly advancing and rising. They covered up the walls, the windows, then whirled around and brushed against him with a careless and needy familiarity.

The ultimate homeless, the saddest panhandlers of all, long dead: Michelle's victims.

How many?

The door to the elevator opened with a buzzing *snick.* A single naked bulb burned orange within. The tiny cage dropped, vibrated, and adjusted itself once again to be level with the floor, as if something had stepped inside.

Something invisible and bulky.

"No," Peter said. "No way in hell."

"Hell," someone echoed, using his throat.

"Hell," said another presence, and "Hell," agreed yet another, all in strangling seizures of his vocal cords. He bit down on his tongue to keep it still, until he could taste blood in his mouth. Muffled groans continued.

They surrounded him, ripples, silhouettes, suggestions, fragments of dead humanity compressed and herded by others, or maybe just one other, not human. Awkwardly, Peter took a reluctant step toward the elevator. His eyes shut involuntarily, he could not stand the small space, and then he was shoved inside.

The bronze meshwork door closed. The interior was even smaller than he had imagined.

The air smelled smoky.

The dim orange bulb flickered. Pulleys and cables jerked. An electric motor whined.

The cage bounced and descended.

CHAPTER 41

PETER LEANED INTO the corner, eyes flickering, trying to keep as much space and distance in front of his face as he could, an illusion of volume, of not being locked inside a coffin. His face was wet with tears and sweat and his heart galloped in slide rhythms.

He knew that if he died, right now, he would be stuck on the freeway, stuck in traffic. He would never get out, never find the off-ramp and move on to whatever neighborhood had been his destination to begin with.

Heaven, staid and orderly and calm, like the Cheviot Hills.

Or out into the night to just fade away.

Peter Russell was determined not to die, not here and not now. His heart slowed and steadied.

The orange light above his head hummed and winked. The cage door slid aside with a reverberant scrape.

He opened his eyes wide and pushed out of the corner with a hasty flinging of arms and scuffle of shoes, as if fanning a cloud of mosquitoes. But he was alone. The crowd in the elevator had gone. The big presence, the invisible grizzly, was not obvious, either; he had no sensation of being accompanied.

They could move faster than he, or did not need to *move* to get out of the way. *Jerk edits.*

He stood with arms hanging and hands clenched on a linoleum floor in a room lined with steel storage cabinets. In the far corner an antique washer and a dryer were half hidden by a stack of wooden fruit boxes, and beyond them hunkered an immense water heater, mounted sideways on concrete piers like a ship's steam boiler. Framed pictures of long-dead actors and actresses lay in toppled piles, blocking the cabinets, dozens of smiles frozen in black and white behind broken glass, strongly handsome and winsomely beautiful faces peering up in false promise of friendship and seduction.

"To Lordy and especially to his better half, Emily."

"To Morty and Frances."

"I owe it all to you."

"XXXXs Galore!"

Cardboard boxes had been dumped beside the stacked photographs. Old scrapbooks, bound in rotting leather, all bore the initials *LT.* One lay opened to a page of curled sepia Brownie snapshots of a slight, smiling blond in a black swimsuit, arms spread, body angled as if ready to leap into a swan dive. Emily Gaumont. Peter turned the page with the toe of his shoe. Other snapshots resurrected pretty young starlets, ingénues all, and stately old cars. A Packard. A Bentley. An antique fire truck.

He flipped back. There was something oddly familiar in Emily's expression, a winning smile but a critical tilt of the eyebrows. Lordy Trenton's young wife reminded him of Michelle. But the picture was more than sixty years old.

"Throw out the old, hang up the new," Peter whispered. Michelle had a passion for redecoration. Joseph had indulged her in everything.

He looked to his right and saw a Dutch door painted yellow and beige. The two halves of the door stood askew. "Joseph, you *fucking* bastard," he said, radiating his fury. The room seemed to vibrate in response. "You brought Michelle here. You brought her here and ..."

He couldn't finish. What lay beyond those accusations was a void, a desert filled with all that he had gone through the last two years, the madness and the searching. What if Joseph had guessed right—what if he had not brought Michelle here, not the essential, commanding part of her? What if that had been at Salammbo already? An ancient creature patiently awaiting the arrival of just the sort of female found around rich, desperate old men—awaiting another naïve and vulnerable young vessel ...

Michelle. Shocked by two murders, her stunned and frightened consciousness had finally shrunk away, hiding in a very deep and dark corner, leaving an almost empty cup waiting to be filled.

Scragg had asked if Peter could provide any more clues, anything that might point to someone familiar, someone who had known them.

As it had to, his anger turned inward. He could not possibly have guessed. Could he?

And now he saw the smoke and scorch marks curling up and around the ceiling above the platform. Whether it was imagination or not—he was inclined to think not—Peter felt a wind blowing out of the tunnel, carrying with it an ancient, acrid smell of barbecue—smoke and burned meat. He could not feel the wind on his skin; it was in his mind. Fragments of thoughts came with the wind like soot falling into a special and all-perceiving eye. Pain, fear. And not just from the victims of the old trolley tunnel fire.

Peter covered his mouth and nose with his hand.

CHAPTER 42

BEYOND A PLATFORM about six paces on one side, the trolley tunnel to Jesus Wept stretched like a miniature subway into murky darkness, lit only by widely spaced incandescent bulbs hanging from a thin black wire. Some of the bulbs had burned out. Piles of lumber, black with char and gray with dust, lay blocking half the tunnel. More boxes cluttered the other side of the small platform, some split and spilling more albums, more photographs, more history. An enclosed trolley car lay on its side in the far right-hand corner, four grooved wheels sticking out from the carriage. Beside the trolley lay an empty toolbox. Dust and soot obscured everything but a trail leading to the tunnel, as if a towel had been swiped with a heavy hand between the piles of debris. Someone had been dragging burdens. Small footprints marred the edge of the cleared path.

Peter looked down at the trail.

Bent over.

Looked closer, not believing what he saw.

Scraps of phantoms lay low to the linoleum, wobbling like plastic wrap or busted balloons, of no material substance but stuck there nonetheless.

Flattened pieces of faces, hands upthrust, fingers in spasmodic motion. Empty eyes in empty skins. Gossamer leavings from so many scavenger feasts, decaying to an indigestible dust that would blow through these spaces and up and out into the world to become fleeting impressions, whims, to stick in dreams like raisins in a pudding, incomprehensible by themselves. Shards of inspirations and hopes. The broken crockery of memories and shapes.

What kind of broom could sweep this away? What kind of wind? There is never an escape; we swim in this all our lives, and cannot know where the impressions come from. Like dust inhaled into our lungs. Explaining ESP, past lives, you name it . . . Trans has just made it visible.

Peter's terror had broken once again on a shoal of the rational. Speculation to the rescue. Yes, he would die; yes, he had encountered unimaginable horrors and would soon encounter more. Bits of what he was would join this crockery, this dust. No doubt. Loss and betrayal. And so? Hundreds of billions had gone before him.

Life was not simple, death was far from simple.

"Let's get this over with," he said. He walked to the edge of the platform. Joseph and then Michelle had come down here and hidden things. He needed to know what.

Who. Other than the two thieves who had threatened to kill Joseph. He stared down into the gloom a few yards from the platform. Saw a roughly troweled slab of newer concrete under some pried-up and rusted rails that had then been laid back down, the bolts left undone.

Sloppy.

CHAPTER 

THE RAILS RAN straight into gloom. Peter walked with mincing steps along the miniature parodies of railroad ties. Water pooled in the gravel between the ties, gray with scum. Black curls of smoke had painted the long, crumbling plaster of the roof.

To either side, he saw hooks and bits of wire and outlines of lighter plaster where paintings now missing had absorbed the pall of smoke. Only one painting remained, the canvas torn down the middle: a darkened, full-length portrait of what must have been Lordy Trenton, without his top hat and made up as a circus clown, but still sporting a long, slender gentleman's cane and wearing his trademark flappy spats. A brass plaque at the bottom of the frame read, DIGNITY, ALWAYS DIGNITY.

Short-nosed, with a little goatee, behind the whiteface and red-dotted cheeks, Trenton looked happy enough, or would have, had he had eyes. They had been sliced out, leaving square pits. Plaster gleamed white through the holes.

Beyond the slashed portrait, Peter noticed brownish markings on the cracked and baked walls. Imitations of claw slashes, downward strokes four or five to a set. Spiral eyes in sketchy masks. All crudely daubed in what could have been blood, now dried. Cave paintings, barely visible in the spaces between the dangling bulbs.

AHEAD, AT THE far end of the tunnel, a gate or door must have been opened, because a real and steady current of air soughed toward Peter, touching the whiskers of his beard. He carefully stepped up to a large, square piece of plywood bolted to another set of carriage wheels. A rope had been threaded through holes drilled in the plywood. The rope hung down onto the gravel, damp and twisted. It was a makeshift dolly, made to roll heavy objects down the tunnel. Blood stained the plywood.

He knelt for a moment. Dolly, trolley. Tunnel. Cave. Awful place, mold and mud. Just to roll people from one house to another, underground, out of the sun, a stunt; too many houses, too many toys, too many greedy and excessive dreams brought to life by money. Money and life faded; the folly remained. Dolly, trolley, folly.

Peter got to his feet and edged around the plywood, soaking his shoes in the scummy puddles. A few yards farther on, a red panel door poked out from the bricks and plaster. A storage closet, a maintenance room, an electrical room. Or Lordy Trenton's bomb shelter.

She—it—could be in there, hiding just behind that door.

Don't want to die down here.

Peter looked back. He had come about four hundred feet. The distance between Flaubert House and Jesus Wept was about a thousand feet, if one took a direct line under the hedge and under the low hill.

A ways to go.

And once more, the knowledge that a large presence was watching and waiting. Behind, in front, Peter could not be sure. Strangely, he did not feel menaced. Just another dread atop a whole stack of them.

He examined the sliding panel. Both red paint and wood had seen better times. Something had gnawed at the bottom edge, probably rats. Fresh grease had been daubed on the wheels and runners. The panel had been opened recently.

Peter's nose wrinkled. Even under the perpetual stink of smoke, something smelled off. He shoved the door aside as best he could without exposing himself to the darkness within. Waited, listened to water dripping. Stooped to look in. A single old bulb had been screwed into a ceramic socket in the wall, yards off and very dim. Might have been left on for decades. Blackness in all the corners. He could not tell how far back the chamber reached.

"Michelle?"

For a startled moment, he felt something peer over his shoulder. Controlling himself, he slowly turned his head. A large shadow slid across the tunnel's opposite wall and ceiling like a vertical sheet of fog.

He recognized it immediately. The grizzly-sized nothingness had returned. It could change shape and *flow.*

"What in hell are you?" Peter asked, but the shadow had seeped back into the plaster and bricks, indistinguishable from smudge. "You don't want me. You could have taken me by now. You've never been interested in me. What *do* you want?"

Then a different kind of tremor struck him. He was starting to laugh, slow and deep, an awful laugh. "Could you at least make yourself *useful?* Fetch me something?" he asked the opposite wall. "Could you at least go back and get me a flashlight?"

He turned back to the space behind the door and the laughter gurgled in his throat. He coughed. His eyes had adjusted as much as they were going to. The chamber beyond the hatch was no more than twenty feet wide but deeper than he had thought. He could not see the rear wall. He stooped again and pushed through.

THE CONCRETE FLOOR was old and cracked and roughly surfaced. He could make out lengths of iron rail propped up in a corner. Along the wall to his right—he tried to orient himself, just to keep his thinking clear—the northeast wall, stood a line of double bunk beds, like those used in barracks. He counted at least eight marching back into the gloom, sixteen beds in all, and all apparently occupied by still, recumbent forms, covered with dusty blankets. Even under the covers, the forms appeared shrunken, diminished.

He pulled back a blanket corner. Dust sifted down over his feet. The bony face beneath the blanket had stringy, bleached-blond hair. Female. Not very large, but an adult, not a child. For that Peter was minimally grateful. The flesh of the face had been gnawed through to brownish skull. What remained was dry and leathery. Dust puffed again as he let the corner drop.

Peter walked on, deeper into the side tunnel. This had to be Trenton's bomb shelter, with accommodations for many dozens of friends. More bunks, more bodies, lined up in the darkness, toothy, grinning, leather-dark faces poking out from beneath rat-filthy blankets.

The bunks stretched along the northeast wall for as far as he could see into the blackness. It was difficult to believe that Michelle could have done all this by herself. How long had she been at it? And how could Joseph not have known? What sort of complicity had been denied, and then shared, as the years went on? Peter realized he might never understand, much less know.

No rats now. That fact struck him. A sinking household.

Peter pressed against the wall, the light bulb to his right like a glowing match head in the gloom, the awful smell of dust and old decay thin and cold in his nose. Worse than the field where they had found Daniella's body. Worse by far than that sunny, grassy knoll in the hills. Scragg had told them that she had not been killed there. Her body had been laid out, as if with some minimal respect, hands crossed over her ruined chest.

Peter stood straight. Reluctant to breathe the foul air, he was on the verge of passing out. He walked back toward the hatch, steadying himself with one hand against the rough, sandy concrete.

A DARK SQUARE had been laid at the foot of the blanketed form in the right-most lower bunk. Peter forced himself to kneel. His chilled fingers touched folded knit fabric. Holding it up, the sleeves and buttoned lapels unfolding, he recognized the one piece of clothing that had never been found. A girl's blue wool sweater, stiff with blood.

A souvenir.

Peter could feel it coming again. The heat behind his eyes. The fear and the love. Between his memory and the blood, the identity of spirit and spilled tissue, between her father and the dust in the long burial chamber, with a clear picture of his daughter and a vivid memory of the way she had smelled, of Daniella's long brown hair . . .

Like a fine autumn mist taking the shape of a little girl, she stood in the open hatchway, yards off, as if reluctant to enter. Barely visible, in this place where she had been taken by Daddy's friend, where she had been killed, she watched him as he held out the sweater.

Peter walked toward her to ask an awful question. "Was it here?"

The shape raised and lowered a refractory outline of a chin. She extended one filmy hand.

Peter reached out instinctively, without a thought for his own safety. Her fingers passed into his. For an instant, he felt youthful surprise and animal-deep panic. Her mouth and eyes darkened and sagged and parts of her gaped like rotten muslin. The ghost of his daughter shared what she had carried for so long, too long, shared how it felt to have the point of a knife slam into skin, punch through with a sound like ripping vinyl, over and over, pain so intense even now it threatened to tear this small ghost apart.

The pain brought Peter to his knees. He voiced the short, hard, dying shrieks of his little girl and his hands ripped at his throat, trying to stop the appalling sounds.

MORE THAN A projection, less than a presence, Daniella pulled back and released him. Clutching the sweater to his face, hiding his eyes, Peter wept, again hoping that his heart would split open. He did not want to live. Too much for any man to bear.

She turned, not all at once—the outer shell of skin rotating first, hints of bones beneath following as if disjoined in time ... Flowed aside, out of sight, toward Jesus Wept.

Again, Peter's strength betrayed him. So much to do. The gashes on his throat soaked blood into his collar. He did not feel it; the memory of his daughter's pain overshadowed all.

PETER LEFT THE old bomb shelter, now a burial chamber, and stumbled the remaining length of the tunnel, passing from the glowing yellowish domain of one ancient light bulb to another, glancing at smears of brown on the walls, finger sweeps and handprints. Not Joseph's large, beefy hand.

Michelle's.

Perhaps the dead could only speak truth.

Joseph had recognized Daniella, once the weather had changed under the influence of Trans. A few days ago, he had seen Daniella and the others and could no longer deny the long-suspected truth about what his woman was, what she had done. Terrors in the night, screams.

Sleep no more.

As Peter walked, shadows like puffs of thin soot followed, darting from side to side. Peter was well aware that he was being tracked, used in a different way this time, by a thing or things that had never been human, that did not speak and had no use for communication as such, little use for matter in and of itself; large, tranquil, and patient, but with an almost unimaginable potential for violence.

He still held the small wool sweater in his right hand. His fingers touched a saturated curve of dried blood and the knife hole in the weave.

Scragg would want it, he thought; in that other, rational world, above ground, away from the suffering of ghosts, Scragg would put the sweater in a plastic bag and send it off for lab technicians to analyze.

Here, in the lower world, at the end of the tunnel and far below the rational, Daniella waited for Peter by the base of a long flight of concrete steps, a daub of crystal and darkness. Air fell down the steps from an open door. He could feel it, cool and fresh, welcome.

A trap.

PETER DRAGGED HIS feet up the last step and gripped the rail with his free hand. No sign of Daniella now. His eyes stung with exhaustion, crust of dried tears, salt from sweat. His collar stuck to his skin. He knew he looked more dead than alive.

The room above was small, cubic, heavy beams supporting the ceiling, a thick black wooden door on one side and a small octagonal window on the other, the window mounted high, above ground level. A faint glow of predawn showed through beveled panes of leaded glass. A workman's light stand faced into a corner, one bright bulb pouring illumination onto the unpainted plaster. A thick orange cord snaked from the stand under the black door. The rest of the room was clean and empty.

The door had been locked from the outside. Peter tried it several times, fingers slipping on the old brass knob. No go. Then he heard a click. The knob turned. The door opened easily.

Another sign of a trap. Michelle would wait for him with the pistol in her hand. *Well, good,* he thought; it would be quick. He would die trying.

* * *

NO ONE STOOD on the other side. The central, circular atrium of Jesus Wept was dark. Even when they were unbelievably ugly, big houses always had big entrances, like desperate old maids showing cleavage. A not very helpful grayness suffused from the high ceiling windows mounted below the dome. To either side of the huge black front door, stairs swept down from the omega-shaped balustrade. Scaffolding and black cloth blocked Peter's view of much of the opposite side of the hall. Workmen had recently come and gone.

Had the killing stopped during redecoration?

One passion giving way to another?

Peter needed guidance. Needed his connection with the reason for being here at all.

"Honey?" he called softly.

From across the main hall, Michelle answered in a brassy, echoing voice, "Is that you, Peter? Are you all right?"

He could not see her. Echoes kept him from tracking her by sound. Peter crossed the wide hallway beneath the high dome, then under the balustrade, between thick, spiraling Moorish pillars and wrought-iron rails, toward the voluminous and unknown rear of the house. He did not see Michelle, but he could hear her breathing, as if she had just been exercising; a pretty intake followed by a little sigh as of gratified weariness. He heard a door close.

"You're running me a merry chase," she called. Suddenly her voice was tiny and she seemed far away.

Peter stopped. Blinked at the sweat, but did not dare wipe his eyes. The temptation to blind himself and see no more was too great. He was a man on the edge of honest-to-God madness, perhaps over the edge, clutching the bloody sweater, still feeling Daniella's ripping pain. He might be capable of anything.

Peter glanced over his shoulder. A dark, thin curtain of smoky gloom rippled and spread to obscure the entire atrium. He had underestimated its magnitude; either that, or like an octopus, it could expand to amazing size.

Whatever, he was not afraid of it. It meant him no harm; he was not its prey. Peter had become a dog following a scent.

Leading a hunter to its real quarry.

"We need to talk," he tried to shout to Michelle. It came out as a husky moan. He lowered his chin to more efficiently use what little voice he had left. "Joseph is dead. I think you killed him."

A door hinge creaked down a long hall, at the end of which a tall window was showing a pale fan of dawn.

"Let's talk it over, just like the old days," Michelle answered. "But stay where you are, okay?"

Peter was turned around now; he had thought the house was oriented east to west, and the sun would rise behind him. Instead, the sun seemed to be coming up directly ahead.

"Why not face-to-face?" Peter hollered, feeling his vocal cords flare.

"You wouldn't like my real face, Peter," Michelle said. "You're in my ocean now. It is so dark down here. You're out of your *depth*, don't you know?"

He did know, but he could not stop.

MICHELLE HAD DROPPED Trans units along the hall. As he walked toward the fanlight window, Peter counted twelve of them, all different colors, like a trail of huge candies. For a moment, he thought the carpet had been stained a pale, milky blue. But as he walked, the blueness parted around his shoes and quickly flowed back. Smooth, odorless, the gassy fluid was pouring from the seams and grill and display of each unit, clinging to the floor like a heavy fog, less than half an inch thick.

He stooped to pick up a unit. His fingers brushed the fluid. Abruptly, the blue changed to yellow and green shot through with veins of red. Shock knocked him back against the wall, not electricity—pain and grief. He slumped and his hands spread to stop his fall. As they touched the fluid, an incredible ache seeped up his arms and spine—pain of loss; guilt; miserable, hopeless frustration; fear of confinement, of being boxed in and beaten and spat upon and clubbed down by men in uniforms with expressionless faces; alone in endless dark with dripping water and roaches and spiders. The catalog ran quickly into varieties of interior and exterior torture he had never encountered in his own life.

Hopeless torment was leaking from the plastic units like oil from a motor. The foulness numbed his ankles, spread up his legs and along his veins like infection. He could feel the anguish creep into his abdomen, his heart, find purchase on his nerves and climb higher, until it bit into his brain like a razor-sharp and rotting tooth.

The swirling mist had turned the color of bloody pus.

Being strapped into chairs, trying to hold a breath against a rising vapor redolent of bitter almonds; tied to hard tables, nostrils widening at the antiseptic whiff of alcohol, the gentle pinch of expert fingers bringing up an artery, the burning sting of the long needle, and every time, all those times, pale faces swimming outside the thick glass, watching, watching in horrified fascination, like visitors to a monstrous aquarium.

Peter pushed himself frantically against the wall and stood. He stared down at the mist. Knew with absolute certainty he was standing in prison soup, thin broth boiled down from the memories and emotions of tens of thousands of incarcerated and executed men and women, the condensation and distillation of all that was cruel and hopeless in human nature.

The lethal heart of San Andreas had subverted the Trans network. It had finally found a way into Arpad's transponder, and now it was free. It could go anywhere it wanted, anywhere there was a Trans.

Confused, he looked to the end of the hall, the closed doors, the fanlight window, the glow of dawn brightening outside. All turned around. No need to even try to understand. A mosquito in a hurricane will never get it right.

"I still have the gun," Michelle called, her voice muffled. "I'll use it if you don't get out of here."

Peter's lips curved in a raw smile. If he found her now, it would all be worth it. From the mist he had soaked up a powerful supply of undiluted *loathing,* enough to top off his tank a thousand times over with high-octane vengeance.

"What part of the ocean are you from, Michelle? What kind of creature are you? The kind that steals bodies for protection, to hide in? *How do I kill something like you?*" Peter's mind easily filled with a thousand scenes of gory violence.

"You can't," she said, almost too soft to hear. "Nobody can touch me."

The shadow rose behind him. He did not turn to look, but he could feel it. He could feel its power and its hunger.

"I've brought a *friend,* Michelle!" he shouted, and for a few moments, everything really did turn an awful red. *It's like I'm bleeding inside my eyes.* That's *rage, all right. Don't give in. If you let it, it will stain you to the core. Your essence will stink. They will have to burn your soul.* "You know all about my *friend,* don't you? You must be old acquaintances."

"Don't come in here," Michelle said, her voice suddenly unsure. No more banter.

They were getting too close.

"What kind of miserable, parasitic creature are you?" Peter harangued, teeth bared, his smile savage. This thief had stolen his daughter. "I think you're a *crab.* A hermit crab, soft and vulnerable, scuttling around looking for empty shells. Well I've found something that loves to dig out hermit crabs. You're it's *prey,* aren't you? Is that what you're afraid of?"

"Just let me leave, let me get out of here," the small voice called. "You'll never see me again. Think of all we shared. Think of what I did for you, Peter."

"Think of all you did for Joseph and Daniella and the others," Peter growled. "How many, a hundred, a *thousand*? They certainly won't like it." It was not his voice alone that spoke now. He twisted; his muscles knotted and he almost fell over. Recovering, bracing against the wall, he felt the pus-colored mist clawing at his insides, trying to form words with his tongue. The dead of San Andreas recognized the creature inside Michelle.

They knew it intimately.

"All the men and women ever put through the gas chamber, they won't like it, either. Can you see them? They're here with us, flooding your precious carpet. All the anguish your kind has caused ... All the killers, the criminals, the sad, empty shells you've filled with murder and pain. That's what I'm wading through, a hundred-proof liquor of hate. Come on out. Let us see you, Michelle, or whatever your name is. Do you even have a name?"

"If you come any closer, I'll do worse than kill you," Michelle shouted, arrogance and assurance trying to return and not succeeding.

"Too late," Peter said, and gave in to a fit of violent coughing. As he recovered, he suddenly understood why Michelle had tried to disperse the Trans units, giving them to all she met. The solution arrived in a spreading blot of induction. For whatever occupied Michelle, the crab in its pitiful shell, it was a matter of survival. A Trans changed the weather. It was like a smoke screen. It provided cover and distraction, making the entire invisible world spark and change.

And that could put a hunter off the scent.

Still, she had not taken into account the side effects.

Nobody had.

NONE OF THE doors were locked. Two of them opened into ordinary rooms, redecorated like model showrooms, filled with ordinary furniture, ordinary if antique wallpapers, common pastel colors. All the masks of normality, of trying to visibly fit in and not raise a ripple of concern.

Nothing more—and in context, nothing less.

He found the right door on the third try.

THE WALLS OF the room behind the door had been torn out but no further work had been done. Just a small, closed room awaiting the decorator's touch: lath and bits of cracked plaster, a dusty parquet floor, a window.

Miasma washed in a thin flood around his feet.

Peter's chest suddenly went hollow. He could not immediately reconcile what he saw and what he felt. He had always been glad to see Michelle. Always interested in what she might say, what anecdotes she might convey about Joseph's rich eccentricities. She had made a very pleasant mask indeed, she had fooled them all.

Perhaps the hermit crab had used something of the real Michelle. He would never know. But that Michelle was gone. What remained was pushed back into the far corner. She wore a shift dress and her arms were bare and skinny, her legs scrawny. Whatever beauty she had once possessed was now less than a memory. She looked just this side of old; face pale, hair spiky and matted.

He could not hate *this.* The mist pulled back from his feet, leaving him in a void, and crept toward the corner.

"Why my daughter?" he asked. "What did she ever do to you?"

"Peter, please," she said, holding up her arms, elbows presented like shields. One hand clutched a black Beretta. Her eyes went to the doorway.

"You said I was your project," Peter reminded her. "You were helping me. Why kill Daniella?" He held up the sweater. "What did my daughter ever do to deserve you?"

"You were my project, not her," she said, shrinking back, dropping her arms, pulling in her strength for one last ploy. "If you take away their most valued things, people only get better." Her eyes narrowed to slits. "How sadness becomes you. How you've *grown,* Peter." Then the eyes expanded, wide, enormous, like a lemur's. She shivered. Peter did not frighten her in the least, but still, she trembled as if with fever.

No escape. She knows it. I almost feel sorry for her.

"Can I talk to Michelle?" he asked. "Is there anything left of her?"

"Just dried strings. *I'm* the one you love, the one you want. I've been at Salammbo, for all of my men, for ever so long." She pointed the gun at him. The air behind her head grew murky. "We played. You learned. Don't tell me you didn't enjoy it, just a little. All that sympathy. Just imagine what your life would have been like if you hadn't been so utterly *charming.*"

Her finger tightened on the trigger. The room filled with painful noise. A bullet whizzed by his head and he smelled burned powder. His eyes stung and his ears buzzed.

"Let me go," she demanded, and tried to pull the trigger again. But her features softened. The gun barrel wavered. Oily flowers like dark liquid glass squeezed from her eyes, her mouth, her ears. The rider, the hermit crab, was trying to make a break, to scuttle away from its shell.

Michelle's body went limp. The gun fell. From all of Michelle's orifices sprang dark, gleaming blossoms. As the gun hit the floor, the hunter shoved through the wall and flooded the room with ribbons of shadow like long elastic fingers. The fingers curled and pinched at the black flowers. They were seized and jerked out, to be instantly and brutally snipped by sudden, scissor-like appendages, then whirled into a mouth like a tangle of razor blades and broken china, a mouth that chewed and cut and spat. The hunter's savor was instantly obvious. The air filled with expanding, glutted sacs, stomachs, receptacles. Bits slopped over in its enthusiasm. Black nubs squirmed, then drifted to the parquetry to be swept up by greedy, urgent black whiskers.

It was over in a few seconds, violent and final. Nothing wasted—nothing of interest to the hunter.

A thin, pale woman with matted, wet hair and parboiled, milky eyes sagged to the floor in the corner of the dusty, unfinished room. Grime caked her knees and calves. A wreath of coiled shadows briefly crowned her damp forehead, writhed, and then vanished. She stared fixedly at her ankles and took shallow, husking breaths.

The room cleared.

The empty woman's head wobbled and tipped. Her face bore the helpless, animal confusion of an imbecilic patient in an old, filthy sanitarium—a raped patient who has just given birth to a stillborn. She glanced up, dazed and listless. Her eyes barely tracked Peter.

The hermit crab, Michelle's rider, a delicacy in the invisible world, had been plucked forth, dispatched, and swallowed. The hunter had left behind only the shell—and nothing else that really mattered.

Not even vengeance.

Peter picked her up in his arms—she hung like an empty sack—and carried her down the long hall, through the atrium, and out of Jesus Wept. The stench that rose from her was finally too much. He deposited her as gently as he could manage on the stone porch. She stood for a moment, legs like frail sticks, then dropped to her hands and knees, rotated like a sick dog, and crawled back inside through the heavy black door. Peter tried to grab her ankle but she turned, eyes flaccid. Her legs flopped and pushed like a frog's. Her teeth clacked and snicked like castanets, and for a moment, Peter thought she would rise up to attack him, all teeth and Michelle's long, thickly painted fingernails.

He jumped back and almost fell down the steps.

The door swung ponderously, then slammed shut.

CHAPTER 45

PETER HAD NOT gotten turned around inside Jesus Wept. The glow through the fanlight window was not sunrise, but Flaubert House. He found a gap in the long row of oleanders and crawled through to stand and watch as the old mansion blew jets of flame from its windows. The roof was already fully engulfed and the northeast corner of the building—where Joseph's body still sat in its chair—had collapsed.

A long tower of smoke climbed above Salammbo.

He heard sirens. Time to make a decision. He could stay on the estate and try to explain what had happened, present the sweater and whatever remained of the bodies in the tunnel as evidence. Scragg would be interested, no doubt.

Smoke puffed from cracks in the lawn, almost beneath his feet. He could feel the heat. The grass, spotted with morning dew, started to steam. Over the hedge he saw a gray haze rise from Jesus Wept. Fire had crept along the tunnel. Lordy Trenton's underground trolley line was turning into an inferno.

Peter's mind worked quickly despite his exhaustion. Evidence was being destroyed. No one would believe him about Michelle—certainly not Scragg, as hardheaded and skeptical as they came. Peter now looked psychotic enough. Why not blame *him* for his daughter's murder?

And all the others as well?

Peter had little faith in justice.

He hoped what was left of Michelle would have sense to flee a fire. And if she didn't . . . he honestly couldn't put together the will or the energy to return to Jesus Wept and find her.

He had what he wanted—or at least he thought he did. Had he actually seen Michelle's rider hunted down and consumed? Or had that just been smoke mixing with the last of a long string of hallucinations? An amazing and convoluted construct of horror and fantasy erected to get around his grief, his self-destructive refusal to work again in the real world . . .

Peter, all by himself, could give the police what they needed to put him behind bars for life. How could he convince himself otherwise, now that he stood under the morning sun, with real flames burning a real house to very real ashes?

Staying for the last of this truly dreadful party would be a bad idea.

Peter climbed into the brick-red Porsche. He laid the sweater carefully on the side seat and looked down at it. Sat upright.

He put the car in gear and backed up. Glanced in his rearview mirror to see if fire trucks or bystanders might witness his departure—so far, so good—then swung left and took a side road around Flaubert House to the rear of the estate. Hidden by trees on the western boundary was a fence secured with a rusty chain and an old lock that dated back to the forties at least. He was pretty sure a tire iron would break it loose. Beyond the fence lay an unpaved fire road that followed some ridges down to the coastal highway.

If the rains hadn't left too many ruts, Peter thought the old Porsche might make it.

CHAPTER 

Sleep no more.

He did not even try. But he rested.

He stripped off his bloody and filthy clothes, but lacked the energy to take a shower. Lying on his bed in the old, familiar house in the Glendale hills, with the sound of wind chimes rising from the backyard, he looked away from the pebbly, diffuse peace of the old popcorn ceiling.

A tired old man stood by the foot of his bed, watching him.

Peter sat up on the rumpled sheets.

The old man was ragged at the edges, but not worn down—not yet. After a few minutes, lying as still as he dared, Peter's legs began to go numb. The old man barely moved—a slow rise and fall of his shoulder, an almost mechanical turn of the head—but Peter thought he recognized him.

A wraith, not a specter. A stray scrap of Peter Russell, but not from the past. Not this time.

"You guys really *like* the foot of the bed, don't you?" Peter asked, indignant. "Why?"

The figure showed some surprise, raised a hand in protest, and then—

with a frightened, focused consternation of empty eyes—faded to a scrim and winked out.

Peter got up and put on his slippers. If Sandaji was correct, seeing himself that way meant he would die soon. "Big whoop," he murmured as he walked on tingling legs to get a shower.

He had never thought he would ever appear so old and gray, but as he looked at himself in the bathroom mirror, he confirmed the resemblance. The scratches on his throat had crusted over. He looked like a bottom-feeder, a freeway bum holding up a cardboard sign.

Stepping into the shower stall and turning on the hot-water tap, he said, in a tired but reasonable voice, "This shit has got to stop."

CHAPTER 

PETER LISTENED TO the radio in the bathroom as he dried off. He had not taken a newspaper for years. The news announcer droned on about a Malibu estate going up in flames, two mansions destroyed, the ruins still too hot to investigate. Reclusive movie producer and real-estate magnate Joseph Adrian Benoliel and his wife, Michelle, were both missing.

The announcer persisted through the bad news of the day. Major telephone companies were experiencing serious outages. Phone and even cellular service had been interrupted for tens of millions of customers across wide areas of the country. No cause had yet been established.

As Peter buttoned his shirt and walked into the living room, he peered down at the Enzenbacher chessboard. Somebody had responded to his move. A knight—a private detective in an overcoat—had been advanced to threaten his pawn.

Peter gazed out the front window at the jasmine. The sky was going gray. He saw someone cross the porch. The Soleri bell tinkled and the door lock turned.

He finished buttoning his shirt and zipped up his pants, ready for whatever.

Lindsey pushed the door wide. "Good," she said. "You're back. The phones aren't working. Mom's half-crazy, she thinks you're dead. Did you know that?"

Peter shook his head and went to hug his daughter. "What did you tell her?"

"I didn't. I just knew it was time to come over." She looked around the living room, biting her lip. "This morning, she showed up again. She looked different. Really thin and weak. Did you do something?" Lindsey's expression lit up, dangerous youth. "Did you burn down Salammbo?"

"No," Peter said, and mussed her hair with one hand. She accepted his touch with a look of adolescent tolerance.

"So why is she still here?"

"She stayed to protect us."

"Against what?"

Peter suddenly hugged Lindsey and shook his head, rubbing his chin against her crown. She did not resist. He could feel her silky hair get caught up in his beard. "No," he murmured. "I did not burn Salammbo."

"But you did something."

"Yes," Peter said.

"And Daniella doesn't need to protect us now?"

Peter looked through the long window. Thought of the key from the bell, white with dust, and the open door. *It's been too long.* "Maybe not."

"She needs to go away," Lindsey said. "I need for her to go away. We all do. Can we do that for her? Let her go?"

"I don't know. I hope so," Peter said. "I took your advice." He pulled away, dragging a wisp of hair over her face. She blew it back. "How did you get here?"

"Rode the bus. Mom's too much of a wreck to drive."

"The bus? In LA? You're a brave girl."

PETER LAID THE sweater on the bed where Daniella had first reappeared. Lindsey sat on her own bed and folded and unfolded her hands in her lap.

"Where did you get that?" she asked him as he sat beside her.

"At Salammbo," Peter said.

"Who killed her?"

"Michelle," Peter said. Explaining was too complicated. Lindsey's eyes widened.

"Mom never did like her. Is Michelle dead now?"

"Close enough," Peter said.

"Is that blood?"

"It's blood," Peter said.

"Daniella's blood?"

"I think so."

"That was her best sweater," Lindsey said, sudden and unavoidable tears welling in her eyes. Peter saw how much she cared under all the brittle armor. "You gave it to her for our birthday."

"I remember," Peter said.

Lindsey jammed her lips together and wiped her eyes. "What do we do?"

"You tell me," Peter said.

"How the hell should I know?"

"You're her sister, her twin. You're closer to her than I am. I think they're attracted to form and memory. DNA and what we remember. Relatives are part of the memory. Especially for a twin. You're the closest thing left on Earth to what she was."

"We're not identical. She used to argue with me," Lindsey said, forlorn. "Maybe she's still mad."

"I don't think so. Tell me what we should do."

"Well, she comes to me when I've been dreaming about her or thinking about her, or sometimes when Mom is crying."

"Did your mother ever see her?"

"Only once, I think. She said she thought she might be going crazy."

"So . . ."

Lindsey shut her eyes and reached for Peter's hand. "What we do is, I guess, we think about her."

They thought and tried to remember.

The room was dark and still.

PETER FIXED THEM a supper of canned soup. They ate in silence. Lindsey watched him carefully, plucking at the chapped skin of her lower lip. After dinner, they did the dishes together and sat on the couch in the living room. Lindsey nodded off and he held her head in his lap, studying the chess set on the coffee table, wondering if this was good, involving Lindsey when touching ghosts might be so dangerous.

But it *was* the right thing, he knew that.

There was a greater place and a greater reality, and in that realm, there were duties and responsibilities known now only to those few who could imagine a time when there had been no electric lights and no candles, no weapons against the dark. When the dead had to be reminded that their time of duty was finished.

Dust wafted up between the coffee table and the window.

Lindsey twitched in her doze and whimpered. Peter stroked her silky hair and watched the dust. Tiny motes waltzed with slow dignity in the glow cast by the porch light through the broad front window.

It took an hour, but even now there was dust enough in the old house.

"Look," Peter said.

Lindsey opened her eyes.

Daniella stood on the other side of the coffee table. In the darkness of the living room, the golden glow in her midriff was obvious, the rest of her less so.

Lindsey sat up, sleepy and somber.

"She's so sad," she said.

Daniella looked over them, a swirl of purposeful dust around a fading hint of sunset.

Lindsey reached out first.

The figure saw or felt the extended fingers. Shifted slightly, as if drawn.

Peter took Lindsey's other hand, and together, they offered Daniella their touch. Daniella did not seem to notice for a moment, then, with a jerk, a bad edit, the whirlpool of dust that was her hand connected with Lindsey's. Another jerk and she touched Peter's.

That made a circle.

This time it did not hurt or shock them senseless, but Peter felt the shadows gathering in the corners and in the hall, the eels and scavengers he had seen before, and for a sharp moment he wanted to stop. He knew what this small ritual meant.

Liberation required sacrifice.

The end of grief and remembrance was freedom.

This was the last, truly the last of any communication with his daughter, in this world, and for all he knew, in any other.

Daniella glanced in Peter's general direction. He felt her vibrancy in his fingers, a tiny electric thrill. Felt the moments they had shared, like faded photos, old tapes. Already she seemed to move her attention elsewhere, as if considering a difficult task. The dust—flakes of skin, fibers of clothing that she had worn—started to sift from her like thin snow, no longer needed and becoming secret once again.

Peter's eyes filled with tears.

"Good-bye," Lindsey said. "We love you."

The sunset glow spread and intensified. For a stunning moment, the living room turned bright as day. Peter saw the bones in his hand, the ghost of his own skeleton and the X-ray haze of the flesh around it.

Deliverance.

Release.

What is it? So beautiful, so powerful. Where does it go? Beyond life, after death, another mystery. Do the mysteries never stop?

Mystery is pain. Why can't I go with her?

Who is she now?

What remained of Daniella was ragged, hollow, sad, without direction. Frayed from its added time, beyond its time, it tried to fasten to them with a desperate and final twitch of old instincts, the last earthly link of Daniella Carey Russell to her father, to her sister, to all of her memories, to the physical world.

Defenseless.

The shadows whirled and plunged as they had since the beginning of life, in the endless dark.

They fed. Cleansed.

Going now: all the summers they had had together, the days at the Santa Monica Pier, getting apple pie and cider in Julian, taking the trams across the California countryside at Wild Animal Park and smelling hot lions lounging in the sun . . .

Picking out a kitten from a squirming, furry litter at the house of Helen's old friend Paulette, in Sherman Oaks, and the expression on Daniella's face when the kitten peed on her . . .

Peter reading *The Hobbit* to the girls before bed . . .

Smelling his daughter's hair as she slept in his lap at age five on a trip to Phoenix to visit their grandmother . . .

Eating ice cream with her sister for the first time at a Baskin-Robbins and getting a surprised look, and then crying, at the cold on her new teeth.

Bringing homework from school and working so hard to get it done on time.

Leaving to walk to the corner market and buy a smoothie.

Asking why boys were different.

Memory is tenacious.

Peter held Lindsey and covered her eyes. But he watched. He had to. It was his way of saying his own final good-bye, I love you, thank you. Of paying respect to a brave young woman who had stayed behind for so long—too long—to protect her father and her family.

* * *

QUIET.

Stillness.

The room had not changed.

Peter heard the Soleri bell jingle softly and sadly on the porch. Lindsey pulled away his hands, looked aside, and said, "Wow."

It was over.

There would never be explanation enough or understanding.

Lindsey cried and then Peter released her and they cried together.

CHAPTER 48

LINDSEY WASHED HER face and looked presentable by the time Helen knocked, or rather slammed her fist on the door. Helen was pale and would not say much to either of them, but she glared at Peter. Lindsey stood to one side, a smaller, slimmer model of her mother, but with his eyes and his own mother's hair, soft and straight.

Helen looked between them and sensed the weary peace they shared. Her eyebrows drew together and she stared directly at Peter. She took a deep breath. "I've been calling and calling, but the whole world's going to hell. I don't know what's happening, and then Lindsey disappears. I've been frantic."

"I'm sorry," Lindsey said.

"What is going on here? What the hell have you two been doing?"

"She'll tell you," Peter said. "You wouldn't believe me."

Helen noticed the marks on Peter's neck. "My God," she said. "Did you get those at Salammbo? I knew it. I should have been here. Lindsey, you should have—"

"We're fine," Lindsey said. "It's over, Mom."

"Not quite," Peter said. "I'm going away for a few days. When I come back, I'll answer any questions. But right now I need some quiet. I'm not feeling very well." His stomach was churning and he thought he might throw up. "Okay?"

Helen looked so sad and lost that Peter reached out with both hands and squeezed her, hard. She was shivering like a frightened colt, and she folded into his arms with surprising ease and no resistance. Even more surprising was how good she felt to him, slight and warm and trembling. Alive.

"You're both cutting me out, and I don't deserve it," she wept into his shoulder. "I want to help. I should have been here, but nobody told me. Please don't cut me out."

Peter held her back and searched her face, appreciating the reversal but not reveling in it. He knew too much about human frailty. "None of us deserved this," he said. "Least of all you."

"Can we all try harder? Really?" Helen asked.

Peter nodded, then let her go and gave Lindsey one last hug.

The parting was slow and a little awkward, as there was much healing to do, and so little time. Not enough time for all the years. It was midnight. Lindsey waved to him as she followed Helen across the porch and down the drive. She waved with the assurance of youth, that the bad part was over and she would see her father again soon and things were starting to look up. Not even sending on the soul of her sister and watching the awful aftermath could dim that vital spark of optimism.

Peter smiled and waved back.

HE SAT IN the kitchen and drank a glass of iced tea. The wind chimes on the back porch were quiet. The air was still and warm.

At one in the morning, he started to pack a small suitcase. He went to the garage and checked the oil level on the Porsche. He would need to stop for gas.

Coming back to the bedroom to pick up his suitcase, he saw someone lying asleep in his bed. The figure turned over, pulling back covers from a bearded, grizzled face, revealing small, amused eyes, puffy with sleep, and a gap between his front teeth. Peter could see the pillow through the man's head.

The man put on an expression of irritated boredom. "You guys really *like* the foot of the bed, don't you?" he asked. "You really like watching us. Why?"

Peter knocked over the suitcase behind his feet and swiveled to recover his balance.

The covers were empty. The loop had closed. His time would be short.

He did not need Sandaji to tell him that.

* * *

SOMETHING IN HIS own weather had changed, and as he drove out of the Glendale hills, out of Los Angeles, over the Grapevine, in the early-morning darkness, he saw the world differently.

The Porsche moved with remarkable speed. At times he was hardly even aware he was driving. Exhaustion had filled him with a gray, dusty calm, his emotions on hold, most of his thoughts on hold. But he could not stop. Peter had miles to go and one last thing to do before he could ever sleep again.

Little fish bring sharks. But in the vastness above and around him, sharks could be just the beginning.

CROSSING THE DRY Central Valley farmlands just before dawn, the windows down, the smell of grass and wind and dust in his nose, he looked up at the starlit sky, down at the rhythmically fleeing stripes of the center divider on the straight black highway. To the east, heat lightning flickered over round hills. The flashes, silent and steady, turned a somber red. The entire sky looked inflamed, swollen.

Storm-sized shadows crossed the stars and dropped dark appendages to the flat valley floor. The shadows marched over the land, then straddled the freeway, cumbrous but determined. Peter zoomed under them, glancing left to see one of the huge limbs touch down and twist like an ethereal tornado.

He drove on with shoulders hunched. Due north, over the Bay Area, the stars had been blocked completely.

Who could ever know what they wanted, what they hungered for? The altered currents of life and death had dredged up ages of nutrients, up-wellings from unknown abysses, rich pickings for these strange, gigantic feeders. More would follow. Visitors not seen in hundreds if not thousands of years would return. The Four Horsemen of the Apocalypse. Dark gods.

Earth's age-old defenses were down. And he hoped he knew what had to be done.

"This shit has got to stop," Peter said, and brought his squinted eyes down once more to track the freeway.

Too late. His jaw throbbed. Pain shot up his arm. His hands went numb and his fingers spasmed. His chest felt as if it would split wide open. The wheel slipped and spun. The old Porsche skidded sidewise, tumbled, bounced along the asphalt, then ploughed the dirt shoulder and leaped a guardrail.

Peter flew through the air like a comet, trailing splashes of brilliant life.

* * *

SOME TIME LATER, standing by the side of the road, confused, he hitched a ride in a battered, colorless pickup. The ashen old fossil behind the wheel smiled. "Pity about your car. Porsche 356C, right?"

Peter nodded, the wind still knocked out of him.

"She's a beauty. And from behind, she looks like booty."

Children giggled, standing in the truck bed and peering in the rear window. Peter had lost his glasses and could not see his benefactor clearly.

"Hope you brought some of that ol' Smoky Joe," the old man said. "Helps you see what you should know. Long tough trip. Hard on the butt. Smoky Joe, twist, blend, or cut."

Light played through the cab of the pickup, wisps and flares of silver. The old man's words and the light made Peter flinch. The children in back watched him curiously, with great sympathy.

CHAPTER 49

THE SKY AND the earth were gray shot through with tiny rainbows.

Peter stood before the gate to San Andreas, surprised to have made it this far. He did not watch the pickup pull away. It had been a nice gesture, the ride, but he could not remember liking that old gray man.

The guard would not look at him or take his name and said nothing, staring nervously at the broad parking lot. Talk around the world had been interrupted. Business was bad. Communication was difficult. Peter could understand. People passing through these gates could be grumpy.

Everyone on edge.

Almost like the bad old days.

Inside the prison, guards lingered everywhere. Perhaps there had been threats from unhappy customers or investors, and that was why there were so many guards, with so many different uniforms. Caps with bills, no caps. Nightsticks, cans of Mace, tasers, cattle prods, rifles, riot guns, shotguns. Gloves, no gloves. Tall boots. Steel-toed boots. Shiny black shoes. They were walking, sitting, standing silently. They watched Peter with eternal suspicion but did not try to stop him. Most were middle-aged and male. The average working life of a prison guard ended before he was fifty, Peter had read somewhere; stress.

The prison was back. But no prisoners; just guards. And him.

The floors were covered with bluish dust. Peter tried not to look down. When he did, the dust flinched and moved in sluggish waves. It turned the color of pus and blood.

He tried to remember the way. It wasn't easy. Nobody wanted to help.

CHAPTER 59

PETER FOUND ARPAD Kreisler on Death Row, wearing a worn-down expression, standing with big shoulders slumped before the gas chamber. His three-day growth of facial hair had advanced to a bristly week or two. He was the only man in the old prison complex who looked as if he wanted to be somewhere else—desperately.

"Business model shot to hell?" Peter asked. Arpad did not respond, so Peter touched him. The effect was immediate: The large man's knees buckled and he swooped aside, jamming up against a broad, shuttered window. Arpad raised his brushy brows in alarm. His eyes focused to the right of Peter, and his breath went wheezy with terror. "Are you a guard?" he asked. Then, looking left, "Who are you?"

"You're going to shut it all down, aren't you?" Peter asked. It took all his energy just to speak. After the wreck, he wasn't his old self. His batteries were running low.

Arpad's forehead furrowed with intense concentration. Peter could not make himself heard. Arpad did not respond. Peter wanted to strangle the bastard.

"Where's Weinstein?" he asked, and reached out to lightly slap Arpad's head. Arpad swerved like a drunken prizefighter, but his lips moved. "Weinstein," he said, Adam's apple bobbing. "He's gone. Guards took him. They took him *here*, yesterday. To the chamber. I haven't seen him since. Who are you?"

Peter had found the way to be heard. He touched Arpad's throat.

Arpad's lips moved involuntarily, and he said, "Peter." Now he saw Peter and showed his teeth in an apish snarl. His eyes narrowed. "Peter Russell ... Is that you? My God, what happened? Are you ...?"

Arpad didn't like the way he looked. Hard to accept, but there it was. Bruised and beat-up from the crash, no doubt. Hours or days in the hospital. But Peter could not remember any of that. And it did not matter.

Arpad tried to back away. Peter enjoyed this little game of cat and mouse.

"You should get out of here," Arpad warned. "There's nothing but guards. The prisoners—they leave as soon as they die. The guards return. They are stuck here. Weird, yeah?"

Peter made him speak some more. Arpad's lips formed more words. "Shut it down."

To this, Arpad nodded vehemently. "Absolutely. As soon as I can get in ..." He pointed to the gas chamber. "It's nasty. Stupid idea, right, putting the transponder in there? Sophomore bullshit. Nerd arrogance. You understand."

Peter was getting the hang of this. Being around Arpad made him feel a little less weary. He had always liked Arpad. And Arpad had seemed to take to Peter as well. The large engineer tracked him with some precision now, frowning so deeply his brows almost covered his eyes.

Peter's perspective shifted with a sudden jerk.

"The guards won't let me leave," Arpad said, speaking to where Peter had been. "Most of our staff ran away a few days ago. It became unbearable. Now the old guards are everywhere, thousands of them. Can you talk to them—convince them?"

Peter could imagine—or perhaps he actually saw—the guards filling the ancient hallways of the huge old prison, milling like rats in a cage—capo rats. The prisoners gone, glad to be rid of Earth and its walls, but the guards in for the duration, the long haul.

Their shift never ends.

Peter touched Arpad's thick neck. "No," Peter made him say. "Shut it down."

Arpad rubbed his throat. "I'll shut it down, I promise," he said, and leaned against a pillar. "How about you? Can you get in? I wouldn't ask, but ..."

Peter looked through the thick glass into the chamber. What he saw did not encourage him. Weinstein was in there, strapped to the table. If he was still alive, he was not moving.

Something apparently made of mildewed gray velvet sat on Weinstein's chest, like the shadow of a desiccated monkey, a very poor bit of taxidermy. It bent over Weinstein's head and pried open his eyes with soft, flabby-looking fingers. The ancient monkey face turned on a wet, leathery ribbon of neck to peer through the glass directly at Peter, no ambiguity, no hesitation.

It had Weinstein's gimlet eyes. It had Weinstein's ingratiating smile. Something dark leaked from its ears.

The transponder equipment, racks of high steel boxes—the heart of Trans—stood in one corner. Green and blue lights blinked in rows across the bottom.

"I can't go in there," Arpad repeated.

Peter did not want to go in, either. He had no idea how much it would hurt, or what he had left that could be hurt. But Peter Russell had never been a coward.

He held his hand against the glass. Even now, it felt cold.

He touched Arpad, used him.

"Open the door," Arpad said on his behalf. Then, with a roll of his eyes, Arpad lifted the bar and spun the wheel on the heavy steel hatch to the chamber. Peter was not certain he needed the hatch to get in, but he took that route anyway. Force of habit, dream logic.

The monkey held up a wizened hand that trailed fumes of stinking night. Peter could still smell, and that astonished him. Dreams were funny that way.

But I'm not dreaming.

Inside the cramped, awful chamber, the monkey with Weinstein's eyes gibbered and danced on his torso. Pus-colored vapor sprayed from its ears, from its nose and mouth.

The monkey on your back. On your chest.

Nightmare, mocker, suffocating the prisoners by night and twisting their thoughts by day . . . feeding off their rot, their prolonged misery.

The monkey spewed the prison's venom, vomited and shat it forth, then, perversely, began to grow like a boil, puffing out, infected, loathsome.

The big one. Eater of souls. The ghost of San Andreas itself.

Arpad stood in the steel doorway. He had picked up a bar of rusted metal. Against whatever sense and judgment he had left, Peter moved in, drawing the beast's attention. It opened its mouth. It had no teeth, no gums, no throat. Something black wriggled behind the shrunken lips.

"It's not a *phone*," the monkey told them in Weinstein's voice, its bony index finger thrust high. "Please don't *ever* call it a *cell* phone."

Arpad swung the bar savagely against the boxes until the last of the lights stopped blinking.

The beast scuttled and skidded around the table. Peter stood aside from the spray of foulness.

Weinstein tried to sit up. He mewled. The monkey, alarmed, stretched out a huge gray paw and pinned him back again.

Arpad withdrew, his arms covered with trailing leeches of shadow. Seeing them, he began to shriek like a little boy.

Peter pushed through the glass, a neat trick. However much it expanded, though, the monkey was a specialist—it could not leave the gas chamber. It was stuck there, along with Weinstein.

The monkey did not seem to mind. It lifted its face and laughed, an awful sound that was no sound at all.

They do have their fun.

PETER WAS TIRED now. He looked up to the high-peaked roof above the chamber and saw a similarity to the atrium in Jesus Wept. He was there for a moment, back at the mansion, surrounded by vaporous walls, confused because he could see the sky. What had happened? Had there been a fire?

Lordy Trenton himself walked through the burned-out, empty ruins, with trademark high hat and flapping spats, forever the drunken, loose-limbed, incompetent fop. Beneath Lordy's truculent eyebrows, someone had cut out his eyes. He felt his blind way with eloquent fingers, their tips worn down to nubs.

I've been going through my scrapbooks, he informed Peter. *Those were the days, weren't they? When everyone, simply everyone, looked at you. Who can ever abandon such an audience?*

Michelle crawled after Lordy on all fours like a wounded dog. She smiled at Peter. *It does show better when it's sunny, don't you think?*

But Peter could not stay.

HE WAS HOME. He knew the place well, though not his place in it. And though he felt some comfort at returning, there was also a sense of guilt. He could not think straight. He couldn't even see straight. Corners seemed devious. The light was uniform, unpredictable. Shadows—real shadows—moved everywhere without warning.

Obviously, after all he had been through, he had finally gone out and gotten smashed—that is, drunk out of his gourd, the mother of all sodden, sopping, liver-dissolving binges. He did have an excuse or two, didn't he? Most certainly did. Time had compressed and slipped away, just as it had during the months he had spent like a lab specimen in a glass jar, soaked in alcohol.

That explained why his head wasn't working right.

The DTs.

He looked down at the chess set, then sat on the couch. Thought about making a cup of tea, a feeble attempt to sober up and die right. Fly right.

A young woman came into the house. Peter watched her with interest, then with some alarm. Who was she, what was she doing here? She stood in the living room, then moved into the kitchen. A man in a beige suit followed.

They were talking about insurance, a will.

It had been a year, two years, he guessed. Could one stay drunk that long? He recognized the young woman. Lindsey was growing rapidly. She was getting to be a real beauty, even more lovely than her mother. No need to bother them. He wouldn't be much help anyway. Like Phil, Peter had never made out a will.

But they did not see him. That was good. Peter understood and approved. Things were getting back to normal.

He looked down at the Enzenbacher chess set on the coffee table. A silver knight, a private detective in his trench coat, lifted slowly over a silver ghost pawn and landed to menace Peter's overextended bishop. The game had progressed quite a ways.

In response, Peter moved the mad scientist back three squares. He felt someone watching him.

PHIL SQUATTED ACROSS the table, pale and ragged, but recognizably Phil. Still carrying the sunset glow that could light up a room, when it wanted to.

"Good to see you," Peter said.

Phil nodded cordially.

"Where have you been?" Peter asked.

Around. Waiting. You're a busy man.

Phil extended his hand over the chessboard. Peter could not see his friend's fingers, but somehow Phil managed to move the silver Dejah Thoris queen into a position of considerable menace. Peter had been outclassed again; checkmate. He was glad to lose, glad it was Phil who had won. Phil had had a tough life, hard luck with women. He had always deserved more.

They clasped hands as best they could, without flesh or touch, hints of thumbs extended in their old victory gesture, from the days when the world had been fresh and full of adventure.

His old friend was here to do more than just finish the game. *We're finished here. We have to give it up, Peter. Time for the Old Farts Cross-country Hot Dog Escapade and Tour.*

Peter tried to deny that. *I want to help Lindsey.*

You already have. It's hard keeping hold of memories now. Believe me, it's time. Dust to dust. Let go of the important stuff.

PETER LOOKS DOWN, looks very deep, and sees the sunset in his abdomen.

This?

Phil nods.

To his surprise, Peter is ready. He has resisted for so long, he remembers that now; first, fighting to be born and to stay alive, to fit in and be social, to do the art thing, to marry and raise children, to protect them all . . .

All the women he has loved, sumptuous flesh and bright doorway eyes, all the men he has worked with and talked with and shaken hands with and gotten drunk with, the films and thousands of cartoons, the ungrateful books he has slaved over, his daughters, born all at once, in a scary rush, beautiful, wrinkled, and pink, changing him forever, the puzzling and painful love he has felt for Helen and Sascha and others, he wonders what they are doing, whom they are loving, and he feels lonely and left out, despairing, but most of all, he sees clearly, too late, his love for Helen, who gave him children and suffered.

For some time now he has resisted giving up all this. And still he resists. Responsibilities and relations, passions and jealousies, the stuff of the living. And only of the living.

There's more to do, so much left unfinished.

Phil will have none of it. *You've crossed the river, Peter. No sense hauling the boat with you. It will just weigh you down.*

So many ties, so many things to protect. The pain comes back to him now, and that's the final goad—the pain of awareness that he is diminished. There is so much he cannot recall. Already he is half-lost and ragged at the edges.

It's over. No going home. No going back.

Finally, following Phil's example, Peter searches for that dreaming release, the unhooking, the ungluing.

We all die with the knack, Phil tells him. *Like an egg tooth on a chick. Can you feel it?*

He can. There are lights across the harbor. A sensation of moving to another land.

Peter relaxes. He drops the luggage, lets go of the boat.

The room fills with light, bright and beautiful, but nobody is there to see it, not this time.

As it should be. Some things are best kept private.

THE LAST OF their memories, like shed skins, play at chess a while longer, a leisurely game without much energy. Because they have no centers, this will take a while. It is becoming impossible to remember what happened a moment before. Moments themselves grow to impossible lengths. The grayness has come down on them with a vengeance, the penultimate desuetude, after which there is nothing, a mercy.

Even now, though, what little is left of Peter will watch and try to protect. What is left of Phil will stick with him. Together, they still have something.

The monster pawns are waiting on one side of the board, the ghost pawns on the other.

I've got your back.

And I have yours.

They will not go without a fight.

A GHOST IS a role without an actor.

Ghosts are like movies—the story goes on, but nobody's home. Like dead skin, under normal circumstances, a ghost lingers just long enough to protect the vulnerable flesh of the living.

Not all that rarely, people are born with nothing inside, or lose what little they have—living ghosts. And when they die, sometimes even before they die, a hole opens up and a bit of the dark world creeps in.

We were all there in that city that draws its paycheck from the manufacture of ghosts. We were there when one man started handing out free talk. And we are there now, sad little dolls made of dust.

Your friends, if only you knew. If only you were smart enough to care. Maybe now you'll listen, though you never have before.

You'll join us soon enough.

You're next.